HER *Sister's* *Bridegroom*

JANE BONANDER

DIVERSIONBOOKS

Also by Jane Bonander

The MacNeil Legacy

The Pleasure of the Rose	*The Scoundrel's Pleasure*

Heat of a Savage Moon	*Warrior Heart*
Wild Heart	*Dancing on Snowflakes*
A Taste of Honey	*Forbidden Moon*
Fires of Innocence	*Winter Heart*
Secrets of a Midnight Moon	*The Dragon Tamer*

Diversion Books
A Division of Diversion Publishing Corp.
443 Park Avenue South, Suite 1008
New York, New York 10016
www.DiversionBooks.com

For more information, email info@diversionbooks.com

First Diversion Books edition January 2018.
Paperback ISBN: 978-1-63576-174-0
eBook ISBN: 978-1-63576-173-3

LSIDB/1711

For my two favorite word wizards:

Dedicated to Randall Klein

In Memory of Edward Swanson

Chapter One

EDINBURGH, 1872

In Edinburgh, a city of layers, Robbie Fleming knew she was currently living somewhere near the bottom. How did she end up here, in a rat-infested rooming house with walls so thin she could hear her elderly neighbor break wind in his sleep? This was not how she had envisioned her life.

Even though she was more level-headed than her sister, Birdie, she still dreamed of a life where she could write the stories that crammed her brain, stories of children and fantasies and animals. Those dreams began early on and they never faded from her mind. Instead, she wrote swill for an underground collection of pornographic stories at night and worked with prostitutes and runaways during the daytime, and only the writing, such as it was, paid anything.

She listened to the wagons lumbering through the street. Pity the days when it was dry and windy, for manure dust blew up from the pavement as a sharp, piercing powder to cover clothing and ruin furniture and race up one's nostrils. Her walk home would be another stressful adventure in trying to avoid heaps of garbage. Ah, what a life.

She studied the girl on the table before her, certainly not immune to her misery, but able to distance herself in order to help her. She had come to the clinic the day before, suffering from the effects of opium and alcohol. She had emptied what little was in her stomach and was now dry heaving, spittle rolling from the sides of her mouth. She was ejecting from both ends; Robbie had difficulty keeping up. Some might have let her lay there in her filth; Robbie couldn't do that. The girl was only thirteen years old, a child, really. In spite of her efforts to distance herself, it broke Robbie's heart. And on top of everything else, the poor thing was pregnant.

As Robbie tried to soothe her, wiping her forehead with a damp cloth, she studied the girl. Thin—painfully so. Her hair was now lank and greasy, but had probably once been a shiny gold. Her clothing was mere rags, hanging on her skinny frame, hugging her pregnant belly.

The girl had told Robbie she was from quite a prominent family, but when the kinsfolk discovered she was pregnant, they made other plans for her.

The name on her registration slip was listed merely as "Bonnie." She had confided in Robbie the night before that it was her stepfather who had gotten her pregnant; he planned to ship her off to the poorhouse, claiming she suffered from hysteria that made her unstable. He could do this with impunity. The depravity of some souls made Robbie's blood boil.

Instead of accepting a punishment she didn't deserve, Bonnie chose her own path, fleeing into the night. Now, six months later, she was here, suffering a new horror inflicted upon her by the man who had claimed to want to rescue her. A pimp, no doubt. But Robbie didn't judge; she had seen many young women in the same position as Bonnie. She wanted to help—the problem was that it wasn't a job that paid. She did it out of compassion for the women who suffered just as Bonnie did, grateful her own father had been a loving and generous parent.

Suddenly Bonnie clutched her stomach and released a shriek that echoed off the thin walls of the shabby clinic room. "Oh God. Oh God," she moaned. "Something's happening!"

Robbie quickly checked the girl and noted the circle of wetness on the flimsy sheet beneath her. "Lydia!" She shouted once again for the midwife on staff. "Lydia, she's ready!"

Lydia, the midwife, a short, stout woman with a no-nonsense manner, scurried into the room.

"Give me something," the girl demanded. "The pain, give me something for the pain!"

Without hesitation, Lydia gave the girl a draught of laudanum, tossing Robbie a worried glance as she did so.

Two hours later they had delivered a dead baby girl, strangled by the umbilical cord. And Bonnie was hemorrhaging. She died shortly after.

Later, after Robbie and Lydia had made arrangements for the bodies, they sat in a quiet corner of the office, each nursing a cup of tea. Lydia had been working since before sunrise.

Robbie gazed solemnly at the pockmarked table, feeling a migraine tap insistently at her left temple. "Things like this happen so much. It makes me absolutely sick inside."

"She had a family. I suppose they should be notified." Lydia studied the tea in her cup. "It breaks my heart when we see girls like her."

"Mine as well. As for Bonnie, her family should at least be responsible for the burial," Robbie added. "It's not as if she has no one, even if they did cast her aside. The poor thing and her bairn should not be buried among paupers. Even though her stepfather was a brute, I can't imagine her mother not wanting to know what has happened." She finished her tea, rinsed out her cup, and went to retrieve her cloak and bonnet.

"I'll have Karl look into it," Lydia promised.

Robbie bade goodbye to Lydia and began the long walk through Old Town to her meager room at the rooming house. A waft of something putrid assaulted her nostrils. She should be used to it by now. If she stayed so long in the slums that she became accustomed to the smells and the filth she encountered daily would be a crime. She lifted her skirt to avoid the offensive piles of nondescript compost in her path, although she knew it wasn't possible. What was another hem stiff with garbage?

After their father died, she and her sister, Birdie, had each inherited a small sum of money. Birdie, always vivacious and flighty, bought a beautiful trousseau, flirted shamelessly with Robbie's beau, Joseph Bean, stole him, and ran off to marry him. It wasn't that Robbie had not cared for Joe, she had. But she was in no way ready to settle down and marry him. It was just another insult from Birdie. Anything Robbie had, Birdie wanted. And she always got what she wanted. Robbie kicked a stone in the street, sending it skidding into a pile of horse manure that the horseflies had begun to feast upon. She chastised herself for her peevish thoughts, for she was certain her sister would not survive the life Robbie now led.

Robbie, always the sensible one, used her inheritance to attend college and become a writer. Actually, that part wasn't sensible at all. Had she imagined she would become the next Mary Shelley? She twisted her mouth into a grim smile. No, more like "author anonymous," considering what she was currently writing to pay the rent.

No one would ever know what she wrote. The underground serials were not the sort of thing "fine" ladies ever read. But were it not for her professor and mentor, Jeremy Greene, she would not be paid for her writing at all. Jeremy had been one of their most prolific writers, and now that Jeremy was dead, Robbie took up the task. They didn't have to know about the change. After all, it was money, and she needed it to survive. And the stories?

She shook her head, wondering what her dear father would say if he knew what she was doing to make a living. But no, it was honest work, just not terribly noble.

However, her two lives often collided. Her real life was so vastly different from the stories she penned. She was really quite innocent in the ways of sex and knew little of the world about which she wrote. The erotic stories of men and women who romped naked and unafraid through the pages were quite foreign to her. Her life, such as it currently was, was day after day in a hell she found herself, unable to claw a way out. She couldn't go on this way, but she could see no opportunity to change things. The indigent, the down and out, and the prostitutes who were taken advantage of needed a champion, and Robbie desperately wanted to be that person but without funds it was not possible.

She blinked, wiping away the tears caused by the coal smoke that hung over the town like a shroud. Some days she couldn't even see the sky.

She trudged through the streets, sidestepping garbage and mounds of compost only to step in more horse droppings as she made her way to her room. Oddly, she never thought of it as "home"—it was merely a place to sleep. She stopped and tried to scrape the muck from her boot by rubbing it on a dry tuft of grass, only to realize it had spread out over the sole.

Cursing mildly, for which she silently asked her father for forgiveness, she hurried along to the rooming house. It loomed up before her like a caricature, really, the upper windows like big, dark rectangular beady eyes, the gable in the front the nose, and the wide, sagging porch the mouth of a creature waiting to take you in and digest you. She shivered and quickly ran down the stairs to her basement room, stepped inside, and kicked off her dirty boots. Cooking smells permeated the thin walls, making her stomach growl. Had she made it home in time for supper? Tossing her cape and her bonnet on the bed, she rushed from the room, up the stairs and into the communal dining room. And her stomach dropped. The table had been cleared.

"Too late for supper." Her landlady, Mrs. Mott, strolled into the room and removed a dish of potatoes swimming in greasy gravy from the sideboard.

Robbie swallowed. Her hunger was palpable. "Are there potatoes left in that dish?"

Mrs. Mott, who looked like she never missed a meal, and whose frizzy gray hair poked out from under her scarf, sighed. "I can't always be doing ye favors, missy. Ye know what the meal hours are, and ye know the rules of the house. If ye can't be here on time, it's your problem, not mine."

Robbie's expression must have been extra pathetic, because

her landlady heaved a dramatic sigh, plunked the dish down on the table and turned toward the kitchen. "Clean up after yourself."

Robbie grabbed up the dish and a fork, and hurried back to her room in the basement. The fact that the gravy had congealed and the potatoes were cold mattered not to Robbie; she ate them quickly, happy to have had something to eat at all.

After she returned the dish to the kitchen, where she carefully scrubbed it clean with leftover dishwater, she returned to her room to write. The installment for the magazine was due tomorrow; she would get little sleep tonight. "All right, Miss Wiggins, let's get to it."

With her lamp lit low, she sat at her small table and began.

Miss Sallie Wiggins was no stranger to sex. She had been peeping through keyholes and windows since she was ten, and although she had seen people naked together in many positions and places, she had never had sex. Well, unless one counted having sex with oneself. And that was pleasant enough; it had been for years. But now she wanted more.

This night, wearing no underthings under her skirt and petticoat, she sauntered out to the stables where the new stable boy, Elijah, was grooming a mare. Truth be told, Elijah was more than a mere boy, he was over twenty, or so she had heard. And he was the color of a caramel candy, all shiny and delicious. Her skin tingled as she watched him work, his brown arms, thickly muscled, moving carefully over the mare's rump. Her mouth watered when she thought about him working those arms and hands over her own rear.

He must have seen her out of the corner of his eye, because he stopped quickly, turned, and gave her a nervous bow. "Evenin' Miss Sallie."

She raised her eyebrows. "You know my name?"

He nodded, innocently rubbing his bare chest. "Yes, ma'am. You be the master's daughter."

Feeling brave, and a tad horny, she announced, "Did you know I'm not wearing any underwear?"

Flustered, Elijah fumbled with the grooming comb and swallowed hard, his Adam's apple bobbing in his throat. "N...n...no, Miss Sallie, I didn't know that."

Confident that she had his attention, Sallie drew up her clothing and showed him her virginal fare. She quickly dropped her skirt and said, "Now you must show me yours." She stared at his trousers and noted with satisfaction that they were beautifully tented.

Elijah stepped away. "Oh, no, Miss Sallie. I don't want to lose my job."

"Oh, pooh," she said with a pout. "No one will see, not if we step back further into the stable."

Elijah threw a look of longing at the back of the stable. "I...I guess we could—"

"Yes, we could," Sallie interrupted. "But it's dark back there. You have to show me yours before we go back there or it won't be fair. After all, you saw mine." She noticed that his penis twitched against the fabric of his trousers, and she felt the luscious swelling and wetness between her legs.

With fumbling fingers, Elijah unfastened his trousers and lowered them past his erection.

Miss Sallie was in awe. He was long and brown and standing as stiff as a flag pole. "Oh my, Elijah, that's a beautiful thing you have there. Might I touch it?"

Gathering courage, Elijah answered, "Only if you let me touch yours first."

Miss Sallie squirmed. "Oh, yes. Please do." She stepped away from the door and backed against the wall of one of the stables and lifted her skirts once again.

Elijah got down on his knees in front of her and pressed his fingers against her mound of glossy fur. Miss Sallie shuddered with anticipation. When one finger slipped inside, her knees nearly buckled. Such pleasure! Such joy!

• • •

Robbie opened her eyes. She knew the sun was up somewhere, but it rarely entered her cellar-like room. In fact, there was always dampness in the air, and her bedding never got aired out unless she did it herself. Unfortunately, she'd gotten used to a number of disagreeable living conditions since she left home. The lack of fresh water for bathing and washing her hair was something she had a hard time adjusting to. She had always been proud of her hair; it was thick and wavy and, as Jeremy called it, the color of Swiss chocolate. Now she kept it in a tight bun, for she had little time to spend on it anyway.

Then there was the room itself: small, dark, dank, and not nearly big enough to swing a dead cat. She did have a nice blanket, thanks to Jeremy, who had seen what the landlady furnished and was so disgusted he went out and bought her one himself. However, there was evidence that the moths or mice (or maybe even rats) had discovered it soon after she got it, for there were holes here and there, not too big yet, but once her toe got stuck in a hole at the bottom, and now it looked as shabby as everything else Robbie owned.

She sat up, slid to the side of the bed, and reached for her father's timepiece, which she valued more than any other object she possessed. Noting the hour, she made a face; if she didn't hurry there wouldn't be any breakfast for "missy" Robbie Fleming.

She splashed cold water on her face, dressed quickly, and ran a comb through her hair before twisting the length into a bun at the back of her neck. Peering at herself in the cracked mirror, she wrinkled her nose, wishing the freckles that stood out like beacons would simply disappear. They seemed to shout, "I say, look at us! We're big, brown spots on Robbie Fleming's nose!" She let out a whoosh of air and hurried up the stairs to the dining room.

As she entered the room, all eyes turned toward her. She slowed her steps and walked to her seat between two young women who worked in one of the local factories. She took a biscuit from the basket in front of her, then reached for the preserves, wondering why everyone continued to stare.

Mrs. Mott entered the room. "I'll be needin' your room, missy."

Ah, so that was it. Robbie slowly lowered the biscuit to her plate. "Why?"

"When I rented ye the room I told ye that I might need it one day for me own nephew, and just happens that he be needin' the room by week's end."

Robbie vaguely remembered such a conversation, but she had pushed it into the attic of her mind, hoping it would never come to that. But it had. Suddenly, she wasn't hungry anymore. She blinked away a sting of unshed tears, angry with herself for the weakness. "You have no other vacancies?"

"Full up." Mrs. Mott, perhaps feeling a bit shabby about what she had to do, put a bowl of fresh porridge in front of Robbie. "Here, now, this is still hot. Better eat up."

Of course, Robbie's first instinct was to say, "Feed it to the dogs!" but she didn't. What she really wondered was, where would she go?

Attempting to eat, she took a spoonful of porridge and forced herself to swallow it. She would need her strength for the days to come.

Later, as she sat at her small table attempting to write, she gave up and simply stared into space. What were her options? Contact Birdie and ask if she could stay with her and Joe for a while? No. Absolutely not. If nothing else it would give Birdie another chance to pity her, clucking her tongue, pursing her pretty lips, and pretending she gave a bloody damn. (*Sorry, Papa.*)

Robbie would just have to get out and walk the streets, hoping for a sign for a vacant room somewhere. Hopefully not in the slums of Cowgate, but if that was her only chance, she would have to take it. The thought made her shudder. She had been in those rooms before; some so crowded with people she wondered how they laid down, much less slept. And even though her current room had only one small window, at least she had one. Some of the rooms in Cowgate were windowless. All those different odors: body, food, filth, all milling about with no place to go. She couldn't imagine the smell.

She threw on her cape, slipped into her galoshes, and left her room, her fingers crossed that she would find lodging.

Three hours later, tired, hungry, and foot sore, she kicked off her galoshes and collapsed on her bed. She had had no luck at all. She rubbed one foot and then the other, noting that there was a new hole in the toe of her multi-darned stocking. Fortunately, she had learned to darn a sock before she had left home; Papa's housekeeper, Mrs. Mann, had insisted on it.

The woman must have had a special insight into Robbie and her sister, because while she insisted on checking Robbie's stitch work for errors, she merely shrugged when Birdie sent hers flying across the room. It was likely that Birdie would never have to sew up a hem or darn a sock. Robbie supposed that was life when you were pretty.

Robbie had dozed off when she was awakened by a knock on her door. She got up and, with a weary sigh, went to answer it. Mrs. Mott stood there.

Robbie swallowed a groan. A visit from the landlady in the middle of the day was never a good thing, but how could things get any worse? "Yes?"

Mrs. Mott took a letter from her apron pocket and handed it to Robbie. "This come for ye by post while ye was gone."

Robbie took the missive and thanked her, then closed the door. She realized her landlady was anxious to know the contents, but Robbie didn't care and she wasn't about to share any more bad news with the woman who was booting her out on her behind.

She went to her desk and studied the envelope, frowning all the while. It was addressed to Miss Robena Fleming. Well, that certainly was her name. She didn't recognize the penmanship, but it was very stately and correct looking. Certainly not from Birdie, whose scrawl was barely legible.

She opened the envelope and pulled out a letter written in the same stately script. She read the contents…and had she not been sitting, she might have fainted dead away.

Chapter Two

She reread the letter to make sure she had read it right the first time.

To Miss Robena Fleming,

I realize that no young woman should accept a letter from a man who is neither a relative nor a betrothed, but I am hoping you will reconsider after you hear what I have to say.

It is possible you do not remember me; after all, we met quite some time ago when we shared the same tutor back home.

I understand what I am about to propose will sound slightly mad, but I've come to a time in my life when I want someone to share it with, and you have never been far from my thoughts. To make things easy for you, one way or the other, I have enclosed an envelope and return postage, so all you have to do is let me know if you will consider becoming my wife. And please, bring a companion with you; I realize it might look scandalous if you do not.

Most sincerely and awaiting your answer,

Gavin Eliot

Robbie clasped her hands together to keep them from shaking. Gavin Eliot, the boy she'd fallen in love with the first time she laid eyes on him ten years before, was proposing to her?

Robbie read the letter a third time. Yes, there was no mistaking it. He had proposed marriage. Stunned, she tried to tamp down her excitement. After all, he had never paid much attention to her back then; it was always Birdie, Birdie, Birdie. All the boys flocked around Birdie; she was like a brightly colored bird with her red curls, deep dimples, and coquettish laugh. Robbie felt like a colorless wren next to her.

But that was ten years ago. She had known even then that Gavin was as infatuated with her sister, as all the boys were, but now perhaps he'd matured enough to realize that Birdie would make a questionable bride.

Gavin was not only intelligent, he was brilliant. That's what had drawn Robbie to him in the first place—his beautiful mind. Oh, it was nice that he was also handsome, with his tight blond curls and his lovely blue eyes. But when Birdie wasn't around, she and Gavin would have the liveliest of conversations. He could speak on anything. His mind was like a trap; he remembered everything he read. But their time together was always cut short when Birdie entered the room, floating along in her gauzy gowns and her pretense at elegance and regal helplessness.

Robbie remembered the time she and Gavin were playing a lively game of chess, their rivalry serious but fun. To Robbie, it had almost been like they were a couple. She had felt so comfortable with him. That was probably because she knew she had no chance to win his affections as long as her sister was around. That day, Birdie flew into the room, pouting because Gavin was not paying attention to her. Of course, that didn't last long, and Robbie was left alone, again. She had gone to the window to watch the two of them leave; Gavin's head bent toward her sister's red curls, as if what she was saying was the most amazing thing he had ever heard. At that moment she realized that boys were every bit as fickle as girls.

But now…Robbie sighed. Gavin could not have timed his proposal more perfectly. Robbie was essentially a positive person; she knew things would look better one day, but she hadn't imagined it would be because of a marriage proposal from Gavin Eliot.

She tipped the envelope upside down and pound notes drifted out, landing lightly on the table. She turned the letter over; there was a note: *In case you agree instantly, I have sent you traveling money and directions to my estate in the country. GE*

It was really happening. She pressed her fingers over her mouth to stop a laugh. She didn't even have to think about it. She quickly drew out a sheet of paper and responded, anxious to get the missive posted.

> *Mr. Gavin Eliot,*
> *It is with great honor that I accept your proposal.*

She added that she would wire ahead when she was on her way, and then she signed it with a flourish.

She was nearly giddy. She'd never felt this way before. And although Jeremy had wanted to bed her many times, she had refused, claiming to want to save herself for the man she would marry. How appropriate now! And how often had she daydreamed that the proposal would come from Gavin?

She grabbed her cape and bonnet and hurried out the door, letter clutched in her hand, anxious to post it. The only thing that bothered her, truly the only thing, was that for once in her life she wished she had something special to wear. She only had one suit, her brown flannel with the velvet collar and leg-of-mutton sleeves. Fortunately, she didn't wear it often, so it would be fine enough as her traveling outfit. But what other clothing did she have that was in any way presentable? Very little, truth be told. She had packed away a few gowns from her life before she left for university, for they were too delicate to wear either in academia or what she was doing now. She would take them with her; at least she wouldn't be carrying an empty valise.

Although Gavin's letter had suggested she bring a companion to stave off gossip, protocol and propriety were far removed from her situation. In truth, she knew of no one she could ask.

After mailing her letter, she stopped by the clinic to see Lydia. As she entered the room, Lydia frowned. "You're supposed to be off doing something fun today."

Robbie laughed. "Oh, my dear Lydia, you can't imagine what

has happened to me since yesterday." She told her friend the story of Gavin Eliot, how she knew him, and what he had proposed.

Lydia embraced her. "You deserve to be happy, dear." She held Robbie away from her and scrutinized her. "Now, don't get upset with me, but I'm thinking you need a bath and a hair wash, am I right?"

Embarrassed, Robbie felt herself flush. "I won't even pretend I don't."

With a conspiratorial wink, Lydia said, "Tomorrow morning is when they come with some clean linen. We'll use the big old tub in the back room and give you a good cleaning, how would that be?"

Robbie collapsed into a chair. "You make me sound like a floor that needs a good scrubbing," she teased. She studied her only friend. "If I knew the circumstances of where I'll be, I'd take you and Karl with me."

"Nonsense," Lydia said with conviction. "Karl and I will be just fine."

But Robbie wasn't so sure. Karl, who suffered from a fairly severe palsy, had developed a thick skin toward the bullies and bruisers in the neighborhood, but Robbie knew that each time Lydia saw him suffer, it broke her heart. The fact that he had been a foundling also made Lydia fiercer when it came to how people treated him.

"When will you leave?"

Robbie stood and hugged Lydia once again. "As soon as I get all cleaned up, and of course, I'll have to check on the coach's schedule."

They said goodbye until morning, and as Robbie made her way back to her room, she wondered what Gavin would think of a prospective bride arriving on his doorstep with little more than a comb and a toothbrush and what she had on her back.

Chapter Three

Gavin Eliot paced the cobblestones in front of the inn, waiting impatiently and nervously for the coach's arrival. When he read Robena's response to his proposal, he'd nearly leapt into the air like a boy. Imagine. All those years and that beautiful young thing hadn't been snatched up and married off to someone else. Perhaps she'd been waiting for him, somehow knowing that he would eventually come to his senses and propose marriage.

He snorted a laugh. Now he was actually thinking like a lovesick boy. He studied his reflection in the inn window, straightening his blue and white striped cravat and smoothing down his dove gray morning coat. He ran anxious fingers over his short, blond curls and ordered himself to relax.

He tried to stop thinking about his new bride-to-be and thought back to the days in Edinburgh when countless young women had been put in his path. The mothers certainly knew that he had a modest wealth, as present owner of a country estate in the Borders near Galashiels, and would make an agreeable husband.

The thundering of hooves brought him back to reality, and he took a deep breath, unable to stop a wide smile, as the coach came into view.

• • •

Robbie held on to her hat and craned her neck, looking out the window at the sparse, hilly countryside. Although it was not green and lush, the smell of the fresh air made her heady. Throughout the drive, she had noticed sheep grazing on the hills, fat and content. There were enormous country houses and even a castle that was going to ruin, the sight making Robbie sad for the days when it must have been lively with people.

The driver shouted the name of the village as they approached the inn, and then there he was, standing in the sunshine, handsome and smiling. Her heart nearly broke through her ribcage, she was so excited. The feeling of love she'd always had for him exploded into shards of light that made her tingle all over. She patted the feather that sprouted from her hat and smoothed her hands over her skirt, suddenly nervous. It was really happening.

The coach stopped, and the door was opened for her. She stepped out into the bright sunshine, needing to shield her eyes from the glare as it bounced off the windows of the inn.

Gavin was at her side immediately, briefly glancing inside the coach, perhaps to see if there were other passengers. Overly eager, she threw herself at him and held him tightly, and then realized how inappropriate her behavior was.

She stepped away. "I'm so sorry for being ardent. I was just so happy to hear from you, Gavin. Please forgive my zeal."

Gavin blinked and said nothing, his eyes not leaving her face. "Your enthusiasm has always been one of your finest qualities," he answered, giving her a slight smile. He turned and ordered his driver to retrieve her things, and she suddenly felt ashamed at the shabby condition of everything. Her valise, her shoes, her traveling suit, and everything she had brought with her was fit for the rag man.

Once settled inside his landau, she talked incessantly, exclaiming over the trees and the wildflowers, the handsome carriage and the fine roads. She sounded like Birdie, unable to keep her mouth shut.

"And I haven't heard from Birdie in months," Robbie went on. "Not since she got married."

Gavin glanced at her. "She's married?"

"Yes, to a nice man. Well, he used to be my beau, but you

know Birdie. She always gets what she wants," she said lightly. "And I don't want to sound mean, I want her to be happy, but she has always gotten her way, if you remember."

Gavin watched the landscape pass by; he nodded but said nothing.

But as much blathering as Robbie had done in the carriage, when they arrived at his country estate, she couldn't speak at all. If she had thought the castle back home was imposing, this mansion was, well, truly a mansion by storybook standards. It was enormous!

"Welcome to Erskine House," Gavin said as they pulled up to the grand entrance.

Robbie glanced up at the bowed windows and wrought iron balconies that jutted from the second story. The only thing she could think to say was, "There must be over a hundred rooms in this house."

Gavin chuckled beside her. "Perhaps not one hundred, but truthfully, I have never counted. In fact, there are rooms I have not even seen as yet."

Robbie put her hands to her cheeks. "I am in awe, truly in awe. I shall make a point of finding every room in the place and letting you know what it could be used for," she said with enthusiasm.

Gavin merely smiled as the footman opened the landau door. Gavin alit and helped Robbie out of the carriage. He gave orders to the footman and the driver, and took Robbie's elbow, leading her up the grand steps to the entry. Robbie stopped.

"What's wrong?" Gavin asked.

"Not a thing. I just want to stand here and breathe this lovely country air. You have no idea how much I've looked forward to that simple thing: fresh air."

The door flew open and a portly woman with rosy cheeks and frizzy reddish hair rushed out, smiling. She took Robbie's hands in hers. "Aye, lassie, I'm sae' happy to finally meet ye. I'm Mrs. Murray, the housekeeper. Mister Gavin spoke of ye so often I feel I already know a bit of ye."

Robbie warmed to her immediately. "Thank you, Mrs. Murray;

21

I'm certain we'll get along very well. And I hope, with your help, that I won't get lost somewhere in this place, beautiful as it is."

Mrs. Murray turned and gave Gavin a knowing smile. "Ye be right; she is a fine young woman with good manners."

Robbie met some of the other help, and was taken upstairs to her room. After her meager belongings had been deposited inside, she strolled to the open window and looked out over the massive gardens. They were impeccably cared for and bursting with so much color it nearly blinded her. And they rambled on and on in a whimsical fashion that made Robbie smile. She wondered how much of the land before her belonged to Erskine House.

She turned from the window and surveyed the room. With walls brightly papered with birds and trees, it nearly begged the sunshine to enter. A slight breeze ruffled the gauzy ecru curtains, and suddenly Robbie felt as though she were in a fairy tale.

She twirled around the room, touching the ruffled edges of the canopy over the big brass bed, the smooth silkiness of the chair fabrics, the lavish pillows. She was in heaven. She removed her jacket and hung it carefully across the back of a chair, then made her way to what she presumed was the bathroom.

She touched the expensive soap, lifting it to her nose and inhaling the scent of Otto of Roses. The bar was so beautifully etched, she was afraid to spoil it by using it. She washed her face and pressed the soft towel against her skin, hardly remembering when she'd felt something so luxurious. She straightened her blouse, tucking in a wayward hem, and smoothed her hair, then left to find Gavin.

On the landing outside her room, she met Mrs. Murray.

"I'm to tell ye that the master will be back shortly; he had an errand to run." She winked at Robbie. "Maybe 'tis to buy ye a special gift, aye? In the meanwhile, come down and have a wee cuppa with me. I know ye must be dry as dust after that ride."

Her heart bursting with newfound love and contentment, Robbie followed the housekeeper down the stairs of her new home, disappointed that Gavin wouldn't be joining them.

• • •

Gavin rode his gelding hard into the village. Birdie was married? His heart had dropped to his shoes when he heard it. He could barely think straight, much less have an intelligent conversation with Robbie. He wondered if she had seen the look on his face when she'd told him Birdie had wed someone else. He hoped he'd hidden it.

He dismounted and tossed the reins over the post in front of the coffeehouse and went inside. His friend, Faith Baker, was serving a customer tea and a scone. She waved at him. Faith was not a pretty woman, but she was attractive. Her best feature, she always told Gavin, was her eyes, which were an enchanting shade of violet. When she worked, she always wore a scarf over her hair, which was so light it barely had any color at all. Gavin had always heard from other fellows that men and women couldn't be just friends. He disagreed; he and Faith were friends, nothing more.

Gavin took a seat at the back of the establishment and waited for her to finish her duties. He and Faith had been friends since Gavin was in college in Edinburgh. Gavin's mentor, Clifford Baker, was Faith's uncle. Both he and Faith were surprised to learn that Erskine House was part of the Eliot heritage, just outside Galashiels, where Faith was born. She had returned to help her widowed mother with the coffeehouse about the same time Gavin had come to Erskine House.

Faith sat down and cocked her head. "Hmm. I thought you'd bring your bride-to-be to town so I could meet her, having heard so many glowing things about her." When she saw Gavin's expression, she frowned. "What's wrong? Didn't she show up?"

Gavin shook his head. "No. She didn't show up."

Faith's jaw dropped. "You aren't serious!"

Gavin crossed his arms over his chest. "Someone showed up— it just wasn't who I was expecting."

An eager listener, Faith rested her elbows on the table and propped her chin in her hands. "Tell me everything."

"In good faith I wrote to whom I believed to be the girl I was thinking of. She had a twin sister—"

Faith laughed, then put her hand over her mouth.

"She had a twin sister," Gavin repeated. "Their names were so much alike, I couldn't remember for sure which one she was, but I was certain she was Robena, and everyone called her Birdie. See? A Robin. Robena. Birdie. It made sense to me."

"And what was the other one's name?" Faith asked, hanging on his every word.

"Well, Birdie, as it happens, was Roberta, not Robena." He was quiet for a long moment, thinking about his faux pas, then added, "I proposed to the wrong sister."

Faith was momentarily speechless. "So, your bride-to-be isn't this vivacious, crimson-haired beauty with deep dimples?"

Gavin merely shook his head.

Faith frowned, but her eyes were bright with interest. "She's not an ogre, is she?"

"No, no. She's a fine-looking woman. I remember her as always being in her sister's shadow, and even though we often played chess together, I could not have conjured up a picture of her in my mind. That's why I was so stunned when she stepped from the coach. I almost didn't recognize her."

Faith leaned back in her chair. "What are you going to do?"

"I don't know." He looked directly at Faith. "She's so excited to be here, so excited to hear from me. From what little she has said, I would venture to say she was in a fairly awful situation in Edinburgh." He rubbed his hands over his face. "What a miserable cad I'd be if I told her the truth."

"But you can't marry her; for the rest of your life you'll be miserable, not having the woman you love. And…and her too," she added quickly, "realizing the mistake."

"Yes. I know." Gavin traced the pattern on the table top. "Honest to God, Faith, I don't know what I'll do. But I should get back; she's probably wondering why I raced off so quickly in the first place."

• • •

Faith watched him leave, her heart light. Well, well. Perhaps there was a chance for her after all. She and Gavin had been friends for a long time, although Faith had wanted more from the relationship from the onset. But she was careful; she knew that if there was even an inkling of how she felt about him, he'd stop their friendship immediately. She had hoped that once they were both living out in the country, he would look at her a different way. Maybe he still would. She envisioned marrying him and having lovely towheaded children. She had also always teased him about his absent-mindedness, and the fact that he could remember names of people long dead but couldn't recall the name of the person he'd just met. This proved to be true. And maybe to Faith's advantage. She went about her work, humming happily to herself.

Chapter Four

The evening meal was prepared specifically for the arrival of Gavin's betrothed. The oval table in the dining room was set with a lovely linen cloth and the finest china and crystal. There was a vase of flowers from the garden on the old oak sideboard and the plush Turkish carpet covered most of the floor. Shimmering candlelight bathed the room.

Everything was so beautiful and perfect. Robbie was sorry she didn't have something equally as exquisite to wear, but she wore what she had, an out-of-fashion, yellow cotton, princess dress that had taken her nearly a half an hour to button.

She was seated next to one of Gavin's friends whose name was Dr. Colin Innes. Dr. Innes, it seemed, often came to stay at Erskine House; he had one of the small apartments, which he called his own.

He gazed at her, his amber eyes filled with mirth. "And now, Miss Fleming, how do you think you'll enjoy Erskine House? Sorry you have to wed this scholarly rascal, but in time you may come to find him a little agreeable."

Robbie enjoyed the banter. "I can't imagine anything more rewarding than living in this fine house, Dr. Innes. And, as for the master of the house," she said, tossing Gavin a coy smile, "I think I can abide his company from time to time. But what about you? Where do you practice medicine?"

Dr. Innes cleared his throat. "To be honest, Miss Fleming, I haven't practiced since I had my accident."

Of course Robbie had noticed his face, which was badly disfigured. A long, jagged, puckering scar ran from his forehead, over his nose, and across his right cheek, where the skin was scaly and pink. It looked well healed. In spite of it, Robbie could tell that before the accident he had been a very handsome man. His hair was dark and thick and wavy, and he had a powerful physique. Since he brought up the subject of his accident, she ventured, "What happened?"

"I dared come between a street cur and his dinner. Of course the cur won." His voice was flat.

Robbie brought her hand to her chest. "Why was it so important to rescue the animal's dinner?"

"Because it was a bairn in a carriage, unattended."

Robbie gasped. "Oh, my goodness. Did he…was the bairn…"

"I rescued the bairn, but not before the dog had bitten through his abdomen. Then he came after me. Fair exchange, I have always felt, except that I couldn't save the bairn's life; infection from the bite set in immediately."

Robbie expressed an honest sympathetic smile. "I'm so sorry, Dr. Innes."

He took a sip of wine, then looked at her over the rim of his glass. "I haven't treated a patient since."

He said the words matter-of-factly, but Robbie detected pain in his eyes. She had also noticed that Gavin had been very quiet during her exchange with the doctor.

They had just finished the soup, a fine scotch broth, and were now being served the main course, which was crisp duckling in orange sauce and roasted root vegetables.

Robbie tried very hard to curb her enthusiasm; she hadn't tasted food like this since she left home. Perhaps not even then! Actually, her stomach sent up some warnings that it wasn't prepared to handle such richness, which made Robbie eat slowly in spite of her hunger. Knowing that she may be hungry later, she stealthily slipped a jam tart into her pocket.

After dinner, Robbie announced, "The journey has truly tired me out, gentlemen. I believe I will excuse myself and go to my room. Goodnight."

27

Dr. Innes bent low over her hand. "Have a good night, Miss Fleming; I'm so happy we will be friends."

"As am I," she answered, waiting subtly for Gavin to speak.

Gavin, too, took her hand and bent low over it. "Good night, Robbie, I'll see you in the morning."

Disappointed by his lack of enthusiasm, she merely nodded and escaped to her room.

Colin and Gavin retired to the library for their brandy.

"She's delightful. Although, not the red-haired siren you had described." Colin accepted the brandy and settled into a wingback chair by the fireplace. Gavin studied his drink, swirling the amber liquid around in the glass.

Finally he answered, "Yes. She is a delightful person."

"Then what's ailing you, man? She's bright and charming and engaging. Quite pretty, really, if not exactly beautiful, and she has magnificent hair, although, again, not red."

After a long and painful moment, Gavin said, "She's the wrong sister."

Colin frowned, his drink halfway to his mouth. He processed Gavin's answer and finally replied, "You mean to say you wrote and asked the wrong sister to marry you?"

Gavin placed his drink on the table beside him and put his face in his hands. "Their names are so alike. Roberta. Robena. If you were to compare one of them to a bright, exotic bird, wouldn't it be Robena, as in a robin?"

"Or Roberta, as in a bird," Colin countered. He expelled a low whistle. "My God, man, you are a menace to society. Everyone who knows you realizes how terrible you are with names of people living. I could probably ask you to name the obscure Scottish poet who was called 'Ettrick Shepherd' of the Borders, you'd undoubtedly know it."

"James Hogg."

Colin threw up his hands in exasperation.

"It was all so spur of the moment," Gavin explained. "I'm not usually like that, but when I get an idea into my head, I act on it. I was so certain."

He lifted his head and looked at his friend, briefly recalling how well Robbie handled Colin's disfigurement. Because he and Colin were close friends, he'd become accustomed to it. Before the accident, Colin had been a fanciful playboy. Now women shunned him. Gavin's friend Faith barely spoke to him, and when she did, she refused to look at him. Gavin didn't know what it would take to make Colin want to practice medicine again.

Gavin thought back to the dinner conversation. Robbie had not even flinched when she and Colin were introduced. How would Birdie have reacted?

"What are you going to do?" Colin broke into his thoughts.

"Faith asked me the same thing."

"So that's where you rushed off to so quickly." Colin snorted. "I'm sure she did. She's probably dancing a lively jig right now over your mistake."

Gavin shook his head. "She's not like that; she just a friend, nothing more."

"Says you," Colin replied. "I'd like to be a fly on the wall of the coffeehouse about now and see what she's thinking... and planning."

"You think everyone has a motive, don't you?"

Colin cocked his head. "Don't they?"

"I disagree about Faith. We're just friends, always have been."

"You mean to say you're not attracted to her?"

"In that way?" He shook his head. "She isn't my type."

Gavin was quiet a moment, and then said, "Roberta, or Birdie, is married."

"Well, that solves one problem, doesn't it?"

"From what Robbie said, Birdie married Robbie's beau."

Colin shook his head. "She sounds like a real keeper," he said with sarcasm. "It looks to me like you've made the most intelligent mistake of your life."

• • •

Robbie had fallen asleep immediately, but awoke when moonlight streamed into the room, over her pillow. Feeling refreshed, she slid from the wonderful bedding, checked her father's timepiece, and noted that it was nearly three in the morning.

She lit the lamp beside her, went to her valise, and rummaged through it to find her writing materials. Noting there was another lamp on the desk near the window, she lit it and settled down to write an episode that was due shortly.

Lady Perlina, dressed up in her short maid's outfit, lifted the breakfast tray and entered the Baron Von Klippen's bedroom. The baron was in bed lounging against lush pillows, reading. His eyeglasses were perched on the end of his nose and his nightshirt was open at the neck, revealing a thicket of black hair that made Perlina's loins tingle.

He looked up. "Ach, fräulein; you bring the baron breakfast, jawohl?"

Perlina gave him a demure smile. "And much, much more." She put the tray beside the bed, leaning over so he could gaze at her ample bosom, which nearly popped from the top of her uniform. His gaze lingered there, and he licked his lips. Perlina noticed movement beneath the covers. Pretending to lose her balance, she fell against him, feeling his hardness.

"Oh, baron," she exclaimed, moving about as if trying to regain her balance, arousing herself and hoping to arouse him further, "I'm so sorry..."

The baron took her wrist and pulled her toward him. "I am not sorry, fräulein." He reached beneath her short skirt and touched her; she was already quite sopping wet, indeed.

Suddenly he threw the covers back, revealing his manly length, long, hard, and pink with its purple bulbous head twitching in her direction. "Sit," he instructed.

Lady Perlina straddled him and thus began breakfast with the baron.

Robbie checked the time. It was nearly five, too early to get up and disrupt the household and too late to go back to bed. But she was craving a cup of tea, and since she and Mrs. Murray had taken tea the day before, Robbie knew exactly where to find what she needed. Pulling on her shabby robe over her nightgown, she pocketed her purloined jam tart, blew out the lamps, and left her room.

• • •

Colin had raided the kitchen and made himself a snack of cold duck between two slices of the cook's excellent bread. A lamp was lit on the table. He heard a sound behind him, and turned to find Robbie standing there, surprised to find anyone else up, no doubt.

"Oh, I'm sorry," she apologized. "I was going to fix myself a cup of tea, but I can…"

"Yes, do," Colin answered. "I could use the company." He looked at her, her fine, wavy brown hair cascading over her shoulders, making her desirable and delicate at the same time. "Couldn't sleep, either?"

Robbie went about making her tea. "Oh, I slept hard for enough hours. Before this, I never got this kind of rest. Either the wind nearly blew my door down or my neighbor's snoring almost cracked my window." She tossed him a warm glance. "It wasn't exactly quiet where I lived."

Colin was interested. "And just where did Gavin find you, anyway?"

"I'm surprised he found me at all, truth to tell." Robbie smiled. "Actually, I had finished university in Edinburgh and, well, had a small, inconsequential job, after which I would go to a clinic and help a friend with her patients."

"Ah, a Florence Nightingale."

Robbie laughed. "Not even close." She brought her teacup

to the table, pulled a jam tart—one he'd seen her pinch from the dinner table—from her pocket and sat across from him. "There are so many young women and girls, even, who roam the streets of Edinburgh, bait for all the criminals who prey on the weak and the lonely." She shrugged. "I just like to help."

Colin was all too aware of the appalling conditions of parts of Edinburgh. "And you grew up with a twin sister, is that right?"

Robbie nibbled on her tart, closed her eyes, and made a sound of satisfaction in her throat, then studied her tea. "That's where I met Gavin. My sister and I shared a tutor with him."

Gleaning interesting information from a willing participant, Colin continued. "And your sister?"

"Fraternal. We look and act nothing alike."

"Is that a good thing or a bad thing?" Colin asked, his tone teasing.

At this, Robbie chuckled. "I used to think it wasn't fair that my sister got the beautiful red curls and deep dimples, making it likely that every boy on the island would trip over himself trying to get her attention."

"And now?"

"Oh, Birdie and I have always had our differences, but she is my sister, after all, and I love her in spite of herself!" This she said with a warm laugh.

"And what became of your sister, Birdie?" Colin knew this as well.

Robbie finished the tart and brushed crumbs from her mouth. "She got married and moved to Glasgow."

"And here you are, going to be married as well," he added.

Robbie glowed. Colin could see that she was very much in love with Gavin, and his heart ached for her.

"I can't tell you what wonderful timing Gavin had. I don't like to dwell on this, but I was two days away from being put out into the street because my landlady claimed my room for her nephew."

Colin narrowed his eyes. "You mean you wouldn't have had a place to stay?"

Robbie shook her head, still glowing. "It's a miracle that this all is happening to me. I can't believe how lucky I am."

Colin took a chance. "This morning Gavin has a meeting in Melrose and I'm going in to Galashiels to pick up my mail. Would you care to ride along?"

Her face lit up. "I'd like that. There are a few things I should probably purchase."

Colin considered her gown. His sister sewed fashionable clothing for ladies in Edinburgh, and he'd seen the shabby cloth of last night's outfit, as well as the shoes, worn nearly to the sole. She probably had few funds. He wanted to take Gavin out and give him a whipping.

"That reminds me," he said. "Gavin said I was to take you to the dressmaker and have a few gowns sewn for you." He winked at her. "A little wedding gift, I presume."

"Oh, how wonderful!" She looked a bit sheepish. "I must admit I came here with very little. I didn't know if he would notice."

Colin knew the owner of the dress shop well enough to tell her to put the items on an account under Gavin's name. Still, he wondered what in the bloody hell Gavin was going to do in the long run. And, Colin had better have someone ride ahead to the dressmaker's shop and make sure they were aware of their visitor in the morning.

Chapter Five

Robbie had worried about what she was going to wear on her surprise shopping trip, but settled for her traveling suit. The pieces were easy to remove for a fitting. Yet another part of the fairy tale—getting new clothes!

Colin picked her up in a chaise and helped her into the seat. "I'll drop you at the dressmaker's, if that's all right, and I'll return after my errands."

Nervous and excited, Robbie replied, "Thank you for being so accommodating, Dr. Innes."

Colin sighed. "If we're going to be friends, you must call me Colin."

"I will," she answered. "And thank you again."

They rode along at a comfortable pace. The air had a slight chill to it but the sky was a clear blue. "What a fine day. It's so incredibly lovely out here. Well, not as lovely as home, but it has a certain beauty," she said with a breathy sigh. "It's like a piece of heaven compared with the back streets of Edinburgh."

Colin nodded. "I've been to those back streets a few times. The smell alone would make a person faint."

"I almost did once or twice, I have to admit."

"I'm curious to know what your 'inconsequential' job was, if you're willing to tell me."

Robbie glanced at her lap. How much to admit? "I...I just write little articles for various newspapers. It doesn't pay much."

"Writing is noble, but misunderstood, I believe." He gave her a quick look. "Would I be looking at a future Brontë sister?"

"Hardly." She didn't add that she couldn't be compared to any of the fine English writers she had read.

They entered the village and he stopped in front of a shop that featured a drawn figure of a mannequin. He came around to help Robbie down.

"The seamstress is expecting you. Her name is Mrs. Ferguson" He tipped his hat and waited until Robbie entered the store before he left.

Robbie had never been in a seamstress's shop before. Even as girls, she and Birdie had worn clothing that was made for them by a croft woman on the island. And when she went on to university, Robbie was very thrifty about what she bought.

The fabrics were so beautiful; Robbie didn't know how she was ever going to decide. Also, it had been so long since she'd had anything new, she wasn't even sure of the styles anymore. Fortunately, Mrs. Ferguson was very helpful, and in a short while, Robbie had been fitted for a number of day dresses in colors that complemented her complexion, a tea gown of ecru linen, a forest green ball gown, and had been shown different styles of wedding gowns!

"I just can't buy a wedding gown, Mrs. Ferguson. Surely I could get married in one of these." Robbie felt terrible about how much of Gavin's money she was spending as it was.

"Nonsense," the woman uttered, fussing with Robbie's camisole. "When a person marries, she wears a wedding gown, like it or not. And," she added, "I don't want to upset you dear, but you may want to order some new underthings."

Robbie flushed. "Oh, I know my things are a bit shabby, but until now I haven't had any reason to replace them. They're still fine."

Mrs. Ferguson shook her head. "I know Mister Gavin, and he would want you to have everything you need, dear."

Robbie finally demurred. "But only what's necessary, all right?"

The seamstress clucked her tongue and made some notes on a pad. "Now, about that wedding dress?"

Robbie had eyed a silk ecru fabric when she'd first stepped into the store. "Well, something simple, then." She went on to explain what she thought was appropriate. Mrs. Ferguson frowned, but when Robbie insisted, the seamstress agreed.

When she'd finished the fittings, Robbie was lightheaded and giddy. After thanking Mrs. Ferguson for her help and her patience, Robbie stepped outside and noticed the coffeehouse across the street. Her stomach rumbled. A cup of tea would be wonderful.

Lifting her skirt, she made her way around a bit of trash and a puddle, marveling at how much cleaner the streets were here than they were in Edinburgh. A little bell tinkled over the door as she stepped inside the shop, and a young woman with very blonde hair glanced at her. She smiled as she approached Robbie.

"Will you have some tea and a fresh scone?"

"Yes, thank you. That would be wonderful." Robbie went to a small table and took a seat. There were potted plants by the front windows and each table was gaily adorned with a single flower. In a short while the young woman came toward her, carrying a tray. Robbie said, "This is a pleasant place."

The woman nodded. "It belongs to my mam. She's been a wee bit under the weather lately so I've been helping out. It's usually buzzing with activity; today is uncommonly quiet." She put the tray down and introduced herself. "I'm Faith Baker. And you must be Gavin's friend."

Robbie chuckled. "I guess you could say we're friends—actually, we are to be married. I just came from the seamstress and ordered my wedding gown."

Miss Baker studied her, her fingers steepled against her lips. "Indeed? And Gavin set up this fitting?"

"Apparently so, or that's what his friend Colin told me."

Miss Baker shivered. "Dr. Ugly. The fellow with the creepy face. It's no wonder he's no longer practicing medicine; who would want to go to him for anything?"

Robbie frowned. "Of course I noticed his scars, but underneath them I discovered the most agreeable gentleman. And it's a shame he doesn't practice," she continued, "because Scotland is in dire need of medical doctors."

Miss Baker lifted a cynical, tawny eyebrow. "Oh, and you know about the need for Scottish physicians, do you?"

Annoyed with the woman's demeanor, Robbie said, "Yes, as a matter of fact I do."

"I see." Suddenly, she asked, "Do you mind if I sit with you?"

Robbie shook her head, but she was surprised and a bit unsettled at the request.

The woman leaned back against the chair and crossed her arms over her chest. She was petite and rather pretty, in a pale, porcelain way. Her skin was so fair and thin one could see the pale blue veins beneath it. "I think there's something you should know."

Robbie took a sip of her tea and replaced the cup in the saucer, surprised to find her hand shaking slightly. "Really?"

"Gavin and I are, should I say, very good friends, if you get my meaning." She gave Robbie a sly look.

Robbie narrowed her gaze, letting the message sink in. "I'm glad he has friends nearby."

Miss Baker snorted a laugh. "Don't be obtuse. You know what I mean."

"Indeed I don't." Robbie refused to be intimidated. "Explain it to me."

Instead, Miss Baker announced, "If, as you say, Gavin arranged to have you fitted for a wedding gown, he's apparently decided not to reveal the truth."

Robbie felt a sudden unpleasant twinge. "The truth?"

"Even if he doesn't want to tell you, I think it only fair that you know he thought you were your sister when he wrote and proposed."

Robbie didn't want to believe it, but the nausea gathering in her stomach told her otherwise. "I don't believe you."

Faith Baker reached across to take Robbie's hand, but Robbie pulled it away. "It's not my intention to hurt you. Gavin Eliot is a very honorable man. I'm sure you know this. He will live with his mistake rather than embarrass or upset you."

Robbie sat frozen, the woman's words stabbing at her like shards of glass. She could no longer hear her speaking; she just saw her lips moving. Whatever else she had to say wasn't important.

The door opened and Robbie looked up to see Colin in the doorway, his forehead creased into a deep frown.

"What have you said to her?"

Faith Baker stood and faced him, her fists on her hips. "I told her the truth. I think she deserves to know it."

He gave her a cold smile. "All to benefit you, I don't doubt."

"Whether that's true or not, I think she deserves to know the situation so she'll be able to handle it. If Gavin actually ordered the dressmaker to make her a wedding gown, then he's more noble than I thought. Neither of them should have to live this lie; she had to be told."

Robbie hoped to see that the woman was not telling the truth written on Colin's ravaged face. But there, Robbie saw that all she had been told was true.

"It still wasn't up to you to tell her anything."

"And let her blissfully believe Gavin hadn't gone a day without thinking of her? How cruel." She pulled a cloth from her apron pocket and began wiping off a table.

"What is cruel is you descending upon her like a jackal."

Robbie had had enough. Finding her strength, she stood and took a deep breath. "No, Colin, I'm actually glad she told me. Obviously Gavin didn't have the nerve to do it; someone had to." She glanced at Colin. "So Gavin didn't order me a new wardrobe?"

Colin studied the floor then shook his head.

If Robbie were transparent at the moment, they both would have seen her heart shatter into dozens of bleeding pieces. Fortunately they could see nothing, for she steeled herself against showing any feelings at all.

She took coins from her purse and put them on the table. "Thank you for the tea, Miss Baker." She walked to the door.

"The chaise is outside. I'll be there in a minute," Colin said.

Once outside, Robbie walked toward the inn where she had been dropped off, hoping that was where to purchase a ticket to Edinburgh. She had no idea what she would do when she got there, but she sure as bloody hell wasn't going to stay here a moment longer than she had to. Under her breath she apologized to her preacher father for swearing, as she always did.

She heard Colin's steps behind her. "Miss Fleming. Robbie."

Bracing herself again, she turned and tried to smile. "Colin?"

He caught up with her. "Where are you going?"

"Seriously," she began, hoping her voice didn't break. "You don't expect me to return to Erskine House now, do you?"

His shoulders slumped and he closed his eyes. "God, what a mess." He took her hands and looked into her eyes. "The coach isn't coming through until tomorrow morning. Come back to Erskine House with me now; at least you'll be comfortable until then."

"Comfortable? Knowing that I'm not the woman Gavin expected? I'm sure they have a room here at the inn," she answered. "I'll be just fine. And Colin," she pleaded, "please do not tell Gavin about this. Just tell him I got a wire from a friend in need, and I'll leave the address with the innkeeper so he'll know where to send my things."

With a heavy heart, she walked bravely away from him, head high, shoulders back, and went straight into the inn, where she nearly collapsed against the closed door.

• • •

All the way to and from his meeting, Gavin's head was crammed with thoughts of Robbie. No, she wasn't vivacious like her sister, and she didn't have hair the color of fire or dimples a man could drown in. But she had other qualities that he certainly had noticed. She took to people easily and appeared comfortable without either needing to monopolize the conversation or sink into a corner and disappear. She conversed well on so many subjects.

Mrs. Murray had told him of her conversation with Robbie over tea, and Gavin had been amazed at what she'd been doing when she'd gotten his missive. Working at one of those pathetic clinics in the slums of Edinburgh? Coming in contact with drug addicts and prostitutes? No wonder Colin's disfigurement didn't bother her. She'd probably seen more hell than any young woman should have to. And Birdie went off and married Robbie's beau. Had he not noticed that quality in Birdie before? Had she really been as selfish and self-involved as Robbie suggested to Mrs. Murray? She certainly hadn't told him that, in so many words, although there were signs.

Birdie would have made a fine-looking wife and mistress of the manor. She was vibrant and beautiful. And he had always loved her. Hadn't he? What was it that he loved about her? Maybe it was her coquettish manner. And surely he was attracted to her physical beauty. All superficial qualities, to be sure. Was he foolishly in love with the idea of being in love? How could that happen to him?

With Erskine House in the distance, he rode on and came to a decision.

Tossing his reins to Ben, the stable boy, Gavin ran into the house; Mrs. Murray came out of the kitchen. "Where's Robbie?"

Mrs. Murray frowned and shook her head. "I ha'ent seen her since she and Dr. Innes left for the village earlier this morning."

Gavin took the stairs two at a time and knocked on Robbie's door. He bent close but heard no movement.

As he made his way down the stairs, Colin came in through the front door. "You took Robbie into the village this morning?"

Colin stood at the bottom of the stairs, his hands fisted against his hips. "I did."

"Is she with you?"

"No. She's not."

Puzzled, Gavin asked, "Where is she?"

"Probably buying a ticket to Edinburgh, thanks to your friend Faith Baker."

Gavin stumbled on the last step but righted himself. "What?"

"While I was doing errands, Robbie decided to have a cuppa at the coffeehouse."

Gavin was still baffled. "So she met Faith; is that a bad thing?"

"Not unless you agree with the notion that Faith told her the truth."

Gavin grabbed onto the newel and lowered himself to the bottom step. "Faith told her I proposed to the wrong twin? Why would she do that?"

Colin snorted. "Why would she do that? She's a conniving young woman, Gavin. She wants you for herself."

"No, she's not like that."

"She is, you know. I don't know what more needs to happen for you to believe me." Colin had a trump card for Faith Baker, and when the time was right, he would use it against her. But not yet.

Gavin put his face in his hands. "God, Robbie must be humiliated."

"Oh, yes, she was. But she didn't show much. She was logical and reasonable all the way to the inn where she probably fainted onto the faded Persian rug. She told me to tell you she'd heard from a friend who was in need, and that you could send her belongings to an address she would leave with the innkeeper."

Gavin had never felt such anguish. His chest hurt and he felt short of breath. He glanced up at Colin. "She can't leave."

Colin's eyes narrowed. "Why should she stay?"

"Because I want her to. I can't claim I love her, but surely we could work something out."

"You're still in love with the sister?"

"Yes. No. I don't know. It doesn't matter."

"It might matter to her," Colin said.

Gavin stood and went to the door, opened it and shouted to the footman. "Bring me the landau."

Colin came up next to him. "Do you think you can handle this alone?" His sarcasm was lost on Gavin.

"I have to. Somehow I have to convince her to stay."

Chapter Six

Robbie tucked her ticket into the pocket of her suit jacket and studied the small room she was able to get until morning. Shabby, but still nicer than her room in Edinburgh. Not wanting to think about Gavin, she thought about her future.

She would go to Lydia and tell her everything. She would sleep on the floor of the clinic if she had to, if Lydia would allow it. That wouldn't be any worse than where she'd been before this. Probably better, knowing how Lydia felt about clean floors.

On the bright side, she still had her job. Ah, but it had been hard enough to write that drivel before; how would she stomach it now? She would have to. She had no choice.

Thoughts of Gavin hammered at her consciousness, insisting on being heard. To be fair, she wasn't totally surprised at recent events. Had not there been one or two occasions when she wondered at his demeanor? Like when he had helped her from the coach and looked into the interior, had he been looking for Birdie, thinking perhaps that Robbie had simply accompanied her?

And he never appeared as delighted to see her as she was to see him. Not once. Colin was more attentive, truth be told. And how foolish she must have seemed! Blithely ensconcing herself into Gavin's home and his life before she'd even seen the interior of the mansion. She was such a fool.

She sagged onto the bed, slid off her shoes and lay down, covering her eyes with her arm. She refused to cry, but tears slid down her face into her ears. Get it over with, she told herself. She didn't need or want pity. She was stronger than that.

Faith Baker's innuendo returned loud and clear. She wondered at the truth in it, but had no reason to disbelieve the woman. What did it matter now, anyway? Robbie was leaving and they could continue their affair without hindrance. She wondered if he would have quit sleeping with the woman if Birdie had actually shown up.

The full awareness of her folly hit her, and she stopped her tears. She was the *biggest* fool, wasn't she? She had just wanted it so badly; she refused to see all of the hints that surrounded her from the beginning. Humiliation. That's what she felt; abject humiliation. And it was her fault; no one else was to blame.

"Stupid girl," she muttered.

It wasn't long before there was a knock at the door. With a heavy sigh, Robbie got up and crossed the room. Probably the inn-keeper, she thought. She wiped her face and opened the door. And looked up into Gavin's beautiful blue eyes. "What do you want?"

He looked contrite. "May I come in, please?"

She opened the door and let him enter, closing the door behind him.

He turned and studied her, frowning. "You've been crying."

She huffed and spun away from him. "You're some detective, aren't you?"

"I know what you must think of me—"

"Oh, let's not go into that," she interrupted. "The only mistake you made was proposing to the wrong sister. I guess that could happen to anyone. I'm the one who should be blamed, for assuming the letter was meant for me when I knew deep down in my soul that you'd barely looked at me ten years ago and that Birdie had stolen your heart."

"I admit that was true. But to be perfectly honest, I'm not sure how things would have worked out had Birdie showed up on my doorstep instead of you."

She swung around to face him, surprised at his answer. "What do you mean?"

"Yes, Birdie was pretty. I wasn't the only lad who thought he wanted her heart. Was she self-involved?" He shrugged. "I didn't know it at the time. It didn't matter. Was she shallow? Probably, but again, a young lad doesn't often look beneath the skin."

"So what are you saying?" she asked cautiously.

"We're all adults now. If Birdie hasn't changed, she wouldn't be the woman I would want as my wife."

Head high, Robbie answered, "And now I suppose you're going to tell me I am."

"Yes."

Robbie stumbled and grabbed the back of a chair, her ears ringing. "You're saying that now you want to marry me?"

"Yes."

Robbie collapsed into the chair, her hand covering her mouth. What could she say? In spite of what he'd done to her, she still loved him. He didn't love her, but perhaps she could love enough for both of them. "Are you certain?"

Now he smiled, one that reached his eyes. He pulled her from the chair and into a warm embrace. "Yes."

• • •

Gavin watched her acclimate herself to the house and the staff. One day he found her tending to a cut on Ben's arm, cleaning it, wrapping it, telling him to make sure he changed the bandage every day, and that if he couldn't do it himself, she would help him.

She went into the garden, but not to pick the flowers. Instead she would sit and weed the patches, sometimes for hours. He would notice that by dinner time, the freckles on her nose had become more pronounced and her face had more color. She was quite fetching, really.

At night, when he made a tour of the house, he often noticed a light in her window when everyone else but him was asleep. He pondered it; he was curious. Couldn't she sleep? He would have to ask her.

During the time Robbie waited for her new wardrobe, she strolled the grounds, investigated the empty wings of the house and spoke with all the staff. She and Gavin did not breakfast together, but Robbie understood that he was busy, and she managed by herself.

She took her breakfast alone in the breakfast parlor where the cook was told to make Robbie anything she wanted. Robbie took a spoonful of the warm porridge and closed her eyes, savoring the flavor. So this was how it was supposed to taste. Warm, rich, thick and laced with honey; a proper feast. She reached across the table for a roll, one she'd come to love, which was called a "bap" but was simply a light, floury roll that melted in one's mouth. If she wasn't careful, she'd get fat just eating breakfast.

As she ate, her gaze wandered around the bright, sunny room. Yellow flowers with lively green stems papered the walls; the ceiling was high and white, the floor was a dark, rich brown wood, probably oak, she thought, like in the dining room. But in truth it was one of her favorite rooms. It was warm and cozy and friendly.

Mrs. Murray scurried into the room. "Your dresses have arrived." She gave Robbie an excited smile.

Robbie's stomach fluttered. Suddenly she couldn't take another bite of food, delicious as it was. She swallowed. "Everything?"

With a knowing smile, the housekeeper said, "Aye, even your wedding gown."

Robbie released a rush of air. "Does Mister Eliot know?"

"He's waitin' for ye in the conservatory."

With more self-confidence than she felt, Robbie took one last sip of tea, dabbed at her lips, and pushed back from the table. Before she left the room, she poked her head into the kitchen and thanked the cook for breakfast.

She had waited for this day, but also dreaded it. Gavin had been nothing but kind and courteous since she'd agreed to marry him. They had supped together in the gigantic dining room, which they both agreed was superfluous. They had even had a few lively discussions about the state of the country, which had astonished Gavin. He admitted that he didn't know many women who were interested in the policies of the land. At times she could feel him watching her. She wondered what his thoughts were. Robbie quietly thought about her writing and wondered what this scholarly man would think of her if he knew. It wasn't a pleasant feeling.

The conservatory was at the far side of Gavin's study. She had marveled at the room weeks before, but since it was virtually empty, she hadn't returned. It was constructed of wrought iron and glass and had cast iron beams soaring into the skylight. She hadn't tended plants much, although as a girl, she had grown some lovely rose bushes that even some of the noblewomen at home had praised.

She poked her head around the door. Gavin stood by the slanted windows, hands clasped behind his back, appearing to study the landscape beyond. She stood a moment, gazing at him, noting his wide shoulders and narrow hips, and a stab of desire rose up inside her. She loved everything about him, down to the tiny mole he had on his left earlobe. She wondered if anyone else had even noticed it. She must have made a noise, for he turned.

"Good, you're here. Come," he said, motioning her to the far side of the room where the sun was streaming in over a leather couch.

Once they were seated, he gazed at her, a look that made Robbie uncomfortable. "Are you ready for a wedding?"

"Aye, I am."

He took a deep breath. "Here's what I thought we would do. Correct me if you want to change anything."

As if she wanted to change one single thing! Oh, maybe just one, she thought, gazing at his beautiful face and feeling her love for him pour through her veins.

He took her hands. "I thought perhaps we should marry quickly then plan a ball and reception for our friends and my family." He studied her a moment. "Is there any family you would like to invite?"

As much as Robbie wanted to shove her marriage to Gavin in Birdie's face, she couldn't do it. "No. Besides Birdie, I have no other family living in Scotland, and if you don't mind, I'd rather not see her just now. Perhaps later." *Perhaps never.*

"I understand. My family, as you well know, is quite large and awfully noisy. I hope they won't annoy you too much."

Robbie remembered them well. "You have the kind of family every girl wants, didn't you know that?"

Puzzled, he asked, "What do you mean?"

"There always seemed to be such joy among you and your siblings. Did you never fight? My sister and I were nearly always at odds. I recall watching your older brother carrying your baby sister on his shoulders, through the streets, not caring that some of the lads heckled him because he was doing 'a woman's job.'" Robbie shook her head and smiled. "Your family was amazing."

Gavin looked thoughtful. "I suppose you're right. I had never really thought about how they appeared to others; I just took the lot of them for granted."

"Do you miss not seeing them regularly?"

Gavin leaned back and rested his arm along the back of the settee, innocently touching the back of Robbie's neck. She was afraid to shift in her seat for fear he would move it.

"I do miss them. I've thought to bring my little sister, Cassie, here, just to give the others a break. She's a precocious one, she is," he finished, giving Robbie a warm look. "But now, of course, I'd talk it over with you before I made the decision."

"Oh, Gavin, I still feel like the interloper. As far as I'm concerned, your entire family could camp out with us."

"I fear their boisterousness would have you running into the woods." He studied her a moment, then slapped his knee. "Now, let's get do some planning. I'm anxious to wed, aren't you?"

Oh, Robbie thought, *you have no idea.*

Chapter Seven

After the festivities, Robbie and Gavin greeted local guests; the cook and Mrs. Murray made sure there was plenty to eat and drink.

Later, when everyone had gone, Gavin walked her to her room. "I'm sorry we won't be able to get away right now, but... well, you understand."

"Had you planned a trip with Birdie?" Robbie was surprised she could even bring up her sister's name on her wedding day.

Gavin shook his head. "I'm not much good at this, as you can see, so perhaps we can plan something a bit later on." He bowed low over her hand, kissed it, and turned.

"Are you coming back?" she said to his retreating form.

On a half turn, he answered, "I'm sure you must be tired, Robbie. I'll see you in the morning."

Robbie flounced into her room and closed the door. Some wedding night. She removed her gown as quickly as she could and carefully hung it back in the wardrobe. She got into her old night-gown and robe. No point in wearing one of the new ones Mrs. Ferguson had insisted she order. But, wedding or not, Robbie had work to do. If she hadn't already been paid for these last few pieces, she would quit writing them all together. And do what? Pine away and moon over a husband who had married her out of obligation? That wasn't her style. She abhorred pity parties. No, he liked her; he wanted her here. That was enough for her—for now.

As she sat at her desk, she was beginning to think this whole situation was unacceptable. But she had work to do.

Pulling out her writing material, she began:

"Oh, please, Elijah," Sallie begged, loving someone else to touch her besides herself. "Quickly, to the back of the stable."

He was close on her heels as they darted further into a darkened corner. When they reached an empty stall, Sallie pulled her dress and petticoat up and threw herself on the hay. Elijah, perhaps more clever than she'd given him credit for, lit a lantern and placed it on the ledge. He then removed his trousers and lay down beside her.

Without having to ask him, she found his big, rough hands on her again, rubbing and moving a finger in and out. Miss Sallie shuddered at the sensations that raced through her blood. She spread her legs wider, allowing him more room, and suddenly he was between her legs, licking her. Miss Sallie Wiggins nearly screamed, the pleasure was so delightful! She grabbed his hair and pulled him closer, pressing his face against her, grinding and grinding until she felt herself coming apart, writhing and bucking against his mouth. When Miss Sallie came back to earth, her ears were ringing and her heart beating solidly against her ribcage.

"Your turn now, Miss Sallie, your turn."

It took no time for Miss Sallie Wiggins to know what Elijah wanted. She was on her knees beside him in a quick moment, finding him thick, hard, and waiting for her mouth.

Robbie's own feelings always caught fire when she wrote this drivel, but she usually just pushed them away. It would be different now; with a man to satisfy her within shouting distance, she wondered how long, if ever, it would be before satisfaction would come. Obviously not this night. An ugly thought poked her. Was Gavin with Faith Baker? She could just envision their meeting.

So 'tis done then?

It's done. Poor wren, all alone in her bed and lucky me, here with you.

Robbie could write a scene with the dialogue, but putting Gavin in bed with another woman was the last thing she wanted to do, even if it was merely on paper.

She lay awake for what seemed like hours, wondering how she was going to fulfill her own desires, not wanting to succumb to the method used by Miss Sallie Wiggins before Elijah took her virginity.

• • •

The next morning she lay in bed and took a moment to see if she felt any different than she had the day before. She didn't.

With a weary sigh, she slid from the bed, washed her face, and put on one of her new frocks. She combed out her hair, returning it to the simple chignon she had always worn in the past. She studied herself in the mirror. Same freckles across her nose, more prominent now that she'd been outside, same heart-shaped face, same blue eyes. And, thanks to Jeremy's description, same bundle of hair the color of Swiss chocolate. Except for the lovely gown, nothing had changed. She was still a plain, unadorned virgin.

And she didn't know what in the bloody hell (*sorry, Papa*) she was supposed to do in this colossal house. She was not the type to sit about and do nothing. She never had been.

• • •

Colin found Gavin in his library, studying a map of ancient Egypt. Gavin glanced up briefly, then returned to his task.

"Well, how are you this morning?" Colin asked.

Gavin gave him a brief nod. "Well. And you?"

Colin frowned. "That's all you have to say?"

"What else do you want me to say?"

"Christ, man," Colin replied, "you're married. You have a bride who adores you. How was last night?"

Gavin looked up, his expression pained.

Colin huffed. "My God. Don't tell me you didn't spend the night with your new bride."

At this, Gavin lowered his gaze. "How could I? She knows I don't love her, how can I ask to bed her?"

Colin sank into a chair and rubbed his hands over his face. "You don't ever plan to, is that it? You expect her to live like a nun for the rest of her life? And what of you? Will you be celibate as well, or will you seek your pleasure elsewhere? You won't have far to go; Faith Baker will always be hovering about."

"You keep shoving her at me. She and I are friends, nothing more."

"Again, I don't think so. She'd bed you in a heartbeat."

"I don't want to bed Faith. And what am I supposed to do with Robbie, walk in there and demand my rights as a husband?"

"Have you ever slept with a woman you didn't love?"

"Yes," Gavin answered, "of course I have. But this is different."

"How, may I ask?" Colin's frustration with his friend was deepening.

"I respect her too much."

Again, Colin shook his head and sighed. "She looked beautiful yesterday, didn't she?"

"Yes. She looked beautiful. In my whole life I had not realized that she could be so beautiful, because I was always blinded by her sister's magnificence."

Colin swore. "I'd sure like to get a look at this splendid creature. No woman can be that spectacular."

"At one time I thought she was. Maybe if I saw her again, I'd change my mind, but old thoughts still bugger me, and I can't seem to get them out of my head. I was an innocent lad, and when a creature like Birdie Fleming came into my life, I thought I'd died and gone to heaven."

Colin felt a stab of disgust. "Wake up, man. Get over this obsession you have for your wife's sister." He walked to the window and saw Robbie throwing a ball for one of the dogs, a long, low-slung Corgi with big ears. When the dog retrieved the prize, he ran back to her and dropped it at her feet once more. Colin had worked hard to rid himself of his fear of dogs after his accident. For weeks he had gone out of his way to avoid any route where he knew there were dogs, either pets or strays. He realized it was foolish; he didn't love them, but he no longer feared them.

Robbie bent over and scratched the animal behind the ears, her face wreathed in a smile. Ben, the stable boy, approached her and said something, and Robbie nodded with enthusiasm, and then threw her head back and laughed.

"Come here," Colin said.

Gavin joined him at the window.

"What do you see?"

Gavin studied the scene. "She's comfortable with everyone. One day she asked me why there weren't any dogs in the house. I couldn't answer her. It had not dawned on me to have a dog in the house even though there were always dogs at home."

"You poor, miserable sap. I've known you for a long time and thought I knew you well, but the depths of your separation from the real world is frightening."

"What do you mean?" Gavin was truly puzzled.

"When I asked you to tell me what you saw, I expected you to say something about Robbie herself, not about the damned dogs."

Gavin retreated back to his desk. "I did. I said she was comfortable with everyone."

"If I were you, looking at my new bride, I'd say something like, 'Just look at her. Look at the way her tresses shimmer in the sunshine, catching rays of red and gold in that mass of beautiful sable hair. I want to see that hair fanned across my pillow again tonight.'"

Gavin gave him a serious look and then went back to his map. "Is that truly what you see when you look at her?"

"What if it is? I'm at least capable of admiring a woman whether she's a friend, a stranger, or another man's wife."

"I can't bed her, Colin." His voice was firm.

"What will you tell your family when they arrive?"

"I'll tell them nothing."

"You don't suppose they're intuitive enough to notice that something is wrong with your relationship?" Colin was getting more frustrated by the moment.

"Things will all work out in the end," Gavin said with conviction.

Colin simply shook his head and walked to the door. "You live in your own little world, don't you?"

As he walked through the door, he heard Gavin say, "I always have."

He retreated to the side lawn, where Robbie was now sitting on the grass, her lap full of wiggly Corgi pups.

"Aren't these the most adorable little things?" She picked one up and rubbed its soft face against her own. "Do you suppose Gavin would mind if I took one for myself? I've never had a pet of my own; Father always said that cats belonged in the barn and dogs in the fields, herding sheep."

Suddenly she gasped and looked up at him. "Oh, Colin. Do you fear dogs now?"

He hunkered down and touched one of the pups. "I did at first; a normal reaction, I suppose. Truthfully, I will probably never have a dog of my own, but I don't have any fear when I'm around them.

"These little ones are herders as well. If you take one, be prepared to be nudged around by its cold nose." How could Gavin not see this woman for what she truly was? He wondered if his friend expected everything to go on as it did, nothing changing. In Gavin's world, that made perfect sense, but Colin didn't think it would make any sense at all to Robbie.

"Gavin is so engrossed in his maps of Egypt I don't think he'd notice if you brought them all in with you."

She gave him a quick glance. "He's a scholar; that's who he is. I've always admired his intelligence."

"Oh, he's intelligent, all right. It's his ability to deal with people that I worry about."

She lowered her gaze and stroked the pups, who wiggled and burrowed into the fabric of her gown. When Robbie looked up at him, she wore an unreadable expression. "Don't give up on him, Colin. He needs your friendship."

At that, Colin actually laughed and started to walk away. "I'd have given up on him a long time ago if he wasn't my best friend, Robbie."

She watched him go, noting that he, too, was tall and well built. She imagined that before his accident Colin had been quite a catch for some girl. Too bad so many women were turned off by his ravaged features; he was a fine gentleman.

Ben returned with the empty box he had brought the pups in. She noticed the cut on his arm was freshly bandaged; she was pleased that he took care of it himself.

"Have the pups been weaned?"

"Aye, mistress. They be weaned."

"Do you have homes for all of them?" she asked, crossing her fingers in the folds of her skirt.

"All but two females; the males go to some of the gentry in the region."

She looked up at the young lad, her expression hopeful. "Do you suppose I might have one to call my own?"

The boy grinned, showing a gap between his front teeth. "Aye, mistress." He bent down and pulled out two pups from the pile in her lap. "These two be females. Take yer pick."

Robbie studied them. "It's so hard to decide. All I really want is a companion."

The stable boy pointed to the one burrowing its way back to her skirts. "I'm thinkin' that one wants to be yours, mistress."

Robbie lifted it into her arms. "Then this is the one I'll have as mine. Thank you."

He put the rest of the pups in the box, nodded, and returned to the barn.

Robbie studied the little face with its white mask and perky ears. "Well, girl, what should I call you?" The pup tried to lick her face and then nuzzled her neck. "Ah, yes. Very affectionate, aren't you? Miss Sallie or Lady Perlina?" The pup cocked her head to one side and appeared to lift an eyebrow. "Ah, yes. Lady Perlina it is."

She returned to the house and Colin was lounging on the steps, smoking a cigar. "So you found one, have you?"

"I have indeed." She frowned. "What do they eat, do you know?"

"I think we could find some dog cakes in town at the livery. That would probably be best when the little thing gets older, but for now, probably biscuits softened in milk."

Robbie brought the pup to her nose, and the pup licked her. "I hope no one minds that I want her in the house with me. Do you think Mrs. Murray will have a conniption?"

"You could bring all the pups into the house and Mrs. Murray would praise you for being so soft-hearted. As long as she didn't have to clean up after them."

Robbie looked up at Colin. "I just want a companion." She gazed up at the immense house, toward the room that was Gavin's office. "I could get lonely living out here," she added.

Chapter Eight

Gavin shoved the maps aside and leaned against the back of the chair. He knew things could not go on as they were; he wasn't an idiot. Of course those thoughts entered his head before he married Robbie, but like always, when faced with an uncomfortable situation, he escaped into his books and maps.

He did want her; he was a red-blooded male, for God's sake. But would she feel he was simply doing it out of duty? Even though he could "rise to the challenge," she was not likely to agree to it.

There was a brief knock on the door, then Colin entered. "I have to leave for a week or so. When are you having the ball?"

Colin and his sister had a townhouse in Edinburgh. The only reason Colin could spend so much time at Erskine House was that his sister supervised the other.

"I've sent my family word that it will be two weeks from tomorrow. I'm hoping you'll be back in time, not only for the ball, but because I know they'd miss you if you weren't here."

"I've always envied your big family. Eve and I pretty much raised ourselves, our parents so busy socially we hardly seemed to matter."

"Interesting," Gavin said. "Robbie said something similar about her family."

Colin turned to leave. "By the way, Robbie has adopted a pup so don't be surprised if you find it in your bed, which I'm hoping will be the case upon my return. If you catch my meaning."

"Will having a dog here bother you?"

Colin gave him a lopsided smile. "Would it matter if it did?"

"Of course it would matter. I won't have my best friend afraid to step out of his apartment for fear of a dog sniffing his pantlegs."

"It won't bother me," Colin replied.

Gavin watched him leave, then shook his head. So there would be a dog in the house after all. Why wasn't he surprised?

• • •

Robbie fed her new little Lady Perlina, and then snuggled her until she fell asleep. She put her on her bed next to a pillow, and watched as the pup burrowed beneath. She sat before the mirror, studying her reflection. Was she such an ogre that her husband couldn't even pretend to desire her? She frowned, turned her head this way and that, and then went to the cheval mirror to look at the rest of her. Truthfully, she hadn't done much to make herself attractive. Her new frocks were lovely, but she looked like she always had: functional.

She pulled at her bodice, trying to lower it to show the tops of her breasts, which were ordinary in size, thankfully not too big, not too small. She pinched her cheeks to give herself some color.

Next she called for Maureen. When her new maid entered, Robbie sat down once again at her dressing table and ordered, "Do something with my hair. Please?"

• • •

Gavin couldn't avoid Robbie any longer. He had to at least tell her about the plans for the ball. It was a start. He knocked on her door and heard her voice telling him to enter.

She sat cross-legged on her bed, her skirt covering her legs and knees. The pup slept in her lap. "So we have a dog in the family."

She gave him a shy glance. "It's a start, isn't it?"

"A start?"

"For a family," she added, lowering her gaze.

Gavin swallowed hard and cleared his throat. He crossed to the bed and looked at the dog. "Corgi means 'dwarf dog.' It originated in Wales in the tenth century, brought here by Vikings and the Flemish, so I've heard."

She continued to stroke the pup. "So you've heard? Is there nothing you don't know, Gavin?" She bent down to give the pooch a hug, and he noticed that the top of her bodice gaped a bit, exposing the top of a slightly rounded breast.

He flushed and looked away quickly, but not before he felt a stab of desire. "I…I retain information for some reason. That's all. You…you've done something different with your hair."

She put the pup on the bed; it woke up and began lunging at her playfully. Robbie stretched her arms and leaned back against them, allowing her pup to pounce on her stomach. When it tried to climb her rib cage, Gavin saw another slight swell of her breasts. "Yes. My life now is so much different than it was before. I thought a little change was due. Do you like it?"

He nodded, rather enthusiastically. "I do. It's very becoming. I, ah, I've come to tell you that we will have the ball two weeks from tomorrow. That will give my family ample time to get here."

"It will be delightful to see them again after so many years." She yawned prettily, and stretched her arms out again. "I thought that having a beautiful and comfortable bed to sleep in would make me sleep like a baby, but it's so big I almost get lost in it by myself." She gave him another shy smile. "That's why I got the puppy. She's someone to cuddle up with."

Gavin raked his fingers through his hair. "Is that why I often see a light on in your room at some ungodly hour?"

Robbie quickly glanced away. "Sometimes I stay up and read."

"I figured as much. Yes, well, I should probably get back to my library. I have some correspondence to catch up on."

"Oh, by all means." She stood and straightened her gown and as she did so, he saw even more of her white bosom. "I don't want to interrupt your busy schedule."

He wondered if she was being sarcastic, but the look on her

face was completely innocent. "Yes, well, then...I'll see you in the drawing room before dinner. We can have a sherry together to celebrate our marriage."

He took the stairs slowly, wondering at the change that had come over Robbie. Her hair was abundant and quite lovely, he realized, now that it wasn't all screwed up at the back of her neck. And had she worn that gown before? Surely he would have remembered.

• • •

After Gavin left, Robbie said, "What marriage?" But a sly smile curved her lips. She had him flustered anyway. At least he had noticed the change in her hair. So this is what she had to do to get her husband to bed her. Act like a girl. Or a woman. Be coy. Be clever. Try to bring to mind all the years she spent with her sister.

It had been so long since she'd even tried to use charm on a man, she wasn't sure if she remembered how. But, she thought, throwing herself back on the bed, charm apparently worked. It was, however, exhausting to work so hard at being something she was not: a coquette.

She had to keep at it. That meant finding a gown to wear at dinner that was even more appealing than the one she had on now. She went to her wardrobe, still marveling at all of the dresses that hung there, and went through them. She settled on a lavender silk with a deep bodice and a slim skirt. Perfect. Although the thought of getting into that corset contraption gave her second thoughts.

Before going down for a drink, Robbie took one last look in the mirror. She gasped when she saw what the corset had done to her bosom. Why, there was more showing that not! Could she be so brazen without feeling like a fool? She hiked up her bodice, which did little good, let out a whoosh of air, and went down to meet her husband for a sherry.

Initially it was harder to converse without Colin's lively dialogue, but Robbie knew that if she got Gavin started on a topic that interested him, things would go well.

"The maps in your study intrigue me," she began, amazed that her breasts hadn't popped out while she ate.

Gavin took a sip of wine. "How so?"

"They don't appear up to date; they seem antiquated."

"They are old. That's what interests me. How narrow and flat the world was back then, yet from those ancient days came some of our most brilliant scientists, physicians, and scholars."

"And artists," she added. "It has always amazed me that those sculptures and paintings from Egypt and Mesopotamia survived the centuries buried beneath the earth."

Gavin's expression grew eager. "Indeed. That's why everything from the ancient world fascinates me."

"I remember that you and your sister, Cassie, used to see who could answer the most questions doled out by the tutor."

He poured himself more wine. "She's a brilliant girl. As with me, she retains most of what she reads and hears. I don't believe it was ever a serious competition between us, but it was lively."

"And what about Louis?" She offered her wine glass, and he filled it.

He settled back in his chair. "Louis was...Louis. At that time he couldn't have cared less whether he learned anything or not. He was too busy carousing."

"And now?" Robbie's tongue came out and licked the rim of her glass before she took a sip of her wine, letting it linger a moment before she swallowed it.

Gavin watched, mesmerized. "He has settled down a bit, but I wonder if he'll ever find a woman who'll have him."

"Why do you say that?"

"He's too hard-headed by half. A trait he got from our da."

"And you? Who do you take after?" Robbie probed.

He pointed to his hair. "Mam, no doubt about it. And she is still as patient as a saint."

Robbie noticed that he pulled on his collar often; she feared he would get a rash. She wondered if it was because of Colin's absence that he was uncomfortable with her.

After dinner, she said, "Gavin, take off your collar. You'll be more comfortable."

He sat back, surprised. "I can't do that."

"Why not?"

"It's just not done."

Robbie rose and went around to where he sat. "Give it a try, will you? Here, I'll help you." She leaned over to detach the collar from his shirt, allowing her bosom to brush his shoulder. When she'd finished, she said, "There. Now, isn't that better?"

Gavin rubbed his hand over his throat. "I feel naked."

Oh, Robbie thought, he made it so easy. "Naked? Really? I'd like to know how you feel when you remove everything."

He wore a flustered expression. "Have you always been so... so bold?"

She sat down beside him and put her hand on his arm. "No. Certainly not when I was growing up in Birdie's shadow. But later," she said, becoming pensive, "when I was at university, and after that when I barely scraped by for a living, I realized that in order to endure I had to become a survivor, and if that meant becoming bold, so be it."

Gavin's gaze probed hers. "You're a woman of many layers, aren't you?"

The conversation had taken a solemn turn, so Robbie just squeezed his arm and answered, "It may not be fashionable, but it's who I am. Now," she continued. "What must we do to prepare for your family, and how many of them will be coming?"

He refilled their glasses again, and Robbie realized she was getting a tad tipsy, but she matched him sip for sip. It did taste wonderful.

While they sipped, he spoke of his mother, Linnea, and his father, Durham, a somewhat staid Scotsman who, when he was a young man on board a fishing vessel, had visited Finland and brought home his bride.

"Oh, that is quite a romantic story."

"So I'm not truly a Scotsman at all; I'm only half a Scot. The other half a foreign Finlander."

Robbie loved hearing about his family. "So we should probably prepare some of the rooms in the east wing, don't you think?"

He raised his eyebrows and smiled at her, the wine obviously loosening him up. "I've already set it in motion. Mrs. Murray has hired some local girls to come in and get the wing ready." At her surprised expression, he added, "I can be useful as well as knowledgable, you know. And by the way, I'm going into Galashiels on Tuesday to help the schoolmaster order some material. He's also asked me to aid in some of his classes."

"Why, that's wonderful! Have you taught before?"

"I did teach a class at Edinburgh, rather something far beyond what these youngsters would be interested in, but I'm excited to get back into it."

"Can I come with you?"

He gave her a quizzical look. "You want to come with me to the school?"

"Indeed. There's so little for me to do here; I'd love the change in scenery," she responded. And, she thought, she had a story to mail.

"All right. The day after tomorrow."

Later, Robbie took her pup outside, then got ready for bed. After putting the pup on one of the pillows, Robbie went to the desk and pulled out her writing supplies. She must post the latest offerings tomorrow, else they wouldn't arrive at the office in time for publication.

Lady Perlina rode the baron like a professional horsewoman, leaning into his erection. They cantered along at a good, steady speed, the baron pulling on Perlina's nipples. Now and then Perlina bent low so the baron could take the tip of a breast into his mouth and suckle it.

"Your breasts are like sheep udders, fraulein," the baron said. "Big with long, lovely nipples. Shall I get you pregnant so we can watch the babe suckle together?"

Lady Perlina rode him harder, the heat from his words adding fuel to her excitement. "If there ever was a man who could make me faithful, it is you, baron." This was a lie, of course, but it made him bigger and harder beneath her, and she felt him so deep inside her, she almost fainted with the pleasure of it.

He reached between them and rubbed her, pulling upward, titillating with the tip of his finger.

Lady Perlina felt it begin, the deep heat that flooded her veins, making her skin tingle and flush and her ears ring. She screamed her pleasure.

• • •

After Robbie had gone to bed, Gavin picked up the rest of the wine. His thoughts centered squarely on his new wife. How she had looked in that gown tonight, how her breasts pushed up over the top of the silk bodice. Once again, desire stirred in his groin. He took another swallow of wine, disappointed when he realized the bottle was empty. He weaved his way toward the liquor cabinet and poured himself a shot of brandy, downing it in one gulp.

He could do this. He could bed his wife. What had made him think he couldn't?

• • •

Robbie was roused from sleep when the door to her room flew open and slammed against the wall. Lady Perlina yipped.

"You're my wife."

Gavin slurred the words.

"I am."

"You prob'ly think because I love my booksh and mapsh I can't make love to a woman."

Robbie sat up in bed, reached over, and lit the lamp. He stood before her, disheveled, blearyeyed, and not at all steady on his feet.

"So you're going to bed me now, is that it?" she asked, her voice rife with sarcasm.

He nodded, making his way toward the bed. When he arrived at the edge, he collapsed into a heap; fortunately his head fell on a pillow, and he passed out. With some effort, Robbie lifted the rest of him onto the bed and covered him with a blanket.

Chapter Nine

The next morning, Gavin sat outside on the front steps with a cup of strong coffee laced with brandy. God, he had such a headache. He remembered little after Robbie had gone to bed, although he vaguely recalled storming into her room.

Embarrassment and shame washed over him. She must think him such a fool. He had passed out for the entire night, not waking until he heard her quietly close the door this morning. There he was, fully clothed in his wife's bed, nothing removed, nothing amiss. His friends and his brothers would roar with laughter.

He had never wished to be like other men. Pierce, his oldest brother, now gone these five years after drowning, had had a presence that everyone respected and was in awe of. Louis, who was the gay blade, loving life and love and everyone around him. Colin, who, in spite of his disfigurement, cut a dashing figure among some women.

And Gavin? Stuck with his nose in a book or hovering over a map older than dirt. Some rake. Some playboy. He pulled out a cigar and lit it, puffing on it until the end was good and hot. It would make him sick, he knew, but what the hell. He couldn't possibly feel much worse than he did at the moment.

He would avoid Robbie today. Surely she must feel as disgusted with him as he did with himself. How had it begun? They'd been having delightful conversations. He remembered the one about the ancient maps, her mentioning the statuary of Mesopotamia... oh, now he remembered. He'd finished the wine and drank some brandy, all the while thinking of her lily white bosom. That's what did it. She had never dressed this way until after they were married. Did that mean something?

He stubbed out his cigar, left his cup on the ledge and wandered down to the Tweed. Maybe a good dose of cold river water would make him feel better.

• • •

Robbie stood at the breakfast parlor window, watching her husband walk toward the river. Poor man, she thought with a grim smile. A hangover to beat all hangovers.

She had studied him after he'd passed out, in the low glow of the lamp. His jaw was strong, as was his chin. He had a wide, smooth forehead and a regal nose. His lips were full but not fleshy. His eyelashes fanned out over the tops of his cheeks like feather brushes. He was adorable. And, if she played her cards right, he would be hers, Faith Baker bedamned. (*Sorry, Papa.*)

Out of curiosity, she left the house and followed him. He strode toward the river. She heard it bubbling over rocks in the distance. The air was heady with the smell of flowering rhododendrons. She stopped behind a healthy bush and watched Gavin sit on a rock and remove his boots. Then he stood and removed his shirt. She should leave, she knew she should, but she stood, riveted to the spot as his broad back came into view. When he unbuttoned his trousers and slid them down his legs, she held her breath. He stood in his breeks; she wondered if he would swim in them or not.

Gavin glanced around, apparently feeling quite alone, and slid his breeks down, kicking them away from him.

Robbie admired the hard, round buttocks, the long, well-muscled legs. And when he briefly turned to the side, she nearly gasped as his package came into view. In truth, she had not seen one before, no matter how often she wrote about the male organ, one she could describe with little difficulty and "use" as it was to be used, she had not set her eyes on one her entire life. And she was not disappointed. Settled into a thick bush of tawny hair was a handsome penis, slightly engorged, and two ample balls. She continued to stare as Gavin waded into the Tweed, watching until he was completely submerged.

She stumbled back to the house, breathless, heart palpitating, and her own desire climbing to a near fever pitch.

• • •

The following morning, she and Gavin went in to Galashiels so she could mail her letter and he could scope out the schoolroom, which was, as at home, attached to the kirk.

As they rode, Gavin started the conversation. "I apologize for my appalling behavior the other night. You must think I'm a terrible cad and a sloppy drunk."

She briefly touched his arm. "It's over. Let's just get on with things, all right, Gavin? I don't think any less of you. Sometimes those things just happen." The image of him naked at the river never left her mind. She hoped it never would.

"I never drink like that. Never. I don't think I've been drunk in my life until you…"

She raised her eyebrows at him, pretending surprise. She knew very well the affect her gown had had on him. "Until I, what?"

"Suffice it to say that I was surprised at the cut of your gown."

Oh God, how proper he was! "Would you prefer that I wear my old things?"

"No."

She hid a quiet grin. "I didn't think so."

When they reached the village, he dropped her off at the inn. "Walk over to the church when you're done."

She went inside and strode to the counter, laying her envelope on top of it. The innkeeper, remembering her, beamed as he came forward. "Aye, miss? What can I do for ye?"

She pushed the envelope across to him. He noted the address and assured her that the next coach would pick up mail in the morning.

Grateful to have the drivel out of her hands, and with only a few more stories to go, she stepped from the inn and made her way to the kirk. Before she could open the door, it opened for her and out stepped Faith Baker, a surprised, rather delicious smile on her face.

"Good morning!" It was such an overly cheerful greeting, Robbie almost didn't answer.

• • •

Faith Baker entered the inn and stepped to the counter where her uncle, Eli, worked as innkeeper and postman. They greeted each other, then Faith asked, "Did a woman just leave here?"

"Aye." He gave her a sly look. "She came to mail a letter."

His expression told her something delicious was about to unfold. "And where was the letter going, pray tell?"

Her uncle looked around to make sure they were alone. "I'm familiar with the address, Faithy. 'Tis not a place I'd expect any nice young woman to even know."

Faith's eyes grew large and she said, "Well, what is it?" When he told her, Faith could barely contain her excitement. She was certain Gavin, sweet, innocent Gavin, had no idea that his wife was corresponding with underground smut.

Gavin had invited her to the party he was throwing for his family. She could hardly wait to inform him of her latest bit of juicy news.

• • •

That evening Gavin was surprised when Robbie didn't show up for dinner. Mrs. Murray told him that his wife had asked to have something sent to her room, if it wasn't too much trouble.

Mrs. Murray had rolled her eyes. "As if anything that sweet girl does would be trouble," she had said.

Gavin was concerned; Robbie had mentioned meeting Faith as she entered the church, but it had not sounded as though it bothered her. He understood that Robbie's first meeting with Faith had not been pleasant for her, but he hoped they all could be friends in the future.

Now, in his bed chamber, he undressed in the dark and slid into bed. He had just gotten to sleep when a whoosh of air washed over him, and then was gone. He got up on one elbow. "Is someone there?" That was crazy, but he felt another presence in the room.

"It's me, Gavin."

Robbie's voice was soft, barely above a whisper. She sat on the bed next to him.

"Do you mind that I'm here?" she asked, her voice shy.

"No, of course not, but—" She got off the bed and he felt a stab of disappointment.

"I'm removing my nightgown, Gavin. I'm getting into bed with you."

A sudden burst of desire fired his loins. He quickly pulled back the covers for her and waited until she was lying next to him and then announced, his heart beating a wild tattoo, "This certainly isn't what I had expected."

She turned toward him and put her hand on his cheek. "I know you don't love me, Gavin. I understand that. But I've loved you forever and I think I have enough love for the both of us. And—"

"Silence, wife," he said, suddenly feeling very virile, "I have need of you."

Her skin was soft and silky, her breasts blissfully full. His fingers moved over the whole of her, learning the perfection that he had not imagined would be there. He traced her buttocks, soft and yielding. He skimmed her thighs, firm and smooth.

She lay there, allowing him everything. He dipped between her thighs to find her bush and lightly stroked it, hearing her swift intake of breath. She parted her legs for him and he found her wet and ready. But he wasn't quite done yet; he stroked her, lightly grazing her mound, dipping inside until he heard her breathing become ragged and erratic. Then and only then did he enter her and find the barrier that made him realize that never in his life had he ever had a virgin before.

"I don't want to hurt—"

"You won't," she interrupted, her voice breathy. "Please..."

He thrust through the obstacle and tried to hold back his orgasm until he knew she was ready for her own. When they came, it was fireworks, and he felt joy when he heard her nearly scream her pleasure.

They slept, Robbie tucked sweetly against Gavin's chest.

• • •

Before dawn, Robbie woke and slid soundlessly from the bed. She put on her nightclothes and, with one last look at her sleeping husband, left for her own room. Poor Perlina was probably beside herself having to sleep alone.

When she entered her room, she found the pup happily chewing on one of Robbie's slippers. "Bad puppy," she whispered.

As she prepared for the day, she thought about the night, and it made her chuckle. No, he was not a playboy or a rake. But he was a gentle and considerate lover. And while she was a virgin, she realized that he probably had not been, for he knew what he was doing. *Silence, wife, I have need of you.*

And she definitely had need of him. Writing her drivel seemed even more unpleasant now that she, herself, was fulfilled. Soon it would end, and it couldn't come quickly enough for her.

• • •

At breakfast the next morning, Robbie was surprised to see her husband sitting in the chair across from her. "You never have breakfast with me."

He looked at her with his teal blue eyes. "Are you disappointed?"

She quickly sat. "Not one whit."

"How are you feeling this morning?"

She had glanced in the mirror before she left to discover whether or not she had changed overnight. She decided that she had; her eyes were bright and her heart was light. "I feel wonderful, thanks to you."

He appeared to puff up a bit, and Robbie was glad.

"I'm feeling pretty good myself, dear wife." He reached for the platter of eggs and sausage and heaped some onto his plate. "My appetite is insatiable." Looking at her over his coffee, he added, "All of them are."

Robbie actually blushed. This was a side to him she hadn't seen before. She liked it. And she would not have to worry about him going off to see that Baker woman. If she had learned nothing else from her writing, it was how to please a man. Although she had to admit she wasn't sure she could do some of the things she wrote about!

She merely smiled and reached for a fresh, warm bap. Not until that moment did she realize she was actually starving. "Pass me the eggs, would you please?"

"So your hunger is as great as mine," he said with a grin.

Again, she felt heat rise into her cheeks. That he was taking the lead delighted her. Yes, definitely a side to her husband she had no idea existed.

Their courtship, as Robbie liked to think of it, continued into the following week, shortly before his family arrived. Although he visited her room almost nightly, they slept apart. Robbie was hoping that would change. Lady Perlina had not been quite the bed companion Robbie had hoped for.

But for now she was happy. Ecstatic, really. Even if he never learned to love her, he cared for her, of that she was certain.

Before they had a houseful of interested family members, Robbie had to know just one thing. At breakfast the day they were to arrive, she asked Gavin, "Is your family aware of the mistake you made?"

He shook his head. "I apologize for not getting that message back to them."

"So they're expecting to see Birdie?"

His expression was so pained, Robbie nearly laughed. "They have no idea."

"Then let us surprise them, shall we?"

Gavin's face changed, and he matched her mischievous grin. "Yes, let's surprise them."

Chapter Ten

The shock on the faces of Gavin's family as they exited the coach was priceless. Robbie stood beside him, greeting everyone graciously, and each returned her greeting with wide-eyed curiosity.

Ensconced in his library with his father, Gavin poured them each a brandy. Durham Eliot was a big man with a barrel chest and a shock of salt and pepper hair. He wore an amused expression as he asked, "So, how did this come about?"

"I got their names mixed up." Gavin took a seat across from his father near the fireplace, which was heaped with fresh coal and glowing brightly.

"Now, my son the bookworm, why doesn't that surprise me?"

Gavin merely shook his head. "It was a disaster at first. Robbie was so excited to be here, having escaped a paltry life in the slums of Edinburgh." He went on to explain that she had gone to university, yet had not found a viable trade, except for writing short pieces for magazines and newspapers. "She has also worked in a clinic helping with prostitutes and runaway girls." He lifted a tawny eyebrow. "She's a woman of many layers."

"How did she discover it was a mistake?" his father asked, leaning forward.

Gavin expelled a deep sigh. "Out of consideration for her feelings, a friend of mine told her."

Durham grunted. "Some friend."

"I think Faith meant well, it's just that I should have been the one to explain."

"Faith? A woman told her?"

"Yes," Gavin answered defensively. "Faith and I are good friends. Nothing more."

"Didn't you know it's not possible to be 'friends' with a woman?"

"That's what Colin told me. He's certain Faith had ulterior motives, but I've never given her any reason to think our friendship is anything but that."

Durham stared at his son and just shook his head. "You're naïve, you know, if you don't think that woman hasn't fantasized about living here, at Erskine House."

Frowning, Gavin asked, "How can you say that, Da? You don't even know her."

"I don't have to know her. I know the type," his father answered flatly. "At any rate, after hearing that you mistook Robbie for Birdie, how did you convince her to stay?"

Gavin explained the meeting he had with Robbie at the inn. "She's not a hysterical sort of woman. She's very pragmatic. She knows I don't love her, but she has been nothing but wonderful."

"So you told her flat out that you don't love her."

"It was the honorable thing to do."

"And she's all right with that." It was not a question. "Has nothing changed since you wed?"

Gavin pondered the question. "Well, she has been dressing more fetchingly, and she has done something different with her hair."

Durham barked a laugh. "Ah, dear boy, you made the most impressive and important mistake of your life."

Gavin swirled his brandy. "That's what Colin said, too."

His father took a look around the room. "And where is that reprobate?"

"He's arriving later this evening. He's anxious to see you; I'm sorry Louis couldn't come."

"He is as well. But the business doesn't run itself, you know."

The family business, a cannery, was a huge ongoing success, mainly because Gavin's father was a smart businessman. Although he had wanted all of his sons to become a part of it, he understood Gavin's need to do something different with his life and sent him off with his blessing. It was a stroke of good fortune involving an old debt that the family came into the ownership of Erskine House. Durham was happy to see his son administering the place.

"And he still hasn't found a wife?" Gavin probed.

"Doesn't seem to be looking," his father replied.

• • •

Robbie and Gavin's mother, Linnea, a pretty, petite woman whose hair was as light as her son's, and her eyes, although warm, were the color of blue ice, sat in the morning room with tea. A strip of meager sunshine tried to penetrate the gossamer curtains. Lady Perlina was curled up at Robbie's feet.

"Your pup is adorable. I always like to have a dog in the house," Linnea announced. "Oddly, all of the children loved to play with them except Gavin. He always had his nose in a book instead."

Robbie loved to listen to Gavin's mother talk. Her speech was a mixture of Gaelic and some nordic language that often made words no one could understand. "She's a scamp, that's for sure."

"What have you named her?"

Robbie thought a moment; how much to say? "She's Lady." Half true.

"I must admit when Gavin wrote that he had proposed to Birdie, I was a bit disappointed. Not that she's not a lovely girl, but…"

Robbie threw her head back and laughed softly. "No need to finish the sentence. Birdie will always be Birdie. Even as an adult she hasn't changed. I will admit to you that she wooed my fiance, who came under her spell like a felled tree. They married and are living in Glasgow where, if I'm not wrong, Birdie is driving all the servants to distraction with her wants and needs."

Linnea's hand went to her chest. "She stole your fiance?"

Robbie nodded. "He was a nice fellow, kind, patient, and

rich." She gave her new mother-in-law a cunning look. "No doubt that last part is what Birdie fell for, but I don't wish her any ill will. After all," she said, looking around her, "I actually have what I've wanted since I laid eyes on Gavin, and I don't mean the fine house." She gave Linnea a shy glance.

"You've cared for him that long, have you?" Linnea took a sip of tea.

"Yes. And in spite of the fact that it wasn't me he proposed to, things are going along quite well."

"How did you find out? Did he tell you?"

"He didn't have to; a friend beat him to it."

"A friend?"

"Her name is Faith Baker, and truth to tell, I'm not especially fond of the way she broke the news to me."

"Hmmm. And Gavin believes this woman is just a friend?"

"Gavin is sweet and a little guileless, which makes me love him all the more."

"It sounds like this Faith Baker is a woman to avoid," Linnea speculated.

"Indeed, but Gavin—being Gavin—invited her to the ball."

Her mother-in-law wrinkled her nose. "I'll have to take a good look at her."

"She is comely, I suppose, and I'm not downplaying her attributes. Her bones are fine and small. She is rather short, and her hair is very much the same color as Gavin's."

"I should be able to pick her out easily, then."

Robbie agreed. "I'll be interested to know what you think of her. Now, on to Cassie. She is absolutely lovely." Gavin's younger sister had taken the little ones to the barn to see the animals.

"She's come a long way, she has." Linnea's light blue eyes were warm with affection. "She's still a handful, don't get me wrong. Gavin has offered to let her spend some time here," she said, then added, "but with you two being newlyweds, it probably isn't a good idea."

"That's nonsense," Robbie answered. "It would be an adventure having her around. Things can get pretty boring out here in the provinces. Or so they tell me; so far I haven't been bored for a minute."

Linnea reached across and touched Robbie's arm. "You are too generous by half."

Robbie drained her tea and placed the cup on the saucer. "I have always envied Gavin for his family. How you kept such a pack in line is beyond me; you seem so quiet and subdued."

Linnea nodded. "Aye, but looks can be deceiving, you know. Truth to tell, I'm the disciplinarian; Durham, for all of his bluster, is just a pussy cat when it comes to his children."

Robbie thought on that. "My family was happy, but since there were just the three of us, it was awfully quiet most of the time. When my sister wasn't throwing a tantrum," she added with a quiet smile.

But in truth, she felt very lucky to have what she had.

Colin's arrival shortly after they had had their tea was met with rousing back-slapping and definite whooping from the children, because Colin had brought them sweets from Edinburgh.

Later, after she'd finished her serial, the writing of which was like pulling teeth, she put on her robe and slippers and crept from the bed where the sleeping pup snored. So much excitement today, it's a wonder she couldn't sleep. Gavin's family certainly made everything lively. Robbie loved the younger ones on sight. Two young lads and a lassie, who, Linnea had told her in private, was a surprise addition to the household, since Linnea had felt she was beyond having more children.

She went quietly to the kitchen to make herself some tea and found Colin there, eating cold chicken.

"We meet here again," he said.

"Is it a bad habit, us meeting this way?" she teased as she fixed herself some tea.

"No. I like to have you to myself now and again."

She gave him a quick look, but even in the moonlight she could see he was jesting.

"How is life going for you, Robbie?"

She settled herself across from him. "It's going well, Colin. Very well, indeed." She could feel him study her.

"I like what you've done with your hair. And the lavender gown you wore to dinner was an excellent choice. You wore it well." There was a knowledgable inflection in his voice as he said it.

Robbie smiled to herself. Colin was intuitive, if nothing else. "Yes, I decided I was far too functional looking to be the lady of such a fine house. And," she shot him a look from under her lashes, "I've learned that a bit of decolletage doesn't hurt when trying to seduce a naïve husband."

Colin barked a laugh. "Robbie, you are an amazing woman. I hope Gavin really appreciates you because if he doesn't I'll have to ferry you away myself."

She took a delicate sip of tea. "Oh, I think there is appreciation there, and if not love, perhaps fondness."

"So you aren't giving up on him?"

"Never." The word came out more fiercely than she'd thought it would. "I will do what ever it takes to be the best wife Gavin could ever hope for."

Chapter Eleven

Faith studied herself in the mirror. She looked grand in her white silk gown with the slight bustle. Almost like a bride. She squirmed under the discomfort of the corset, but she had to admit it made her waist look so very, very tiny. She was like a delicate little bird, fragile to look at but…Her smile turned suggestive. She was anything but fragile under it all. She had put padding under her breasts, held in place by her corset, to make her bosom appear fuller. One little misstep and she would expose a nipple. She grinned wickedly into the mirror. How much excitement would that cause?

She glanced at her dressing table where the letter sat, the one Gavin's friend (she refused to call her his wife; that was to be Faith's role) had thought she mailed. Of course Uncle Eli was an honest man and would not have given it to her, so Faith had to sneak it out of the bag when he wasn't looking.

Faith had steamed it open and her jaw dropped when she discovered what it was. My God! Robbie Fleming (again, she could not give her the Eliot name) actually wrote smut for those publications! The content itself not only titillated Faith, the very idea that the woman was pretending to be something she wasn't was almost as exciting. Think of how Gavin would react when she showed it to him! He was almost hers.

She straightened her gloves, picked up her fan and, tucking the letter into a pocket on the side of her gown, gave herself one last admiring glance before making for the ball.

• • •

Robbie sat before her mirror and gazed at herself. The bodice of her gown, the incredible forest green satin that she had picked out all those weeks ago, fit her like a second skin. Her neck looked long and sleek, making the bare expanse of the bosom almost blinding. The long, white gloves felt strange next to her skin; she couldn't remember ever having worn them before. She had told Maureen to take the rest of the evening off, attend the party, have some fun.

A rap on the door startled her. "Come in."

Gavin entered, looking very handsome in his black dress coat and trousers. He wore a white vest, and when he brought his gloved hands from behind his back, he held a small box in them. Apparently very pleased with what he saw, he said, "Robbie, you look especially beautiful tonight."

Grateful for her decollete, she thanked him. "As you do, my husband."

"I have something for you; Mother brought it for me to give to my bride."

"Then I'm lucky that I am that woman, aren't I?" She did still feel a knot form in her abdomen when she thought about Birdie, who would have been the recipient had Gavin been a more observant man.

He opened the velvet box, and there lay the most beautiful pearl necklace Robbie could ever have imagined.

"Oh, Gavin, it's too exquisite for me to wear."

"Nonsense. And since I'm the first son in the family to marry, it's yours." He lifted it from the satin bed it lay in and put it around her neck, lifting her hair to fasten it. His touch made her tingle, and she thought she might cry she was so happy.

"It suits you, Robbie."

She touched it with delicate fingers. It complemented the bareness of her skin, bringing out sparkling highlights in her hair that she had no idea were there. "Oh, my," was all she could say.

"Indeed," he replied, smiling down at her. "Now, are you ready to meet the world?"

She picked up her mother-of-pearl fan—something else she

was unaccustomed to—and her dance card and took his arm, so excited that again she thought to pinch herself to make sure it was all real.

The ballroom was richly decorated and well lit, giving the room an ethereal quality that lent itself to the occasion. A young woman in a sweet pink moire frock played "Amazing Grace" quietly on her harp in the background. Robbie felt an immediate surge of emotion, for it had been her father's favorite.

Robbie recognized a few of their neighbors, but there were a number of couples there she had not met. It was an eclectic gathering: farmers, tradesmen, and gentry. Her dance card was quickly filled, save for the dances she would reserve for her husband.

He bowed before her and kissed her hand, then led her onto the dance foor. The musicians opened with a waltz. Even though the instruments were of a rustic sort, the fiddles, the flutes, and the whistles made the waltz from *Swan Lake* recognizable. Gavin swept her around the dance floor. He was amazingly light on his feet, and she allowed him to whirl her across the wide expanse of the room, his hand at her waist and their fingers gently clasped.

Later, after she had danced with Colin and Durham and a number of her neighbors, she begged to rest and stood by Linnea, who was watching Cassie and her father twirl around the floor in a spritely quadrille.

At that moment, something caught Robbie's eye. She made a face.

"What is it?" Linnea asked.

From behind her fan, Robbie announced, "Faith Baker just strutted into the room."

"Wait," Linnea said, "don't tell me, let me guess." Three women entered, one the wife of their nearest neighbor and the other her young daughter. The other was Miss Baker.

"The one who swaggered in like she's the belle of the ball? Or a bride? Isn't it rather gauche for a guest to wear white to another woman's wedding ball?"

"If it isn't, it should be," Robbie answered, narrowing her gaze at the woman.

"And I notice that she is unchaperoned." Linnea tsked. "How audacious!"

Robbie thought of her own unchaperoned path into Gavin's life, so curbed her tongue. They both watched as she glided directly for Gavin, who was in conversation with another neighbor. He turned to greet her, and she stood on tiptoe and whispered something in his ear. He frowned, looked around the dance floor, but his gaze did not find Robbie. He looked a little peeved, but took Faith into his arms and joined the quadrille.

"Now there's a young woman who has no sense of propriety, and I don't like the looks of that," Linnea murmured.

"Nor do I," Robbie answered, her stomach a tad uneasy. When the dance had finished, Gavin walked her toward them. "She's coming this way."

Gavin leaned toward Robbie and whispered, "I will be back shortly. We still have another dance."

After he left, Faith stepped right up to Linnea, completely ignoring Robbie. She made a little curtsy and then said, "You must be Gavin's mother." Her smile was saccharine. "I am so pleased to finally meet you; Gavin speaks of you fondly, and often."

Robbie tossed a sideways glance at her mother-in-law, who had a faux smile painted on her face. "I didn't catch your name." Her response was polite, although not particularly warm.

"Oh, I beg your pardon," she said quickly. "I'm Faith Baker; Gavin and I are very good friends. We met at Edinburgh, where my uncle taught. We spent many evenings together at my uncle's townhouse, where they would have the liveliest of discussions. He was Gavin's mentor, you see." She finally looked at Robbie, a shrewd look on her face.

"I see. Well, it was nice to meet you." Linnea's posture clearly told her their conversation was over. She turned to Robbie. "Shall we visit the refreshment room, Robbie dear?"

Robbie stopped a grin. "By all means; let's do." Both she and

Linnea turned and walked away from Faith Baker. Before they entered the refreshment room, Robbie glanced back to see Faith Baker making a quick exit out one of the glass doors.

The room was filled with heady, delicious aromas. A table of tea, coffee, and ices was positioned to one side. Biscuits, cakes, bon bons, cold tongue, and a variety of sandwiches were beautifully placed on another.

They each filled a small plate and took a seat by the windows. "I noticed Faith whispering to him during the quadrille. What do you suppose that means?"

"I don't know, but it can't possibly be good."

"I've only just met the woman, but I'd venture a guess that she plans to meet Gavin somewhere. Are you going to follow them?"

Robbie nibbled on a biscuit. "At some point I'm going to have to trust him." But did she? She felt a headache begin in her left temple.

● ● ●

Colin had watched the contact between Faith and Gavin. Something was happening, and he didn't like the looks of it. He went the back way to the path that led to the patio and saw Faith sitting on a bench, a letter or packet of some kind on her lap. He crept up behind her and pulled the epistle from her, startling her so that she nearly screamed.

When she saw him, she said, her voice dripping with disdain, "Oh, it's you. Give me my envelope."

Colin put it in the inside pocket of his jacket. "I don't think so."

"It's not your business."

"Anything to do with Gavin's happiness is my business," he answered.

She gave him a superior look. "So you believe learning that his *wife* writes smut for an underground magazine would make Gavin happy?"

Ah, so that's what it was. No wonder Robbie was so evasive when he asked her about her writing job.

"Well, apparently you were going to prove to him that she does," he countered.

She raised her chin. "He needs to know."

"Do you know what he really needs to know, Miss Baker?"

"Oh, do tell me, you wretched-faced degenerate." Her voice dripped with poison.

"My, my, namecalling. How very mature."

She shrugged one shoulder and glanced away, hoping to see Gavin coming up the path.

"What Gavin really needs to know is exactly the kind of woman you are."

She cocked her head. "Really? And what kind of woman is that?"

"One who had an abortion at a backstreet clinic three years ago. You're lucky you survived it."

She froze, then turned slowly, giving him the kind of look that wished him dead. "Even you wouldn't be that low."

Colin lifted his shoulders. "It would prove to him once and for all that you are not what you pretend to be."

She crossed her arms over her chest and tapped one foot on the stone. "So it's blackmail."

He patted his jacket pocket. "So it is. Now leave, Miss Baker, and stop trying to interfere in Gavin's life. He's married. He's happy. If you truly loved him, you would want him to be happy."

"He could have been happy with me."

Colin grunted a laugh. "I don't see how."

She threw him another deadly glance, then turned and hurried down the path to a waiting carriage.

Gavin appeared beside him. "Is that Faith? She's leaving?"

"Yes. Apparently something to do with her mother," Colin answered. He turned to Gavin. "And what are you doing out here anyway? Shouldn't you be keeping track of your wife, instead of the woman who wants to tear your marriage apart?"

Gavin looked uncomfortable. "She said she had something to show me and that it was crucial to my marriage."

"Don't believe her, Gavin. Concentrate on your wife. Nothing

Faith Baker has to say is important enough to risk Robbie's happiness, and yours."

When both men returned to the ballroom, they saw Gavin's mother leaving the refreshment room alone.

"Where's Robbie?" Gavin asked.

Linnea strolled over to them. "She claimed a headache. She asked me to tell you that she's so sorry to leave the party, but in order for it not to turn into something worse, she has to lie down in a dark room."

Disappointed, Gavin said, "Maybe I should see if she's all right."

Linnea put her hand on his arm. "No, Gavin. Let her be. She'll be fine in the morning."

Colin left the ballroom and made his way up the stairway to Robbie's room. Perhaps it wasn't correct of him to talk with her in her chambers, but he felt it was necessary. He rapped softly on her door.

A moment later, she opened it, her pup in her arms. Surprised, she said, "Colin? Is something wrong?"

"No, not now. But," he said, sliding the envelope from his pocket, "I thought you might want me to mail this in the morning."

She gasped and nearly dropped the dog. "Where did you get that?"

"Faith Baker was going to use it to try to drive a wedge between you and Gavin so she could have him for herself."

Frowning, Robbie said, "But I mailed it at the inn."

"The innkeeper is Faith's uncle. I don't believe he would have given it to her willingly, so I assume she snatched it when he wasn't looking."

Robbie's gaze narrowed. "That evil witch."

"She is that, you know. She's wanted Gavin for herself for as long as I've known her, and I knew her in Edinburgh when she visited her uncle."

"Thank you for this, Colin. I don't know what I would have done if..." The sentence fizzled out and Robbie looked away.

"I'm aware of the address, Robbie. Just so you know." He looked both ways, and then asked, "Is there somewhere we can talk?"

Robbie opened the door wider. "Come in here. It's not proper, but I think you deserve an explanation."

The small parlor off the bedroom was dimly lit. When they were seated, Robbie told him the story.

"So your mentor died before he could finish the stories he had promised the magazine."

Robbie nodded. "And I needed the money desperately. It wasn't much, but it was all I had; I could have been out on the street."

The look she gave him nearly broke his heart. "You want to write, is that it? I mean your own stories?"

"Of course. Ever since I was a girl I scribbled stories on backs of paper used for packing. I didn't care where I wrote, just that I could write. Even as a young lassie I preferred getting writing tablets as gifts rather than dolls or fancy dressses."

Colin studied her, his expression sympathetic. "You are a complicated woman, Robbie. But I don't think you give Gavin enough credit. He's not a saint, you know, although he often acts like one. He might find it exciting to have a wife who has such knowledge."

Robbie laughed, short and humorless. "All I did was use the wording Jeremy had used in the serials before I got them. I know where all the parts are, but I don't know how to use them," she said with a cynical smile. "And I've said too much." She stood, an invitation for him to take his leave. "I would appreciate you mailing it, though. I have just a couple of pieces I need to finish before I'm done with the drivel forever."

After Colin left, Robbie sat down and tried to write.

Lady Perlina took the baron's balls and gave them a squeeze.

Nothing else came. She crumpled the paper and tossed it on the floor. She started another.

Miss Sallie Wiggins sat squarely on Elijah's firm brown... Beyond that, she had nothing. That, too, ended up a crumpled heap on the floor.

After several more attempts, Robbie went to bed, disgusted with it all.

Chapter Twelve

When Robbie didn't join the family for breakfast, Gavin went up to her room. He knocked, and when he got no answer, he opened the door. The room was empty. He noticed that all around the wastebasket were crumpled sheets of paper. He bent and picked one up, smoothed it out, and studied the script. He picked up another.

Miss Sallie Wiggins and Lady Perlina. An image popped into his head. Weren't they two characters from...? When reality set in, he slowly picked up the rest of the papers and read them.

Why would Robbie...was this her writing job? The one she had been so vague about? He certainly wasn't a prude, but—Robbie? Writing smut? He couldn't wrap his mind around the idea.

He stepped from her room and ran squarely into Colin, who saw the papers in his hands.

"So, you've figured it out, have you?"

Still confused, Gavin asked, "What do you know about this?"

Colin took his arm and steered him back into Robbie's room. "I didn't know anything about it until last night, when I took a letter that Robbie had thought she mailed from your friend, Faith Baker. She was going to show it to you to make sure you ended your marriage because of it."

"But why is Robbie writing this?"

"I could tell you, but I think she should tell you herself."

"No. You tell me, and tell me now." Although he sounded demanding, Gavin had never felt so powerless.

"All right, I will, if only to keep you from having a stroke," Colin said.

Colin shared what Robbie had told him the night before. Gavin's first question was, "Why didn't she tell me?"

Colin snuffled a snort. "And admit to you that the only way she could survive in Edinburgh was to write smut? How would you have reacted if she had approached it that way?"

Gavin turned back to his friend. "I don't know. I don't understand how she could write this stuff. She was still a vir—" He stopped, embarrassed that the word nearly slipped out.

"That should tell you something, Gavin. It wasn't as if she was experiencing it; she was merely using the words her mentor had used for the same twaddle. And we both know we've read all of it ourselves."

"But, Robbie. My *wife*."

"You're more concerned about that than you are about the fact that Faith wanted to break up your marriage so she could have you for herself? Don't try to deny it; she admitted it to me last night."

Gavin sank onto a tufted velvet settee and picked up a little ball meant for the dog. "Am I that naïve, Colin? Do I see only what I want to see in people?"

"Yes."

"It's who I am. And I prefer to see the best in others."

"That's fine. Just listen when more than one other person begs to differ with your opinons. You know more about the ancient world than any man alive, but you still have a lot to learn about life."

Just then the pup came bounding into the room, Robbie not far behind. She stopped and stared. "What are you two doing in my room?" When she saw the papers all smoothed out on the writing table, she moaned, "Oh God," and covered her face with her hands.

Both men went toward her. "Robbie—" they said in unison.

Her eyes blazing, she pointed to the door. "Out. Both of you, please just get out."

She'd known it would happen sometime. But even so, she wasn't prepared. All the excuses and reasons in the world that she made for having to write smut didn't seem to be enough to keep her from feeling unclean. She shut the door behind them and leaned against it, her eyes closed, her heart pounding hard against her ribcage.

Now what? Her secret was out. The jig was up. Would she end up back in Edinburgh anyway? Gavin would have a perfect right to divorce her, or at the very least ask for an annulment. And she couldn't blame him.

She glanced around the fine room, taking mental pictures of the lovely things she had use of for such a short time. All fairy tales don't end happily, do they? She feared this one wouldn't.

Gavin's family was leaving tomorrow. Robbie wondered if she could avoid them altogether. She also wondered if Gavin would have gone right downstairs and told them what he'd just learned about his wife. Morbid embarrassment. Far worse than being booted from her shabby room at the rooming house. That was a piece of cake compared to this!

She went to the window and looked out onto the fading summer garden, memorizing each and every flower and shrub. She must begin packing. She glanced at her bulging wardrobe. What in the devil (*sorry, Papa*) would she do with all of the gowns, capes, hats, and geegaws that seemed necessary for a country estate's mistress? Leave them? She certainly would have no use for most of them back in Edinburgh. And that was where she would go, wasn't it?

She dragged out her battered valise and began folding necessities, like her underthings, into it. She fingered a finely spun cotton corset cover with a pink grosgrain ribbon threaded through the bodice. She certainly thought she was something, didn't she? As if fine underwear and fancy gowns made her something other than what she really was. A poor—but educated, she reminded herself—purveyor of pornographic passion and verbal vomit. Oh, she was a fine example of "the lady" of an estate. Hogwash.

A knock at the door startled her. She tossed the camisole cover into the valise and opened the door. "May I come in?" Gavin sounded tentative.

She turned away and walked toward the window, looking out at the garden.

"Robbie, just explain it to me." He closed the door behind him. "Explain why this was the only means of making a living."

She whirled around, angry. "Do you think it's what I wanted to do? Don't you think if I could have sold beautiful fiction or children's stories, I would have? I have tablets of stories I have written that no one seems to want to publish. And Colin asks, all innocently, if he's looking at the next Brontë sister. Ha!"

"But couldn't you have done something else?"

She rounded on him. "Like what? Clean up after the ill at the poor house? Oh, don't think I wasn't tempted. But whatever you think I am, Gavin, I am a writer. And a writer writes because she must, even if it doesn't pay well. And if she is fortunate enough to find a writing job that pays something, she grabs it before someone else can, because believe me, someone else as needy and eager as she is, will."

He was quiet for so long, she finally said, "I'll pack up as soon as your family leaves."

"You'll pack up?" He raised an eyebrow at her. "And go where, may I ask?"

"Well, thanks to Colin, and no thanks to your friend, Miss Baker, I still have a job, and even though it isn't decent or noble or proper, it pays something."

He took a turn around the room. "Don't be a fool."

"Oh, now I'm not only a smut peddler, I'm also a fool."

"Robbie!"

His voice was so harsh she nearly stumbled backward. She had never heard him raise his voice to anyone, much less her. He hadn't even scolded her pup when it had an accident on the morning room carpet.

"I don't want you to leave," he said.

"Why would you want me to stay?"

"Because I like having you here. I want you here, with me."

"Even though I peddle smut?"

"Stop saying that. I do understand why you did it. But I don't want you to do it anymore."

She sat down on the bed. "Just like that?" She snapped her fingers. "What about the pieces I owe them?"

"If, as you say, there are all these would-be writers roaming the streets Edinburgh, I'm sure the editors, if that's what they call themselves, won't have any trouble filling your position."

This was all so baffling. "What am I to do with myself, then?"

"I want you to write what you have always wanted to write."

She stood there, taking in his words, with her mouth hanging open. Then she bounded off the bed and threw herself at him. "Oh, Gavin, thank you, thank you!" Tears rolled down her cheeks and off her chin. "I'm getting your shirt wet."

"Now," he said, "my family is probably wondering what's going on up here. I'll leave it to you to decide whether or not to tell them about—"

"No. I'm putting it behind me, Gavin. Let's start fresh."

Chapter Thirteen

In the weeks after Gavin's family bade them farewell, Robbie dug into her trove of partially written stories, reading through them, trying to decide how to continue. Then, one day as she watched Lady attempting to make friends with one of the stable cats, a thought came to her. And she began to write. The story was about a Corgi named Oscar and a regal, yet scruffy looking cat named Madeline, both of whom could speak to Oscar's owner, but no one else.

She couldn't write fast enough. Things popped into her head so quickly, she had trouble getting them down on paper, afraid she would forget. Even a time or two at night, she awakened with a wonderful thought, lit the lamp, and scribbled on a paper she kept by the nightstand.

She was so busy and engrossed in her work, she hadn't even realized she had missed her menses two months in a row.

And that's when her new perfect life began to fall apart.

She and Gavin were in the breakfast room when Mrs. Murray hurried in with a note. "Come by messenger, it did," she explained.

Gavin opened it, read it, and looked across the table at Robbie. "We're about to have a visitor." He handed her the note.

Robbie looked at the words and realized that until this moment, her life had been too good to be true. Birdie, true to form, was interrupting Robbie's idyllic existence.

"It doesn't say why she's coming, or if she's coming alone," Gavin said.

Robbie's only hope was that Joe accompanied her. Otherwise, why would she come to see Robbie?

She and Gavin had been getting along so well. He was kind and attentive, and they had a wonderful life together, even though Robbie knew he still didn't love her.

She touched her abdomen. And now, sensing she was pregnant, she wondered how that would change things. Although Gavin visited her room frequently, he never stayed the night. Now, with Birdie's arrival, would he visit her bed at all?

"So we're to expect her, or them, tomorrow before tea. We'd best get one of the small apartments ready," Robbie said, gritting her teeth. As much as the thought of her sister's appearance irked her, she was not one bit surprised.

. . .

Birdie's arrival was led with as much fanfare as Robbie expected. She came with a companion who looked after her needs—for the time being. Birdie was blind. And Robbie was stunned.

"Oh, it was terrible, just terrible," Birdie lamented. "The carriage hit a large rut in the road and it tipped over and killed my poor Joey. And this," she said, pointing to her face, "is what it left me. Without sight."

Robbie placed a hand on her sister's shoulder, her own heart thrumming against her ribs. "Joe is dead?"

"Isn't that what I just said? Aye, now I'm not only a widow but I'm blind as a bat." She pulled a delicate handkerchief from her pocket and dabbed her nose.

Poor Joe, Robbie thought. Along with her own shock, Robbie was sympathetic. "What do the doctors say?"

Birdie gave her a little pout. "They told me there was nothing wrong with me. They called it 'hysterical' blindness." She huffed. "Apparently they feel that the trauma of the accident and losing my poor Joey has rendered me temporarily blind."

"But that's good news, isn't it?" Gavin placed his hand over hers, and Birdie squeezed it and smiled.

"Oh, optimistic Gavin; always looking on the bright side."

Suddenly, though, she frowned. "I was truly surprised to learn that you and Robbie got married," she said, her expression concerned. "I don't remember you even talking to her all those years ago."

Gavin cleared his throat, and everyone was uncomfortable. "Things have a habit of changing, don't you think?"

She sighed. "I suppose, but…well…" She sighed again.

Robbie watched the exchange and bit the insides of her cheeks. As had become a ritual for her, she rubbed her hand over her stomach.

"The problem is that my companion must leave in the morning, and I'll have no one to care for me," Birdie bewailed, dabbing at her dry eyes with a handkerchief.

"Nonsense," Gavin said. "You can stay here with us, isn't that right, Robbie?"

Robbie nearly lost her lunch. In truth, she was still nauseous from the morning. "Why, yes of course. Where else in the world would she go?" She hoped she kept the sarcasm from her voice, but she wasn't sure she succeeded, nor did she care.

"Well," Birdie began, "it is bad news. Joey's family got a solicitor and took all of his holdings, leaving me with nothing." Tears, perhaps crocodile, perhaps not, rolled down her cheeks.

At least she hadn't ended up a rich widow after stealing her beau, Robbie thought. That would have been the perfect ending, though, wouldn't it? The fact that she's no longer able to make people scrape and bow is probably the worst thing that had ever happened to Birdie.

But Robbie did have an idea. Thoughts of Lydia and Karl had not been far from her mind. She would bring it up to Gavin once they were alone—if, in fact, they were ever alone again.

• • •

That night after her companion had helped Birdie get ready for bed, and when Robbie was sure her sister was asleep, she met Gavin in the library.

He lifted his gaze from the map he was studying as she entered. "Well, who would have thought of this turn of events?"

She tried to smile. "Who, indeed?" She sat in a wing chair across from him. "I have an idea."

He looked up, giving her his full attention.

"There is a woman, a nurse and midwife, I worked with at a small clinic in Edinburgh. She has a teenaged son with an affliction, a palsy, that affects his speech and movements, but his mind is sharper than most his age." She paused, waiting to see if Gavin had a question.

"If you would agree, and, I suppose we'd have to check with Birdie as well, I'd like to write and offer her a position as Birdie's companion. The woman is patient as a saint, and I believe that's what Birdie is going to need, to be honest."

Gavin leaned against the back of his chair. "I guess I hadn't thought of her future care; she would be easy enough to appease, though."

Robbie almost blurted, "'easy to appease'?" but held her tongue.

"Contact this woman. If she's been working in the slums of Edinburgh, she might jump at the chance for a change. As for the boy, the country is a good place for him. I do understand bullying, Robbie. Believe it or not, I was bullied in school."

She could see him, retreating into his books and maps after being teased. Perhaps that was what had made him such a recluse. "Thank you, Gavin. I've thought of her situation so often since I've been here; she deserves more than she had when I left her." And even Birdie wouldn't complain if there was yet another person to cater to her.

Chapter Fourteen

Colin's return to Erskine House couldn't have come at a more opportune time, according to Robbie.

He strode into the morning room, well dressed and relaxed, and his first words, when he saw Birdie sitting on the settee, were, "And who is this charming creature?"

"This is my sister, Birdie," Robbie announced. She watched the different emotions inch over his face as he looked at Birdie. He was bemused, then enlightened, and then, finally smitten. Robbie knew the look well. It rarely took the male of the species to come to that conclusion any faster.

He joined Birdie on the settee and took her hand in his. "It's my pleasure to meet you, madam. I have heard so much about you."

Delighted for the attention, Birdie tittered. "It's nice to meet one of Gavin's friends, sir. And might I say, you have the most calming voice. Are you a preacher?"

He laughed, apparently delighted with her, and said, "No, madam, I am a doctor."

Birdie perked right up. "A doctor? Well, now isn't that most interesting. Where is it that you practice?"

He glanced at the others, and then answered, "I'm currently not practicing medicine, madam. I'm on a hiatus."

"And where did you practice before, may I ask?"

"In Edinburgh. I was a surgeon."

Birdie let out a great, huge sigh. "Oh, if you could perform a miracle on me and heal my sightless eyes."

Robbie rolled hers. "Apparently Birdie suffers from hysterical blindness, Colin."

"I see. Tell me how it happened."

Birdie, happy to be the center of attention, told her story again, embellishing it here and there to make it more dramatic for her new conquest.

* * *

Later, in the library, Colin sat almost speechless, a glass of brandy in his hand.

Gavin waved his hand in front of his friend's face. "Hello? You in there?"

Colin blinked and focused on Gavin. "She is exquisite."

"I did tell you that, didn't I?"

"I couldn't imagine any woman having such perfect features. She is completely symmetrical, did you know that? One side of her face is not more beautiful than the other; they are both perfection."

Gavin raised one cynical brow. Considering Colin's own ravaged features, Gavin wasn't surprised that it was something he would notice. "I guess I hadn't detected that." He watched his friend. "So now do you think I made the most intelligent mistake of my life?"

"I won't lie to you. She would have been quite the beauty on your arm. But, after getting to know Robbie, I still think it was a mistake in your favor."

"Why, so you can step in and become Birdie's hero?" Gavin said it with humor, not malice.

Colin grunted. "Like that would be possible. Imagine her horror if her sight should return at some point when she was sitting with me. The shock might blind her for good."

"You're too hard on yourself. She might surprise you. Anyone can change, you know."

"How about you? Are you sorry now that you didn't send Robbie packing when she arrived?"

Gavin was quiet for a moment, then said, "I've become very

fond of Robbie. We fit well together. There is no drama, no theatrics. I'm not sure I could handle that sort of thing in my life."

"But you think about it, don't you?" Colin asked with a sly smile. "Don't tell me the moment you heard that Birdie was coming, you didn't feel a twinge of excitement?"

"Actually, what I felt was curiosity. Strange, I wasn't knocked for a loop when she walked into the room. Yes, she is beautiful, I won't deny it. But I was more curious as to how Robbie would react to her sister being here."

"And how did she react?"

"I think she was feeling far more than she let on. She was polite and sympathetic, and I believe they were honest reactions. But remember, Birdie took her beau. Was she thinking that perhaps Birdie would try to steal me away as well?"

Colin nodded. "Just imagine what Birdie would do if she ever discovered the truth."

"God forbid," Gavin replied, a shiver racing up his spine.

"Robbie worked with a nurse in Edinburgh whom she feels would be a good companion for Birdie. She has a young son with palsy. This might be just the place for them."

"Palsy," Colin repeated. "I've always been interested in it. What causes it and all that. Is it an accident at birth, or is it something that happens very early on in the growth stage of the fetus?"

"Ah, if you stick around, you might be able to pick the chap's brain," Gavin remarked.

"Indeed. I guess I've always preferred being here rather than in the city." He was quiet a moment, then asked, "Is Birdie aware you have already taken control of her life?"

"It's Robbie's plan; it's a good one. No matter what Birdie is or is not, I can't imagine her not feeling grateful for such a proposal."

"But seriously, Gavin, you don't expect her to stay here indefinitely, do you? Live right under your nose? Be present at every evening meal? Surely Robbie wouldn't be comfortable with that."

"No, I don't imagine she would. And truthfully, neither would I. This is all so sudden I haven't really thought of a future plan. But until I do, we must be absolutely sure that Birdie feels welcome. This is my home, and I will insist that she be taken care of until something else can be worked out."

• • •

Robbie sent off a missive to Lydia immediately, telling her of the position and explaining that both she and Karl were most welcome. To ice the cake, she sent coinage enough for them to travel by coach to Galashiels. She did not go into detail about her sister's personality. But even at her worst, Birdie would be easier to care for than the girls whom she had treated at Lydia's little clinic. Or so she hoped.

One day as she passed through the hallway near Birdie's apartment, Mrs. Murray came barreling out of her room, carrying a load of laundry, steam coming out of her ears.

"What is it, Mrs. Murray?"

The woman stopped. "What is it? What *isn't* it? That sister of yours has a never ending list of chores for me to do." She huffed. "I wouldn't be surprised if her poor Mr. Bean didn't throw himself under that carriage just to get away from her."

Robbie bit her lip. "I'll talk with her. Please, you aren't her servant. I'll take care of her until her new companion arrives. You just stick to the job you do so incredibly well."

Mrs. Murray studied her. "Are ye sure the two of ye are related?"

Robbie gave her a wan smile. She found Birdie in her apartment, fanning herself with an elaborately decorated Japanese fan.

"It's me, Birdie."

"Oh, Robbie. Come," she said, patting the space beside her. "Sit with me."

Robbie obliged. "Tell me about your life before the accident."

A rare embarrassed smile curved Birdie's mouth. "I took him away from you."

"Yes," Robbie answered, "You did." She wanted in the worst way to add that everything Robbie had ever had was the one thing

Birdie wanted, but she held her tongue. Instead she asked, "Were you happy?"

Birdie blinked repeatedly, something Robbie had noticed she did now that she couldn't see. "I suppose I was. He had a lovely townhouse in Glasgow. Three beautiful floors with fine-looking furnishings and servants." On a sigh, she added, "I loved it there. The help treated me like a queen, and Joey made sure I had everything I wanted." A wistful look spread across her face. "Now I suppose I'll have nothing. Nothing at all." She sniffed and dabbed at her nose with a lacy handkerchief.

"He also had a small country house which he loved more than the house in town, but of course, I didn't care much for being in the country. What was there to do? Rarely was there a ball or a party, and if there was, they were all country bumpkins. I had nothing in common with them. And to make matters worse, it was quiet all the time." She lifted one delicate shoulder. "You know how I hate it when there's no excitement."

How well I do. "But he was kind to you?"

"Oh, yes. Joey was a kind man." She frowned. "Rather bland, however, don't you think?"

"He and I had lively discussions about Scottish politics," Robbie explained.

Birdie made a face. "Oh, pooh. I can't stand it when men talk politics. When Joey tried, I feigned exhaustion and went to my room."

Poor Joe, Robbie thought. Poor, besotted Joseph Bean. Perhaps Robbie really had dodged a bullet. Perhaps Birdie had actually done her a favor. And, she thought, a wry expression on her face, perhaps Joe did purposely throw himself under the carriage.

"...and to leave me penniless. What am I to do? Who will care for me?" Again, the expensive lacy, linen square went to dab at her nose.

Robbie was grateful her sister couldn't see, for her own expression was less than pleasant or sympathetic. Birdie had not reformed. Robbie changed the subject by telling Birdie about Lydia.

Birdie frowned. "You mean you have hired this woman without my knowledge? How do you know I'll like her? Maybe she'll be mean. Maybe I'd rather just stay here with you." She gave her sister a pretty pout.

Robbie took a deep breath. "Birdie, Lydia is a trained nurse. She will be a wonderful companion, and since you need the care, surely you can't decline this help. Gavin is busy at the school, and I have duties here as well." Well, her writing was a duty, wasn't it? "It wouldn't be fair to leave you to your own devices, since you aren't able to see. But I do hope you'll work at becoming a little independent," she finished.

Birdie sat with her arms across her chest and her chin upturned. "Colin could help me."

"Colin isn't always going to be here, Birdie, and he isn't a lap dog, so don't go relying on him to keep you entertained."

"Don't scold me, Robbie," she whispered. "I am blind. I can't do things for myself."

"But surely there are some things you can learn to do," she countered.

"Like what? Read? Take a walk? Travel to Edinburgh alone? I think not," Birdie answered, her voice tight.

"But how about learning to get around without having someone always with you? Do you have a cane?"

Birdie tsked. "I'm not crippled. I'm blind."

"A cane would help you 'feel' your way. It could be used to detect things in front of you that you can't see."

"So would a dog," she said. "I'd rather have a dog."

Robbie chewed the inside of her cheek. Ever since the arrival of her sister, her cheek had gotten raw. "But Lydia Dunn will be here within a week, and I'll not have you treat her shabbily."

"Oh, all right," Birdie said with a huff. "I hope she can read. I may not have been the scholar you are, Robbie, but I did love to read before this," she said, waving her hand over her eyes, "happened."

Suddenly Lady Perlina bounded into the room, making straight for them as they sat on the settee. Exuberant as always,

Lady jumped onto Robbie's lap and immediately stuck her wet nose in Birdie's ear.

"Oh! Oh, what…" Birdie reached out, her hand rubbing against Lady's fur. "Oh, Robbie, it's a dog. A sweet dog. Remember when Papa forbade us to have one because they didn't belong in the house?"

Robbie was amazed at her sister's reaction. For some reason, she had thought Birdie would scream and leap off the couch. "I do remember him saying that. This is Lady," she introduced.

Birdie's features actually softened. It was the first time Robbie had ever seen her sister so serene. "Lady," she repeated, allowing the pup to lick her hand. "Will she sit with me, do you think? I would love to have her sit with me."

Once again, Robbie had something that Birdie wanted. But how could she refuse her? And what harm would it actually do? "She's still a puppy, Birdie, she's not really trained, so I can't promise she'll do as you want her to."

Birdie bent and put her face against the puppy's fur. "She smells just like a dog. It's an earthy smell, don't you think?" Lady was lavishing Birdie with kisses. And Birdie didn't squirm away. How very unusual, thought Robbie.

"Yes, she certainly smells like a dog. I've bathed her a few times, but I always seem to come out wetter than she does," Robbie said with a laugh. Then, "Birdie, I have some work I must get to. Will you be all right here alone?"

"With Lady? Of course. Go. Do your work. And if you see Gavin anywhere, tell him I'd like to see him. And, also, tell that Murray woman I need fresh bedding—"

"Mrs. Murray isn't your personal servant. That's why I've hired someone. If you need your bedding changed, I'll do it myself." She turned to leave.

"But, Robbie?"

With a patient sigh, she said, "Yes?"

"After you've changed the bedding, could you get me some tea and biscuits?"

"Of course." Robbie left in a hurry before her sister could demand anything else. She prayed Lydia and Karl had no obstacles to overcome that would keep them from arriving on time.

In the hallway, she met Colin.

"How is she doing?"

Robbie took a deep breath. "She's being typical Birdie, demanding something from everyone. I think she's even confiscated my dog. Whatever Robbie has, Birdie wants, was always my chant as a girl, and things don't seem to have changed."

Colin merely chuckled. "What can I do to help?"

"Read to her. She misses it, and it would keep her occupied for a spell."

"Done," he said with a nod. "I'll pick something from the library and go right in."

"You're a saint, Colin, thank you."

Later, a rider came with a message. It was addressed to Robbie. She recognized Lydia's handwriting, and her stomach flipped. Inside, it said:

> *Awful, terrible news, Robbie. I'm bereft! My Karl was put upon by thugs last evening and they beat him terribly. He died in my arms. I am unable to travel at this point.*

Robbie sank into a chair in the foyer. Oh, my God. For this to happen to Lydia! Poor, sweet Karl; he never had a chance.

She rushed into the library where both Colin and Gavin were conversing over Birdie's care. They both looked up.

"Robbie? What's wrong?" Gavin stood immediately and went to her side.

She handed him the note. After he read it, he said, "Has she other family?"

Robbie rubbed her hands over her face. "No. No one. She and Karl were so very alone in the world." Tears threatened, not because she now wouldn't have Lydia to care for Birdie, but for Lydia's pain.

"Perhaps you should go to her," Gavin suggested.

Robbie's head came up. "How can I do that?"

He gave her a patient smile. "Quite easily. I have a carriage, a driver, and a very good friend," he said, looking at Colin, "who could accompany you on the journey. I would go myself, but I have promised the students we would do a special project this next week. I don't want to disappoint them."

"Splendid idea!" Colin said. "And we can stay at my town-house. Eve will be delighted."

Robbie was stunned. "Both of you would do this for me?"

Gavin shrugged. "I think that's what we're here for, don't you agree, friend?"

Colin nodded. "We should probably go quickly. Pack a bag, and let's get on the road."

This was all happening so fast! "What about Birdie?"

"Ah, yes," Gavin answered. After a moment he said, "What if we ask your maid, Maureen, to be with her until we can figure something out? With you gone she won't have so much to do anyway. I'd even pay her extra to do it."

With everything apparently settled, soon Robbie and Colin were on their way.

Chapter Fifteen

It was odd. Although Robbie hadn't been gone for more than a few months, she felt like a stranger in Edinburgh. She hadn't realized how much she loved the country until the smoky fog of the city loomed over her once more.

Colin had sent a rider on ahead to inform Lydia that Robbie was on her way. She met them at the door of her little clinic and immediately fell into Robbie's arms, sobbing quietly.

"I'm so, so sorry, Lydia. What can I do?"

Lydia stepped away, sniffed and wiped her face with a handkerchief. "You shouldn't have made such a long trip, Robbie. There's nothing to be done now but bury the lad."

"Then that's what we'll do, right, Colin?"

Colin stepped down from the carriage and introduced himself, failing to mention that he was a doctor. "I have a friend who is a mortician, Mrs. Dunn. I would be honored if you would let me take care of the entire process. I understand how difficult and overwhelming this is for you."

Lydia's lower lip quivered. "I have very little money—"

"Nonsense," Robbie interrupted. "Everything will be taken care of. I know that Gavin would be more than happy to pay for the burial."

Now Lydia smiled through her tears. "So all is well with you and your new mister?"

Robbie raised her eyebrows. "There will always be something for us to adjust to," she said with a little laugh.

Leaving Gavin at home with Birdie was not something Robbie wanted to think about. But think she did, all the way from Erskine

House to the outskirts of Edinburgh. Her darkest thoughts centered on the fact that Birdie had already commandeered her dog and her maid; what was to keep her from trying to do the same with her husband?

They took Lydia with them to Colin's townhouse where they met Eve, Colin's spinster sister. She looked nothing like her brother. Although her eyes were warm and her smile sincere, she was a very plain-looking woman who, Robbie thought, was probably well past thirty. But she took Robbie and Lydia in, scooting them along in front of her like they were a couple of chicks being tended to by the mother hen.

Later, as Robbie and Lydia were ensconced in a room together, Lydia told Robbie what had happened.

"They cut him, Robbie."

Robbie took her hands in hers. "Cut him? Where?"

Lydia took a deep breath and gave Robbie's hands a squeeze. "From what Karl said before he...before he...passed on, the thugs told him that he should—" She sucked in a breath. "They told him he was an abomination and that he should never have children."

Robbie gasped, realizing what Lydia meant. "Oh, my dearest. I'm so sorry. What's this world coming to when an innocent young lad can't even be left alone to live his life? How could he possibly have been a threat to them?"

"He threatened no one. A gentle soul, he was," Lydia whispered, close to tears again.

After a moment, Robbie said, "I don't even know how to begin to ask you to leave here, knowing that Karl will be close by."

"I have no reason to stay in this despicable city, Robbie. Karl and I were excited about a new spot; if you still want me to come, I'll come gladly."

Relieved, Robbie hugged her. "I'm not sure you'll be so glad you've come once you've met my sister."

Lydia pulled away and put her hand on Robbie's cheek. "If she's your sister, how difficult can she be?"

Hiding a smile, Robbie thought, *how difficult, indeed?*

Feeling the need to let Lydia know the whole story of her "fairy tale romance," Robbie filled her in on the mistaken proposal and everything that came afterwards. She told her she thought she was pregnant, but she wanted it kept between the two of them. She wanted Lydia to have a full picture of the household she was coming into.

The funeral was small, but Karl had touched many lives in his short one. A nun from the poor house came, the one who had found Karl on the steps those many years ago. She embraced Lydia, and they spoke quietly together after the service and the interment.

After packing Lydia's meager belongings and giving her a moment to look around one last time, they bade goodbye to Eve and set off for Erskine House.

• • •

They were met by a frazzled Mrs. Murray when they entered the foyer.

"Thank the Lord ye be back!" Her scarf was askew, and her clothes looked as though she'd slept in them.

Oh no. "What's happened? Is something wrong?" *How foolish of me to ask.*

"I sent Maureen home for a few days; the madam was running her ragged. Sweet girl, though, she offered to stay in spite of it, but she took a fall carrying the madam's laundry and turned her ankle. I thought it best to send her where she could get some rest."

Robbie winced. "Oh, Mrs. Murray. Please don't let her drive you away, too," Robbie pleaded. She pulled Lydia beside her. "This is Lydia Dunn. She's the nurse that we've hired to care for Birdie."

"Praise Jesus," Mrs. Murray said, making a sign of the cross over her chest. "Ye've got yer work cut out for ye, that's for certain."

Lydia stepped forward. "Now, now, things can't be as bad as all that. Let me get right to work. Show me my charge."

Robbie had been holding her breath. She exhaled, relieved, and took Lydia down the hallway into Birdie's apartment.

They stepped into the room. "Birdie?"

"Robbie? You're back. Good. That housekeeper of yours sent Maureen away, just when I was getting her acquainted with my needs. Now that you're home, you can get her back, can't you? Mrs. Murray doesn't like me, I know she doesn't. She can barely stand to come in and take care of things I need done."

Robbie glanced at Lydia, relieved not to see fear or even distaste on her face, although there was a hint of amusement. "Birdie, I've said this before. Mrs. Murray is not your personal servant. She's the one who keeps this whole place going, so you have to remember she has many other duties. And," she added, "I've brought you your own nurse."

Lydia sat down next to Birdie and touched her hand. "I'm Lydia Dunn."

Birdie frowned. "Your hands are rough."

Robbie shook her head and rolled her eyes.

"Aye, they are that," Lydia answered. "Hard work does that to a person."

Birdie released a petulant sigh. "Well, I suppose I can give you a try, since you've come all the way from Edinburgh. But I am quite helpless, you know."

"You have very pretty hair," Lydia commented.

All smiles now, Birdie said, "I know. And it needs washing. That can be your first task."

Lydia sat back, surprised. Or appearing so. "Do you mean to say you aren't even able to wash your own hair?"

"How can I? I can't see!"

"But you can feel, can't you, dear?" Her voice was soft but stern.

"Of course I can feel, but I don't know where anything is. I need help finding the bathroom."

Lydia tsked. "You mean to say you've been here for this long and you haven't learned how to find the bathroom? How do you manage?"

"Someone takes me by the hand and leads me there," Birdie explained.

"Oh, my dear. Wouldn't you rather be able to find it yourself, rather than counting on someone to be around when perhaps they aren't and cannot be?"

Exasperated, Birdie said, "Robbie? I don't think this is going to work."

"It's going to work, Birdie. You have to learn to do some things for yourself, and Lydia can teach you and help you."

"But she's—"

"Stop. No more whining, Birdie, I'm serious."

Birdie sank back against the settee. "Where's Gavin? I want to talk to Gavin. And where's my dog? Lady!" she shouted, and lo and behold Robbie's pup came running and jumped into Birdie's lap, not even giving Robbie a look. "Now send me Gavin. And did Colin return with you? I want to see him as well."

Robbie curtsied; fortunately Birdie couldn't see the whimsy.

● ● ●

Robbie and Lydia sat in the breakfast room having tea. "Now do you see what I mean?"

Lydia stirred her tea, then took a sip. "She's always gotten what she's wanted, hasn't she?"

"That and more, I believe," Robbie answered.

"Even as a youngster? Wasn't anyone stern with her?"

"No. Papa catered to her, and our housekeeper tried to handle Birdie once, but Papa intervened. I guess he didn't do her any favors."

The door swung open and Gavin entered. "Here you are." He took a chair next to Robbie and gave her a peck on the cheek. "I'm happy you're back." He looked a bit frazzled himself. When introduced to Lydia he released a sigh of relief.

"How are things at the school?" Robbie asked, so pleased to see him she wanted to drag him off to bed.

His forehead creased into furrows. "I didn't realize how difficult children were to control. I had no problem with my students at university; they were there because they wanted to be." With a puzzled shake of his head, he added, "There are a few boys in the class who continue to disrupt things for the rest of the students."

"How does the schoolmaster handle them?"

Gavin made an unpleasant face. "He takes a switch to them. I've never thought that did anything but make the child angrier and more apt to rebel, but they are his students, not mine."

"How have you handled them?"

"I've sent them home."

"That's probably what they wanted you to do," Lydia answered.

"I realize that," he said, "but I don't believe in corporal punishment for children."

Robbie watched as Lydia studied her husband. "You are truly a kind and patient soul, aren't you?"

Gavin let out a harsh laugh. "Between Birdie and my students, both kindness and patience have been sorely tested, believe me."

"Oh, no. What did she have you doing for her, anyway?" Robbie asked.

"Playing referee, mostly. At one point Mrs. Murray was close to quitting," he said.

"God, what kind of plague have I set upon this household?" Robbie asked. "So far no one has been able to control Birdie. You," she said to Lydia, "are our last hope."

"I'll do my best, but mind, it might not be pretty."

Chapter Sixteen

As a way to release her frustrations, Robbie wrote. Her story about Oscar and Madeline was coming along well, but it needed an antagonist. And who more antagonistic than a prim, wily, spoiled parrot named...Birdie? Robbie pondered that decision. Perhaps it wasn't right, but it was true that Birdie was the perfect antagonist.

Suddenly she heard a crash, and a wail. *Oh God.*

She raced to Birdie's apartment to find the porcelain water basin on the floor, in many pieces. She turned to Lydia. "Where's Birdie?"

One eyebrow raised, Lydia said, "Flailing her arms and legs against the mattress, she is. I thought we were doing well; she could find the bathroom by herself." Lydia pointed to the floor, "Then this happened."

"It was an accident?"

"Aye, if she'd done it on purpose, I'd have given her something to cry about."

Robbie's gaze settled on Lydia; she almost pitied her. "Are you sorry you came?"

Lydia's chin came up. "I am not a quitter. Truthfully, this is the most difficult patient I've ever dealt with." She gave Robbie a knowing look, "And I've known many difficult patients, as you well know."

Robbie helped Lydia clean up the mess, then went to check on her sister.

Just as Lydia said, Birdie was on the bed, face down, pounding on a pillow.

"Birdie?" Robbie prayed for a sympathetic tone.

Birdie rolled over. "I can't do this. I just can't. I've always had help, even when I could see. How does that woman expect me to do things blind when I didn't even do them when I had sight?"

Robbie lifted an eyebrow. "You were always capable of using the bathroom by yourself."

"Oh, you know what I mean." She blinked repeatedly, as she often did now. "Am I so hard to look after?"

Robbie sat on the bed and stroked her sister's arm. "I think you could use a little patience when you speak to others. In spite of how you might feel, you aren't alone in the universe."

Birdie sighed and sat up, swinging her legs over the side of the bed. "If I thought I had it hard before, this is far worse than anything I could have imagined."

"When did you ever have it hard?" Robbie couldn't help it; she needed to ask.

"The minute Joey was dead, my life became miserable. Not only was I blind, but I was poor." She screwed up her face and her lips quivered. "That was hard."

"We were never anywhere near wealthy, Birdie," Robbie reminded her.

"But I never wanted for anything. Papa gave me whatever I asked for." She stopped a moment, then frowned. "Except for that pony I always wanted." Then she gave Robbie a sly smile. "I didn't really expect to get it, though."

"You sure put up a big enough fuss," Robbie answered, remembering the incident well.

Birdie lifted her shoulders. "It was expected of me."

"Are you going to act your age now, when Lydia asks you to do something?"

"I'll try. I can't promise anything."

With that, Robbie left and went in search of her husband.

• • •

She found him behind the barn, chopping wood. Without a shirt. She stopped and stared. He was beautiful.

He glanced up, aware of his lack of modesty, and stopped working long enough to grab his shirt.

"Don't," Robbie said, taking it away from him. "You are handsome."

"Robbie, I—"

"Shh," she answered. She stepped close and ran her palms over his chest. It was hard and well muscled with just a salting of blond curls across his nipples. "I've wanted to do this, you know."

He didn't move, but she saw confusion and perhaps even a little desire in his eyes. "But we're outside..."

She smiled, continuing to touch him. "Yes, we are, aren't we?" She looked around. "But no one can see us back here, Gavin." She bent closer and inhaled his scent, now mixed with sweat and brawn.

"Robbie, I—"

"I'm going to kiss you, Gavin." Not giving him a moment to react, she stood on tiptoe and pressed her lips to his. She took his arms and placed them around her; she felt a thrill as they tightened.

He opened his mouth to say something, and Robbie put her tongue against his teeth.

When they separated, he said, "You know, you're quite a naughty girl."

She gave him a winsome smile. "Thank you." She put her arms around his waist and held him close. "Have you ever had sex outside?"

He threw back his head and laughed. "No, minx, I don't believe I ever have."

She pressed herself against him, feeling him stiffen. "Would you like to?"

He glanced around. "I don't see any place suitable."

She took his hand and tugged him along into the trees. "Suitable isn't what I'm looking for." She saw a small shed beyond the barn. "What's in there?"

"Your guess is as good as mine," he answered, taking the lead.

He shoved the door open; it smelled musty and earthy. The

floor was hard-packed dirt and there were some old tools leaning against one wall.

"The floor is too dirty," he said.

She shoved him against one wall. "We don't need the floor." She began undoing his breeches, finding him long and hard, waiting for her. In a matter of seconds, her underwear was on the floor and she hiked herself into his arms, hugging his waist with her legs, impaling herself on him. He held her easily, and they stood there a moment, simply savoring the feeling. They kissed again, face to face, their breaths mingling, their hearts pounding.

And then they began to move; not much, just enough so Robbie could feel his shaft rubbing against her. For her, the feeling came on so quickly she almost wanted to stop it and savor it, but she had no control over her hunger, and she squeezed him inside her and felt him explode just as she felt her own release.

Breathing hard, he lowered her to the floor. "You are a woman of many contradictions. You never cease to surprise me." He pulled up his breeches.

She climbed back into her underwear and gave him a hooded look. "Good. I hope you like surprises."

"Like this?" He took her chin and tilted it toward him. "How could I not?"

"I still haven't had a good look at it, you know." She didn't mention that she'd seen him at the Tweed.

He gave her a half grin. "It's always been dark."

"It's not dark now," she teased.

"Right now he isn't much to look at, not after you took such good care of him."

She stepped close and put her hand over his crotch. "I want to see."

"Only if I can see yours," he tormented.

"Any time, but now it's my turn." She undid his breeches again and tugged them over his naked hips. His penis was still at half-mast, and it was nestled into the beautiful, thick, tawny bush she'd seen briefly before. She was almost dizzy. "Oh, Gavin, he's beautiful, just like you are." She touched it and saw it move, then touched it again. And again. She glanced up at him and cocked an eyebrow.

"He's got a mind of his own," he murmured.

"And what is he saying right now?"

"He's telling me he wants you again, so drop your drawers, wife."

• • •

Robbie met Lydia on the foyer stairs; her expression was pained until she noticed Robbie, then she smiled.

"Having problems with Birdie again?"

"She's a handful, I'll admit that."

Robbie shook her head. "How are things otherwise?"

"Colin is reading to her now. She really seems to enjoy his company."

"Well, of course she does," Robbie countered. "He's probably the only one who caters to her every whim."

"That could get old."

"I know it already has for me," Robbie answered. "But men never seem to tire of my sister. She has some kind of hold over them. It's almost mystical."

"As long as he's entertaining her, I'm going to help Mrs. Murray in the kitchen."

• • •

Robbie went down the hallway to Birdie's apartment and listened at the door. Yes, Colin was reading.

She opened the door a crack and peeked in. Birdie was nestled close to Colin on the settee, her eyes wide, a tiny smile on her face. And Lady, once Robbie's sweet pup, was asleep on her lap.

Colin glanced up, and Robbie put a finger to her lips. Colin turned the page.

"'I resisted all the way: a new thing for me, and a circumstance which greatly strengthened the bad opinion Bessie and Miss Abbott were disposed to entertain of me.'"

As quietly as she could, Robbie stepped into the hallway and closed the door. Bless Colin and his willingness to keep Birdie occupied. *Jane Eyre* was an exciting read for anyone.

Chapter Seventeen

A letter arrived from Gavin's mother for Robbie, thanking her for her hospitality.

> *We did so enjoy our time with you, getting to know you and seeing how well you and Gavin get on. I couldn't be happier as a mother to know that my son has found such a wonderful, kind, and lovely young woman to marry. We, too, are thankful for the mistake! Gavin has always had his head in the clouds. Both Durham and I want the two of you to come visit us soon. The children keep asking when they can return to Erskine House! You are a fine hostess.*

Robbie put the letter aside, intent on writing Linnea of their latest adventures: caring for her hysterically blind sister and the accident that killed Joe, her husband.

She stood and felt dizzy, something new in her pregnancy. She should see a doctor, but there wasn't one locally, and she didn't want to raise any questions by asking to go into the city. And Colin? She wasn't ready to tell him her news, especially when she hadn't told Gavin. The dizziness passed quickly, and she was on her way to her writing room when she met Colin in the hallway.

"So it's *Jane Eyre*, is it?"

Colin rubbed the back of his neck. "She likes it."

"Of course she does," Robbie responded. "She'd like it if you read her Mrs. Murray's grocery list."

He chuckled. "At any rate, she wants to see you."

Robbie pulled in a deep sigh, releasing it on a whoosh, and pushed open the door. "Birdie?"

"Robbie. Come," she said, patting the place beside her, "come sit with me."

Robbie took a seat and gave her pooch, Lady, a scurrilous look. The dog wagged its tail.

"You know," Birdie began, "it's been a puzzle to me how you and Gavin even knew each other well enough to marry. It was obvious that he had a huge crush on me, but, as far as I can remember, he didn't know you were alive."

Blunt. Very Birdie. "Time changes things," Robbie said. "We happened to meet at university," she said, pleased with the quick lie.

Birdie raised her eyebrows. "Oh, how interesting." She seemed to ponder a moment, and then said, "I wonder what would have happened if I had gone to university too."

Robbie reached over and scratched her disloyal pet. "But you didn't. You bought a lot of fancy clothes, and got married." She wanted to add, "to my beau," but at this point it didn't matter anymore.

Birdie's face creased into a frown and said with a woeful sigh, "And now you have all this. And I have nothing. I can't see anything, but I know the house is beautifully appointed. I have felt the furniture, their coverings are soft and expensive. And it isn't just some little cottage in the woods; I swear it took five minutes to walk to my apartment from the front door."

Robbie didn't know how to answer. "Is there anything you want?"

Birdie closed her eyes and rested her head against the back of the settee. "I want your life, Robbie." She turned to Robbie and smiled, overly bright. "You know I'm kidding. A nice cup of hot tea would be lovely."

Robbie left, knowing she had to tell Gavin about her little lie. And also knowing Birdie meant every word she said.

• • •

It was two weeks before Robbie got Gavin alone; he'd been back home clearing up some legal issues regarding Erskine House.

In that time, Robbie had felt the quickening, very slightly, but she knew what it was. It really was time to tell Gavin what was happening with her body. When she heard his carriage arrive, she hurried down the hallway past Birdie's apartment, and suddenly the door opened swiftly, the knob catching Robbie directly in the stomach.

As she bent over, cradling her abdomen, Birdie bursted from the room, waving her arms and ranting.

"I don't care! I can't stand being cooped up in here a minute longer."

Lydia came out behind her and saw Robbie bent over. Alarm registered on her face.

"Get back inside, Birdie, please."

"I'm going crazy in here by myself. I want to be out where everyone else is," she shouted.

Lydia gave Robbie a worried look, but Robbie pressed a finger to her lips and shook her head.

"I promise you can, truly I promise. But for now, would you please, just for me, go back into your apartment? I'll bring you fresh sweets and some tea."

Birdie huffed. "Oh, all right. But hurry. Robbie is always promising to bring me tea and she never does. I'm starving, and I'm bored."

When Birdie was inside, Lydia went to Robbie. "What happened?"

Robbie continued to hold her stomach. "The doorknob hit me in the belly."

Lydia ushered Robbie down the hallway into the parlor and made her lie down on the settee. "We'll have to see if it did any harm."

"How will we know?"

"The only way we can. You'll have to monitor things, like if you start to bleed, let me know immediately. And cramping. I hope to God you don't have any cramping."

"Would that mean I'm going to miscarry?" The thought weighed heavily on Robbie.

"Not necessarily, but we would take some precautions." She stood a moment, her hands tented over her mouth. "I'm thinking we should let Dr. Innes in on our secret."

"I suppose, but I must tell Gavin."

"You mean to tell me you haven't told him, and he hasn't figured it out for himself?"

"These past weeks have been so hectic, with Birdie here and all, and then Gavin had to go home. We just don't seem to have any time alone."

"Pardon my frankness, dear, but not even at night?"

"I haven't wanted to worry him." But was that the truth? Robbie didn't know how he would react, for she still wasn't convinced he would ever love her as she wanted and needed to be loved. Knowing she carried his child could send him either way, she thought.

A sudden cramp made Robbie wince, and Lydia said, "I think for now you'd best stay put. Go to your room where it's nice and peaceful, and try to rest."

Robbie sat up slowly. "So you're going to treat me like an invalid?"

"Why not? There is nothing going on in this place that needs your specific attention. When I see Dr. Innes, I'll send him up. I want you to tell him."

"I doubt he knows all that much about pregnancy," Robbie murmured.

"Well, I wager I've delivered more bairns, but surely he knows the basics." With that, Lydia took Robbie's arm and walked her to her room.

· · ·

They were all ensconced in Robbie's suite, the men looking quite baffled.

"Robbie is with child," Lydia announced.

Silence.

Suddenly Gavin's face lit up. "But, that's wonderful. Isn't it?"

Robbie felt a rush of relief.

"It should be and probably is. She was walking past Birdie's apartment when the door flew open, and the knob hit Robbie in the stomach."

Colin understood immediately. "How far along are you?"

Robbie counted back. "Four months, I believe."

"Four months?" Gavin nearly roared. "Why haven't you told me?"

"Things have been so hectic, Gavin, and well, I guess I don't really have a reason."

His frown turned to worry. "You're not happy about this?"

"Of course I am, but to be honest, I wasn't sure you would be."

Colin intervened. "All right, so now everyone is happy. Robbie, I want you to keep to your bed, maybe a week or two, to make sure things are all right."

"What am I supposed to do with myself?" Robbie groused.

"Finish that book you've been working on," Gavin said with a knowing grin.

"You know about that?"

He reached out and touched her hair. "You talk in your sleep."

Before everyone left her alone, she asked each of them for a favor. "Please don't tell Birdie how this happened. She couldn't see me, after all. Tell her anything, but don't tell her the truth. And Gavin, be warned: she asked how we got together, and I told her it was at the university."

He gave her such a warm smile she felt teary. "Good to know."

When she was alone and resting on her bed, she thought that wasn't it perfect that Birdie would be the one to possibly terminate her pregnancy, inadvertent though her actions had been? Robbie had a strong feeling that if Birdie could change places with her and have Gavin's baby herself, she would do it. It would be the ultimate prize; all other things she had taken from her sister were nothing compared to this.

Chapter Eighteen

It had only been a few days, yet Robbie was beginning to understand Birdie's need to escape her apartment. At least Robbie could see. But what? Four walls, a window, a few pictures hanging here and there, and not even her own Lady Perlina had come to stay.

The day before Lydia had brought Birdie in for a brief visit. Birdie had Lady Perlina on a makeshift leash; the pup pulled against it and jumped around, clearly uncomfortable. But Birdie was curious as to why Robbie was confined to her bed.

"Will you be here long, Robbie?" she had asked. "Is it the influenza? Have you a fever? I daresay I probably shouldn't get too close to you; I don't do well when I'm feeling poorly."

Lydia and Robbie exchanged wry glances.

"Why do you have Lady on a leash?"

"Colin and I are training her," she said. "She already knows a few commands. Watch." Birdie blinked repeatedly. "Lady, sit."

The rambunctuous dog did as she was told, her tail wagging. Birdie reached into her pocket and brought out a small bit of oat cake, which Lady took delicately. "Good girl. See?" Birdie was clearly excited. Robbie was impressed.

"It does give you something useful to do," Robbie pondered. She was still a bit resentful about her sister hijacking her dog.

"It won't be long before she'll be my eyes, will it Lydia?"

"I don't think you should go getting your hopes up, my dear."

Robbie added quickly, "But one never knows how fast a pet will respond, does one, Lydia?"

Understanding Robbie's meaning, she answered, "I guess one

truly never knows. And," she added, "Lady is a smart little critter. She's a fast learner."

"Birdie, would you mind if she came up onto the bed? I'd like to pet her." *She's my bloody dog; she should be here with me.*

Lydia lifted the pup next to Robbie, and she sniffed Robbie, then licked her face. "So you haven't forgotten me altogether, have you?"

Birdie released a little gasp. "Oh, dear. I have completely taken over the control of your puppy, haven't I, Robbie?"

Yes, you have. Like everything else in my life. Robbie shrugged. "I guess it's all right. At least she's learning something. That's important."

After the little visit, Robbie felt weepy. If Birdie hadn't waltzed back into her life, she would still have a dog. And a good life. And peace. At this moment she was grateful that Birdie had no idea how close she had come to being the current Mrs. Gavin Eliot. Some solace, anyway. She stroked her stomach, wincing as she felt another twinge in her belly.

• • •

In the dim light of the library, Gavin and Colin each nursed a brandy.

"How long do you suppose this will go on?" Gavin asked.

"Since there's apparently no reason for her blindness, I would guess it would take some kind of incident, traumatic or otherwise, to snap her out of it."

"I hate to say it, but I do believe Birdie enjoys being waited on hand and foot."

"And I, for one, enjoy being her slave. Undoubtedly it will end once her sight returns." He ran his fingers over the scar on his cheek. "When she sits next to me while I read, it almost feels like we're a couple. Until I come to my senses."

"I don't even like to think about what my life would be if I hadn't asked Robbie to marry me by mistake."

"Having Birdie as mistress of Erskine House? I don't know, I realize she is self-centered and spoiled, but perhaps she would have changed, knowing that she would have everything she has ever wanted."

"Perhaps, yet…"

"No sense contemplating the future, my friend. Drink up. We have some books to go over."

• • •

In the hallway outside the library door, Roberta Bean, née Fleming, was so surprised at what she heard, she released Lady's leash. The dog pushed the library door open and bounded inside.

Birdie felt her way into the room; suddenly she could see shapes of furniture and light coming from the fireplace.

"I'm sorry." She thought quickly. "Is anyone here?"

"Gavin and Colin," Gavin said. "Is there something you need?"

Birdie stood perfectly still. "No. No, I was walking Lady along the hallway, and she pulled from my grasp. Is she in here?"

"She's here," Colin said. "Come, you rascal, we'll tether you up again."

As Colin got close, Birdie could see him almost as clearly as if it were daylight. What she saw nearly caused her to faint. Blinking furiously, she said, "Here, let me take the leash. If one of you could help me get back to my apartment, I'd be so very grateful."

"Come, my ladies," Colin took her arm, "back to your kingdom."

Had Birdie not been a woman who could feign any feeling she wanted, she may not have been able to pull off her pretense. But as they got closer to her apartment door, she could see more clearly than ever. But she couldn't let on. No, not yet.

Her apartment door opened, and Lydia stepped out. So, that's what the taskmaster looked like. Short, dumpy, a peasant if there ever was one. "Lydia, are you there?" she all but shouted.

Lydia took her arm and led her inside. "Thank you, Dr. Innes. She's getting tired of being cooped up."

Birdie used her sight to look at Colin through a veil of lashes. Ghastly. She recalled what Lydia had told her about Colin's accident, but Birdie had no idea it was so severe; a small scar here and there would have been nothing. She thanked him and went inside.

So here it was. Gavin, the poor, mild-mannered bookworm, had gotten her and Robbie mixed up. Birdie almost chortled. Well of course he had wanted to marry her! She had yet to meet a man who hadn't toppled head over heels for her. If what she heard was correct, it was she and not her sister that Gavin had proposed to in the first place!

Her heart pounding, she felt her way through her apartment, although she could see a little. By the time she reached her bedroom door, she knew what she had to do.

And the more she thought about things, the more upset she became. She closeted herself in her bedroom, explaining to Lydia that she wanted to rest, then went to the window. There were gardens outside, very pretty, too, if one cared about such things. She turned and studied the room. It was pleasant, she had to admit. She was anxious to see the rest of the house, but of course would have to bide her time. No telling what Robbie would convince Gavin to do if they found out she was no longer blind.

No place to go. She had absolutely no place else to go. Her eyes narrowed and a tiny smile ticked the corner of her mouth. This place was rightfully hers, anyway. That thought made her angry. Had Gavin not been such an absentminded fool, she would be mistress of the house at this very moment. And how much better that would have been than having to pretend to enjoy Joe's company or even his touch. She shivered. Thank God she never got with child. At least Gavin was handsome; she could live with that, even if he was bookish.

And what about Colin Innes? She made a face. Too bad he was so badly maimed. He was, after all, a physician. A surgeon, no less. But in truth, she had merely been shocked to look at him that first time. If he ever went back into practice, he might make a good living.

But now, she had to focus on herself. Keep up the pretense of blindness. Be watchful. If she was a clever girl, she could keep everyone fooled for as long as she wished.

• • •

Robbie drew her gaze away from the pile of sheets she had rolled up on the floor. So, that was it. She should tell someone, Lydia perhaps. Maureen would probably faint dead away if she was told there was a dead bairn in the bedding.

Her lips quivered, and she bit down on them. *Dead bairn.* The words were as heavy and morose as they sounded. No way to make it better, was there? *The bairn is up in heaven with the angels, Papa would say. The bairn is in a better place, Papa would say.*

Sorry, Papa. Robbie didn't think it was that easy. Well, perhaps it was, but it didn't take the pain from her heart.

Once again her gaze went to the pile on the floor. It had to be removed; she couldn't stand it any longer. Not wanting to alert everyone to her dilemma, she inched from the bed, feeling the strong discomfort between her legs, and put on a fresh nightgown that Maureen had put at the end of her bed. She bent and hauled the bedding into her arms and made for the door. That was as far as she got.

• • •

"She's coming around."

Colin's voice.

"Robbie? Can you hear me?"

Gavin.

She opened her eyes and found them at her bedside. Momentarily confused, she asked, "What are you doing here?"

"We might ask you what you were trying to do," Colin scolded.

Robbie blinked and moved her legs. And remembered her loss. "I…it's…I was…"

Gavin took her hand. "We know, Robbie. You should have called someone. Instead, you took it upon yourself and fainted dead away."

"You made quite an awful thud as you fell," Colin said. "The bedding cushioned you, thankfully."

Lydia scurried in. "I took care of the laundry." She gave Robbie a kind and gentle look. "I'm sorry, dear heart. I'm so sorry."

Tears sprang from Robbie's eyes; she couldn't stop them. "It's just one more thing my sister has taken from me," she said softly.

"If it were me," Lydia said, "I don't think I'd be quite so rational about it."

"I'm too tired to be anything else," Robbie answered. She gave them all a weak smile. "Maybe later."

Gavin took her hand in his and squeezed it. "That's my girl."

She looked at his handsome face, strong jaw, dimpled chin. He smiled at her as if he was proud of her. Did he mean he was proud because she wasn't the kind of person who would retaliate against such an outrage? Or did he mean he was proud because she would do what had to be done when she was stronger? He might be surprised. Robbie had taken about as much from her sister as she could. Something had to be done. Unfortunately it would have to wait until she was stronger, and Birdie could see again. And knowing Birdie, she knew which would come first.

Rather mean-spiritedly, Robbie wondered if Birdie would even tell them when she saw signs that her sight was returning.

Lydia broke her reverie. "I wrapped the bairn in a towel; what do you want to do with her?"

Robbie started. "It was a girl?" Tears came again.

"Aye, and whether she was fully formed or not, I expect you'll want to bury her."

"There's a small family cemetery on the south side of the house, away from the wind," Gavin explained.

Robbie nodded, a lump in her throat. "Yes. We'll put her there."

"Will ye name her?"

"Hope. She will be Hope." Robbie glanced at Gavin and saw that his eyes were shiny with tears. Hers came again.

Suddenly there was a shout from downstairs. "Hello? Where is everyone? Lydia? You promised me tea and some sweets. Hello?"

They all looked at one another, then Lydia threw up her hands and went to wait on the "poor blind girl."

Chapter Nineteen

After they buried little Hope Eliot, Robbie spent another week in bed, for her bleeding wouldn't stop. She was truly getting tired of being on her back, although she had finished the first draft of her book and for the life of her she couldn't change the name of the haughty, snotty parrot, so Birdie it was.

A knock at the door brought her out of her reverie. Lydia entered and closed the door softly behind her. She crept to the bed, sat in the chair beside it, and looked at Robbie. There was an odd expression on her face.

"What's wrong?"

Lydia took a deep breath. "I think your sister's sight has returned."

Robbie sat up, alert. "Why do you think so?"

"I've wondered about it for a while. Shortly after she and I visited you the last time, she changed."

"Changed. How?"

"She makes sweeping gestures in an attempt to find things. She didn't do that before. It's as if she's pretending."

Robbie rested against her pillows, a slight headache forming behind her eye. "Now why doesn't that surprise me?"

"What should we do? We can't let her go on indefinitely, having us acting as her hand maidens."

"It sounds a bit mean, but perhaps we should set a trap. Nothing drastic, nothing that could hurt her, but something to catch her in her lie." She gave Lydia a stern look. "You're sure about this?"

Lydia nodded. "I've been watching carefully, and she's just not the same person she was before."

Robbie's fingers drummed the bedding. "I wonder what she's waiting for?"

"I wish I knew."

"Did anyone tell her I was pregnant and lost the bairn?"

"As far as I know she still thinks you have the grippe, but since she can see, Lord knows what else she has discovered."

"Do you suppose she sneaks around the house at night? That would be my guess, knowing Birdie as I do."

"What, listening at keyholes?"

With a shrug, Robbie said, "Why not? What better way to find out what's happening in a house this size, especially if no one is telling you anything."

"So, what do you want to do?"

"Bring her here to visit again. I'll think of something."

• • •

Gavin stepped into Robbie's room; she was asleep. He saw her finished manuscript on the floor, picked it up, and read through it. It was delightful and insightful. He chuckled quietly a few times; her humor was well placed. And how appropriate was the name of the parrot!

A thought occurred to him. Hopefully it would be something to lift her spirits. He tucked the manuscript beneath his waistcoat and went to pen a letter to a friend.

He met Lydia on the stairs.

"Might I speak with you, sir?"

"Indeed," Gavin replied. "In the library?"

"Nae," she answered. "In the solarium, if you don't mind."

Curious, he followed her down the long hallway, past the kitchen, morning room, and dining room, and into the large, empty solarium.

Gavin glanced about, realizing that he had done nothing with this room; it looked a bit neglected. "I've been meaning to bring in some plants—"

"'Tis not plants I'm thinking the room needs," Lydia interrupted.

Interested, he asked her to explain.

Lydia moved about the room, her stout legs taking longer strides than Gavin had thought possible. "You'll think me disrespectful, but I have an idea."

"Go on," Gavin encouraged.

Lydia took a deep breath. "Well, seems to me our doctor friend does little when he's here. I've seen him bored even if you haven't. He caters to Miss Birdie like a lap dog, but I'm thinkin' he needs more to do than that."

Interest piqued, Gavin urged her to continue.

"There's no doctor in either Galashiels or Melrose, is there?"

"No," Gavin answered. "One travels through from time to time, but not as often as the townfolk would like, I imagine."

Lydia's gaze was intent. "What if we were to set up a little clinic in here? Would the doctor be interested?"

The idea was sound, if surprising. Gavin was quiet for a few moments, and then said, "Lydia, you have taken me by surprise."

"If I'm going to stay on here, sir, I'll need something more to do than babysit your wife's sister. I'll be ready for the madhouse long before my time if that's what will keep me occupied."

Gavin tented his fingers against his lips. "Let me bring it up to Dr. Innes, feel him out on the idea. It's fine with me, but then, I'm not the doctor." He lifted a tawny eyebrow in her direction. "Methinks that means you'd like to work with him."

"Aye. I'm an excellent nurse and midwife," she replied.

"All right then," Gavin said, leaving the solarium to pen his letter, "we'll have much to discuss later."

Lydia drew in a deep breath. She felt good about this. Now, however, she and Birdie needed to make a little visit to the real patient.

• • •

Birdie stepped into the room, blinking repeatedly. "Robbie?"

"Yes, I'm here, Birdie. I'm still in bed. You remember where the bed is, don't you? Just follow my voice." She watched Birdie carefully. Lydia came into the room behind her.

Suddenly Robbie doubled over, pretended to have a severe cramp. "Oh, Lydia, please bring me some towels from the bath; I think I might be losing more clots." She winced and let out a series of little cries. She peeked at her sister and found her watching her, eyes wide.

Lydia hopped to it, scurrying off into the bath.

"Oh, oh, I need...I need that basin on the bedside table, please, Birdie hand it to me or I might be sick in the bed. Oh, God! And...and would you go into the drawer of the night table and get me a clean handkerchief? Thank you, you're such a dear."

Birdie gave her sister a quizzical look; their eyes met. Robbie saw it; the evidence that her sister could see.

Birdie narrowed her gaze. "All right. So I can see. What of it?"

"How long?"

Now Birdie looked like the cat that swallowed the canary, or the nasty little parrot in her story. "The night I happened to over-hear Gavin and Colin talking about the mistake he made when he asked you to marry him because he thought you were me."

It all comes out now, Robbie thought.

Birdie swung around, flinging her arms. "All of this should be mine. All of it." She gave her sister a hateful look. "When did you discover he'd made a mistake, and why in God's name did you stay?"

"Because he asked me to."

Birdie snorted. "I'm surprised he didn't come looking for me when he discovered his blunder."

"I told him you were married."

She frowned, her face ugly with furrows and wrinkles. "That must have given you great pleasure."

"I merely told him the truth, that you absconded with my beau."

"If Joey had actually cared for you, I wouldn't have been able to sway him."

"But you did. You did. And now, here you are, rather in a predicament and, I might add, an unusually ugly temperament, even for you."

Birdie studied her sister for a moment. "You think just because you carried his bairn he'll stay with you." She snorted again. "I heard them all whispering, like I was both deaf and blind. My God, Robbie, it wasn't even fully formed yet. It wasn't even a baby! And you named it and buried it." She put on a sarcastic pout. "Buried in the Eliot plot, as if it really had been something."

Heat and anger rose up in Robbie, her cheeks burning with a rage she could barely conceal. "She was something to me. She would have been fine if…if—"

Birdie cocked an eyebrow. "If what?"

"Nothing. It's nothing," Robbie answered.

"Oh, yes it is." Lydia came out of the bath. "It's your fault she lost that bairn, you selfish girl."

"My fault?" Birdie placed her fists on her hips.

"In your eagerness to get out of your apartment, you accidentally pushed the door open, and the doorknob hit your sister in the stomach."

Again Birdie's eyes narrowed. "If you're trying to make me feel guilty about something just because I couldn't see at the time, forget it."

"That's right, Lydia," Robbie said softly. "Let's forget it."

Lydia swore. "No, let's not. I've seen the pattern here. Birdie does something hurtful, and everyone excuses her. Birdie suddenly acts the victim, and everyone pities her. Birdie pouts when she doesn't get her way, and everyone lets her have it."

The pan Lydia was carrying landed on the floor with a thud. "I've been silent long enough. What this girl needs is a dose of reality."

Birdie stood, arrogant, her arms folded across her chest. "And just what might that be?"

Lydia studied her through slitted lids. "Maybe I'll shave your head."

Birdie squeeked and touched her precious hair. "You wouldn't dare!"

"Oh, I would dare, missy; maybe one night I'll come into your bedroom while you sleep and shave off all of those curls you value so much."

Birdie whirled toward her sister. "You wouldn't let her do that, would you?"

"I'll need Robbie to hold you down," Lydia replied.

Birdie was nearly speechless. Breathing heavily, she turned to her sister. "Robbie? You couldn't do that, I know you couldn't."

Robbie hid a smile. "At the moment I don't have the strength, but give me time."

With a frustrated huff, Birdie stormed from the room.

Chapter Twenty

In the next days while Robbie was still confined to her room, she would occasionally see Birdie outside, attempting to train Lady Perlina. Teaching her to fetch. To stay. To come. Lady was a perfect student—most of the time.

At one point even Lady had gotten tired of work and jumped on Birdie with such vigor, she knocked her off balance and she fell to the ground. Instead of being upset, Birdie allowed her to playfully snatch at the ribbon of her gown.

That day Mrs. Murray stood beside Robbie as she watched. "'Tis like she be two different people, don't it?"

"I think I like this Birdie better, don't you?"

Mrs. Murray had snorted an unlady like laugh. "Do ye have to ask?" She waited a moment and then said, "What's to be done?"

Robbie inhaled, expelling her breath slowly. "I wish I knew. I suppose it isn't unreasonable to expect her to stay here, with us."

"But Lord Almighty, I hope that don't happen."

"It's not all that unnatural for sisters to live together," Robbie mused, albeit not happily.

She turned to find the housekeeper studying her. "Well, it isn't."

"There be only one person who wants that, and she's outside, playin' with *yer* dog, being the sweetpea for a change. It won't be long before she'll be back to her sourpuss ways."

Robbie knew she was right. And she rather liked the expression. A sweetpea and a sourpuss, always one or the other. Both of them were too dramatic by half.

The door swung open, and Gavin looked in, his face wreathed in worry. "There's been an accident."

Mrs. Murray and Robbie waited for him to explain.

"The small stove in the schoolroom exploded; the kirk is on fire and there are children and adults needing attention. Colin is already gone. I've got Lydia waiting in the foyer."

Robbie turned toward her wardrobe. "I'll get dressed—"

"You'll do no such thing," both Gavin and Mrs. Murray said.

Gavin crossed to her. "Please, Robbie. I know you want to help, but how can the rest of us do what we need to do if we're still worrying about you?"

"Nicely said, Mister Eliot," Mrs. Murray praised. "I'll put together some supplies and follow you in the wagon. Maureen can stay here; no need to leave you alone, Robbie, dear."

"What about Birdie?"

Both of them looked at her. "What good would she be?" It was Mrs. Murray's observation.

"Oh, please, just take her with you. Knowing Birdie, she'll stay out of the way to protect herself, and who knows, she might even be helpful."

"And if she refuses?" Gavin asked.

"I'm sick of her theatrics. Tell her she'll have to find other lodgings if she doesn't do as you ask."

Under his breath, he murmured, "It will be my pleasure."

• • •

There was fire and chaos everywhere. Birdie had never seen such turmoil. Of course, she hadn't seen much havoc in her life; she always tried to avoid it. But suddenly she was thrust in the middle of people shouting, children screaming, women wailing. She briefly pressed her hands over her ears, almost wishing she were blind again so she wouldn't have to look at what was before her.

"Please."

Birdie looked down. Beside her was a young woman, a girl, really, whose face was blackened with soot. One arm hung lifelessly at her side, and in the other she held a baby, small enough to tuck close to her body.

"Here, please, I beg you, take the bairn." She thrust it at Birdie, who took it hesitantly.

"What am I to do with it?" Birdie held down her panic.

"Keep her safe." The girl struggled on.

Birdie peeled back the dirty blanket. A pair of big, blue eyes looked back at her, serious as sauce. Birdie glanced around, looking for someone to pass the bairn off to, but everyone was busy, and she did not see Lydia anywhere.

Uncertain as to how to proceed, Birdie found a bench far from the chaos where she sat and studied the infant more closely. She cocked her head as she considered the lass, who appeared to study her as well. All at once the child giggled and smiled, and Birdie gasped, so surprised she nearly dropped the armful.

"Well," she said softly, "who are you, little lassie?" She put her finger to the child's cheek, and it was instantly taken into the baby's mouth and sucked on.

The most unusual feeling coursed through Birdie, one she had never ever experienced before.

"Birdie!"

She looked up and saw Colin rushing toward her. "What have you there?"

She opened the blanket and showed him.

"Whose is it?"

"I don't know. Some poor wretch shoved the child at me and told me to keep her safe."

Colin watched her, his gaze tender. "Will you be all right for now?"

Feeling embarrassed, which was a new sensation for Roberta Bean, née Fleming, she merely nodded. When she looked up at him, despite the ravaged scars on his face, he almost appeared handsome. "What shall we do with her?"

"I think it's a perfect job for you; stay put and keep her safe. We'll find out who she belongs to after all of this is over."

Birdie swallowed. "That means we'll have to take her back to Erskine House, doesn't it?"

"Yes, unless someone claims her before the night is over."

Birdie felt an odd rush of excitement followed by an instinctive realization of how her sister would feel upon hearing the news.

Isn't it just like Birdie to find a baby to care for right after I've just lost one? She could hear Robbie's voice in her ears, and it rang true.

In the meantime, she let the baby suck on her finger, knowing that sooner or later that would not be enough. Then what? Thank God for people who knew how to care for babies. She certainly didn't, nor did she think she ever wanted to. How does one concentrate on oneself when there's someone so small who constantly needs tending?

Suddenly Lydia was beside her. Her hair was askew and her face and clothing were covered in soot. She looked very tired. "Dr. Innes just told me." She peered into the little face. "I'm thinking it will need more nourishment than your finger very soon."

"I thought that very thing just before you came," Birdie answered. "What shall we do?"

Lydia looked back at the mayhem. "I have to get back and help. See that coffeehouse over there?" she asked, pointing to the little building across from the dress shop. "They must have milk or something."

Birdie watched Lydia hurry back to the accident site, then she wrapped the baby up tightly in the dirty blanket and crossed to the coffeehouse. Surprisingly, it was open. She dashed inside.

A young woman with hair almost as white as Gavin's looked at her, alarm registering on her face when Birdie showed her the baby. "I need to find something for her to eat. Or drink. I don't know, but soon she'll tire of my finger."

The woman studied her, a small smile marking the corner of her mouth. "It's your bairn, then?"

"Oh, God, no," Birdie answered. "Some young woman gave her to me." Birdie shrugged. "I have no idea what to do with her."

Appearing to consider the situation, the young woman went into the back of the shop and returned a bit later with a bottle.

"It's goat's milk," the woman explained. "Try it."

Awkwardly, Birdie took a seat and prepared to feed the infant. She glanced at the woman and said, "I'm surprised you're not out there with everyone else."

"They have plenty of help. My place is sort of a haven where people like you can come for support."

Her explanation sounded reasonable; at least Birdie was glad she was open. She touched the nipple to the bairn's mouth, and in spite of Birdie's inexperience, the lassie latched and began to suck. Birdie looked up at the woman and grinned. "Well, look at that."

"You're new in town?" the woman asked, sitting down across from her.

Birdie nodded. "I'm staying at Erskine House. Oh, I'm sorry, my name is Roberta Bean. I recently lost my husband. I'm...currently staying with my sister."

"So you lost your husband, what a shame," the young woman appeared sympathetic. "I'm Faith Baker. I know Gavin Eliot well; we were friends in Edinburgh."

Surprised, Birdie asked, "I haven't heard him mention you, I'm sorry. You see, I've just recently been able to see; after my husband was killed before my eyes, I lost my sight for a few months."

The baby finished the milk, and instinctively, Birdie raised her to her shoulder and patted her on the back. After a healthy burp escaped, Birdie continued to stroke the bairn.

Miss Baker threw her head back and released a quiet laugh. "Oh, I know all about you, your sister, Gavin's mistake..." She seemed unnaturally pleased with her knowledge.

Oddly, Birdie felt a wave of protection for her sister. That was new. "She was in a terrible predicament when that all came about. You see, she was living in the slums of Edinburgh—"

"I know that too. And I also know how she made her living."

The babe fell asleep against Birdie's shoulder. "She was doing some kind of honest work, I'm sure. If my sister is nothing else, she's an honest person. Perhaps the most honest one I know." Again, Birdie found herself defending her sister, and it was a new sensation.

"Oh, indeed she was." Faith Baker laughed again. "Only I'm not sure exactly how 'honest' it was."

The door flew open, and Colin stepped inside, his gaze traveling between the two women. "Things are settling down, Birdie," he said, not taking his eyes off Faith. "At least for now, I think you and Lydia should take the bairn back to the house."

As they left, Colin said, his voice low and threatening, "Mind yourself, Miss Baker. Mind yourself."

He helped Birdie into the wagon next to Lydia. Mrs. Murray climbed in as well, taking the babe from Birdie and snuggling the child close.

Birdie felt an odd sense of loss. Good God, she was losing her mind. To feel bereft of something she'd held only briefly? She then remembered Robbie. "What's Robbie going to think of this?"

The wagon lumbered along, Lydia at the reins. "What do you mean?"

"I mean, she's just lost a bairn, and here I come, rescuing one from a fire."

Lydia looked straight ahead; the lantern on the side post giving them enough light to see the road. "She'll be grateful you were there, I suspect."

"But…you don't think she'll be upset?"

"If she is, she won't show it," Lydia answered.

Birdie glanced at Mrs. Murray, who was humming a soft lullaby that Birdie recognized from her childhood, as they made their way home.

• • •

The injured were put at the inn. There were more than a dozen there. Gavin bent over a boy he recognized from school. His name was Bernie Kostner. "Bernie?"

The boy's face was covered in soot, as Gavin was sure his own was. He opened his eyes. "Mr. Eliot?"

"How are you doing, lad?"

"Me leg hurts real bad," the boy told him, fighting back tears.

"Dr. Innes will be here very soon. He'll take care of it for you. In the meantime, is there anyone you need to contact? Where's your mam and your da?"

"I don't know where they are." Tears slid down his cheeks.

Gavin understood the lad's fears. He saw the innkeeper and his wife trying to give water to some of the patients who were alert. He caught the innkeeper's wife's eye and motioned her over.

"Are you familiar with Bernie's family?"

She nodded. "Aye, I'll try to find them," she said without being asked.

Soon after, Colin came in carrying supplies. He put them on a table and hunkered down beside Bernie. "How are you doing, young man?"

"It hurts real bad."

Colin had prepared something in a vial and told Bernie to drink it down. The boy did as he was told, and it wasn't long before he was drowsy enough for Colin to begin his work.

"Fortunately the break didn't go through the skin," he said to Gavin. "I can brace it temporarily, and then tomorrow I'll look in on him at home and fix it up right."

The door slammed against the wall, and a portly woman hurried in, her face creased with worry. "Bernie, my Bernie!"

Gavin took her over to see her son, who was now sleeping peacefully. "He'll be fine, Mrs. Kostner. Dr. Innes has put a temporary splint on his leg."

She was wringing her hands. "Can we take him home, then?"

Her husband, even portlier than his wife, came in behind her. "The rig be ready. 'Tis time to take him home."

Gavin and Colin gently lifted the boy and carried him out to the family wagon and settled him in the back.

As they watched the wagon roll away, both men knew that although they were exhausted, their night was only beginning.

Chapter Twenty-One

Although she'd been ordered to stay put, Robbie luxuriated in the fact that she was nearly alone in the big house. It was more quiet than usual, and even Lady Perlina had come to stay for a bit, snuggling up with Robbie in her bed.

Maureen had brought her a light supper, which she shared with Lady, and then they both settled down for the night.

Early in the morning, before the sun peeked through her curtains, something awakened her. She sat up and listened. It sounded like...a baby? Or perhaps it had come from outside, one of the farm animals.

No, there it was again, and it was definitely a bairn's cry. Without further thought, she slid from the bed and into her dressing gown and headed for the door, her heart pounding.

In the hallway she met Maureen, who had a breakfast tray for her.

"Is that a bairn I hear?"

Maureen's eyes lit up. "Aye, mistress, 'tis."

"What...who..."

"'Tis from the fire," Maureen explained, putting the tray on a table outside Robbie's room.

Robbie relaxed. "For a moment I thought I was going mad."

Maureen gave her a sympathetic look. "Should ye be up?"

"I think it's high time I'm up and about. I've been in that room and in that bed for so long I'm not sure I want to see either of them again any time soon. But now," she said, taking Maureen's arm, "show me the way to that bairn."

"'T'was your sister what found it," Maureen clarified.

142

Robbie smothered a sad laugh. Of course it would be Birdie who found a baby. There would be no irony in it at all if someone else had.

They ended up in the kitchen, where Mrs. Murray was heating a bottle. And surprise of surprises, Birdie was holding the bairn, looking quite content. She glanced up and caught her sister's gaze. "I'm sorry, Robbie."

Robbie frowned. "Sorry?"

"I know it must seem cruel for me to have been given this bairn when you just lost yours, but in truth, that's exactly what happened. Some poor wretch handed it to me. What could I do? I couldn't refuse to take her."

Fresh pain rolled over Robbie. "So it's a girl?"

"Aye," Mrs. Murray said, handing Birdie the bottle, just in time before the little thing had a chance to really let out a wail. "And she got a proper set of lungs on her, too."

Robbie sat across from her sister and watched her feed the babe. She looked natural. Robbie was a pragmatic person; she didn't believe in good luck charms or bad luck omens. But she discovered she didn't want to study the infant, either.

"We found some little things for her to wear; apparently someone at some time had a babe here to care for," Birdie said.

"Aye, and 'neath that dirty blanket was a robust lassie, dressed in the softest of fabrics," Mrs. Murray said, her eyebrows raised.

"And on that soiled blanket was a very delicately stitched 'A,'" replied Lydia, who walked into the room carrying a stack of soft flannels to use as clouts. "And on her tiny left thigh there's a birthmark in the shape of a daisy. What do you think of that?"

"Well, we can't call her Daisy," Birdie reflected. "Sounds like a maid."

Maureen had just entered the room with fresh linens, her eyes down obediently.

Lydia said, "Nothing wrong with being in service, Birdie. It's an honest occupation."

"Yes, but still."

"So her name begins with an A, or it's the letter of her last name. What was the woman like who gave her to you?" Robbie asked Birdie.

"She was plain, I didn't really notice how she was dressed, but one arm wasn't functioning well; she held the bairn with the other."

The four of the women sat at the table, each studying the infant.

"What will we do?" asked Birdie.

"I imagine we should send someone into the village to see if anyone has asked for her," Robbie said.

Birdie's eyes were big. "And what if no one does?"

"Don't get yer hopes up, missy," Mrs. Murray warned. "'Tisn't likely a babe like this will go unnoticed if she's missing."

All this time Robbie studied her sister. It was as if someone else had control of her body, someone who could converse without demanding something. Someone who could actually care about someone other than herself. It was an incredibly fast and amazing transformation. Robbie wondered how long it would last.

"Well, I for one think we should keep her. After all, this girl, and she was just a girl, gave her to a complete stranger. How sensible is that? If she's that reckless with a bairn, perhaps she doesn't deserve to have it."

Ah, thought Robbie. Birdie had returned.

"And, just suppose no one claims her, who does she belong to? There must be a law about this somewhere in Scotland. People can't just give their bairns away, can they?"

Lydia answered, "People give their babies away all the time, Mrs. Murray. My Karl, rest his gentle soul, was a foundling.

"She needs to be put on a feeding schedule," Lydia continued. "And since there are three of us, we should take turns. Undoubtedly she'll wake during the night, and I don't think any of us want to be the only one in charge for as long as that could go on."

"I hadn't thought of that," Birdie mused. "But since she was given to me, I think I should be able to request feeding her only during the day. After all, I'm still recovering from blindness."

Robbie tossed Mrs. Murray a look. "Sourpuss has returned."

The sentence went right over Birdie's head.

Colin stepped into the room. "And how is the patient?"

"Oh, I'm fine, really. Thank you for asking. I don't seem to have any ill affects from the blindness at all," Birdie blathered on.

Robbie caught a smile. "I think he means the bairn."

"Actually," Colin said, "I was talking about you." He took a seat between Robbie and Lydia. "You sort of took it upon yourself to get up and move around, didn't you?"

"I'm fine. If I'd had to stay in my room another day, I'd have found a way to escape."

Colin shook his finger at her. "Don't start doing everything right away. And, by the way, Gavin went into Galashiels to see if he could discover who the bairn belongs to."

Birdie squeaked a little gasp. "I don't think he'll find anything."

Colin now gazed at Birdie, his eyes warm. "You mean, you hope he doesn't find anything."

The babe, who was now asleep against Birdie's chest, was the focus of everyone's attention. Except Robbie's.

"Did you treat a woman who had an injured arm?" Birdie asked him.

Colin frowned, concentrating. "There were burns and breaks, lots of trauma, but I can't recall a woman with an injured arm."

"There, you see?" Birdie said, beaming. "She's what Lydia calls a foundling. I found her. She's mine."

"You can't be serious," Robbie said. "Taking care of a babe is nothing like taking care of a pup, Birdie."

"How much difference can there be?"

Robbie thought of the single mothers she had encountered in Edinburgh, woman whose husbands had died or merely left, or women who had no husbands in the first place. She understood that caring for a child was difficult enough for two parents; for one, it was overwhelming, often impossible.

Gavin poked his head into the kitchen. "So here's where everyone is."

"Did you find out anything?" Robbie asked.

Gavin shook his head. "Not so far. Of course, there are a lot of estates within a few miles radius, it's possible the woman came from there. Birdie, was there anything special about the girl?"

"Nothing special except that funny arm of hers that just hung at her side."

Gavin frowned. "Which arm?"

"I don't know, maybe the right one?" She frowned. "Maybe it was the left. I don't really remember, she had a pretty face, I think, but I don't remember much. Her hair was long and dark and she covered it with a scarf."

"But what on earth was she doing in Galashiels, all alone, at night, with a child?" Lydia asked.

"That's a good question," Gavin answered.

Birdie gasped. "Maybe she stole the bairn and was going to run away with it. She got caught up in the accident and knew she'd never make it after she was injured."

"And where did she steal the babe from?" Mrs. Murray probed.

Now Birdie's eyes got big. "Maybe she was a servant and the babe was hers all along, and the father was some big important laird who wanted to take it away from her or get rid of it so there wouldn't be evidence besmirching his reputation."

In spite of her weariness, Robbie bit back a laugh. "'Besmirching'?"

"Well, it means dirtying, doesn't it?"

"You've always had a fertile imagination, Birdie, but that sounds like something that you'd read in a book."

Birdie scowled. "Have you got a better idea?"

"We don't even know her name," Lydia murmured, her eyes not leaving the infant's sweet face.

"It must begin with A. I'll call her Adrianna. How's that?" Now Birdie smiled.

"Well, I suppose we have to call her something. But you know, naming anything, whether it be a pet, a farm animal, a horse, or a baby, means you get too attached to it when reality comes knocking at the door." Colin's voice was firm.

"Well," Mrs. Murray said, taking the babe from Birdie and burping her, "I was thinkin' maybe Alice."

Birdie wrinkled her nose. "Sounds old and plain."

"I'm thinking you're both crazy," Robbie interjected. "Any minute now someone could show up on the doorstep, asking for their little lassie."

"They'd have to prove she was theirs," Birdie said.

"Or we could just hide her." Mrs. Murray's suggestion.

Colin and Gavin looked at each other.

"Do all women have such devious minds?" Gavin asked, actually perplexed.

Colin snorted a laugh. "Of course. It's the nature of a woman. And ladies, I mean no disrespect."

"In the meantime," Lydia said as she stood, "the cradle is ready. We can't simply take turns holding her all the time."

"Why not? I think it's my turn," Birdie said, reaching for the child.

"You just fed her," scolded Mrs. Murray, turning away from her.

Birdie released a sigh. "Wouldn't this be just like a fairy tale? An abandoned baby girl, left alone in the wilderness among the animals when a beautiful princess comes along and saves her." She gave them all a glowing smile.

Mrs. Murray said, "Well, if we're goin' to give the babe to anyone it should be Robbie. After all, she the one who lost her own."

That was it. Robbie had had enough. She stood. "No one here is going to claim that baby at all. Not now, probably not ever. She obviously belongs to someone who loved her and cared for her. She's healthy and she's..." She clamped her lips together, fearing she would start to cry. "And," she said, moving toward the door, "just because I lost my own bairn doesn't mean I want another to replace it. You can't replace children. You just can't." She left the kitchen in a rush and hurried to her room, slamming the door behind her.

Chapter Twenty-Two

Gavin saddled his mount and rode straight back to Galashiels. He strode into the inn. Eli Baker, the innkeeper, was sorting mail. He nodded a greeting.

"Did a stagecoach come in last night?"

Eli stopped working and thought a moment. "Aye, 'twas later than usual, but just before the big accident."

"Do you remember how many were on the stagecoach?"

"Aye, I have it written here, somewhere." He rummaged around on the counter and came up with a sheet of paper. "Here 'tis." He handed it to Gavin, who studied it and felt a sinking sensation in his stomach.

"Did any of them get back on the stagecoach when it left?"

Eli stroked his beard. "Might have, can't say for sure."

Gavin pointed to a name on the list. "How about her?"

"She had a bairn with her," Eli explained. "And she had a bum arm. The wife complimented her on how well she dealt with it all, with only one arm."

"I see. But did she take the stagecoach out of here?"

Eli studied another list. "Looks like she did."

Gavin swallowed the lump in his throat. "Did she have the baby with her when she left?"

Frowning, Eli said, "Can't say fer sure. I didn't see her meself." He shouted for his wife, who poked her head around the door to the kitchen, and asked her.

"Nae, Mister Eliot, she didna' hae a bairn with her when she left here," Mrs. Baker assured him.

"But I do have a letter here for you."

Gavin's heart lifted. Hopefully it might be information about the baby.

The innkeeper checked around, hunting here and there, then put his hand on his stubbled chin and grunted. "Can't find it. I know it's here someplace."

Disappointed, Gavin said, "If you find it, have someone bring it to the house, if you please."

Promising to do that, the innkeeper continued to check slots and drawers until Gavin finally left.

Gavin swung onto his mount and made for home. Now at least he knew who the baby belonged to, or he was almost certain of it. The question was, why had she come here, and why did she leave the bairn?

• • •

Robbie had escaped to the room she'd been confined to for weeks, suddenly glad she could have some solace. She thought she'd had time to process all that she'd been through, but she was wrong. She was pretty much healed physically from the miscarriage, but in her heart there were many emotions she had never dealt with before, and they created havoc inside her.

A scratching at her door prompted her to open it. Lady Perlina trotted in as though she'd never left.

Robbie crossed her arms over her chest and gave the dog a stern look. "Traitor."

Lady hopped up on the bed and settled in, her tail slapping the bedding.

Robbie sat on the bed and scratched the pup's ears, reliving the past few days.

How was it possible to feel so much for something that was barely formed? Even Birdie had that right—it didn't make sense. But Robbie felt such a sense of loss, even now, that she wanted to scream and weep and carry on like a fool.

Lydia had told her she might be depressed. Might? If what

she was feeling wasn't depression, she couldn't define it. If she didn't watch it, she could easily crawl into bed, pull the covers up over her head, and sleep for a month. Maybe then she'd wake up feeling better.

• • •

Gavin found Colin in the library. Although it was early in the afternoon, he was nursing a brandy. Colin raised his glass wearily.

"What in the hell do we do with a bairn?"

Gavin poured himself a drink and sat down across from his friend. "I think I know who it belongs to."

Startled, Colin put his snifter on the table beside him. "You found something in Galashiels? You didn't say anything earlier."

"It wasn't until Birdie described the girl that I got to wondering. The long, dark hair, the bum right arm...I know it sounds crazy, but I had to find out for sure."

Colin leaned forward, his interest fed. "And?"

"I checked the passenger list at the inn. I'm quite certain Darla Dean was on the stage that stopped shortly before the accident."

Colin sank back. "Darla? You mean that girl you tutored before you came out here? The one from Edinburgh?"

Gavin nodded. "Even though she listed her name as Darla Samuels, the innkeeper and his wife described her. It fit with what Birdie said. And the strange thing is," he continued, "she left on the stage without the bairn."

Frowning, Colin asked, "If her name was Samuels, how do you know it was her?"

"Because her father's name is Samuel Dean." He shrugged. "Of course I can't be positive, but everything fits."

"Why would she bring it out here?"

Gavin let the question sit in the air.

Suddenly Colin sat up straight and pinned Gavin with a stunned glare. "You don't think that—"

"That the baby is mine? Good God, Colin; I'm no degenerate. The girl was barely fourteen."

Still puzzled, Colin repeated, "Then why would she bring it here?"

"That's what I'm going to find out." He raked fingers through his thick, tight curls. "She was such a sad young thing, overprotected by her parents to the point of suffocation." He paused, and then added, "Mrs. Dean's young nephew, Lyle, also lived with them for a while. He was a student at university; I suppose he was eighteen or nineteen. He was often put in charge of her when they went out, or entertained at home." A vile thought penetrated his gut.

Colin raised his glass. "What are you going to do?"

"I have to go to Edinburgh and find her, talk with her. I need to know why she would leave a baby with me, if that was her intent."

"Did she have other family out this way?"

"Not that I'm aware of. And right now I have a wife who lost a baby, who is probably feeling alone and rejected, and I have to leave her."

"And I get to referee the hens. A thankless job, to be sure." He raised his snifter to his lips and swallowed the remainder.

• • •

Gavin slipped into Robbie's room. She had crawled into bed and faced the window. Her pup was curled into the arc of her legs. He went to her bedside and gazed down at her. Her eyes were closed, but he noticed there was puffiness around them. She'd been crying.

He smiled as he remembered the day he had told her to stay and marry him. She had been crying then too, and her answer when asked was "you're some detective," or something like that. Saucy, she was, when she wished to be.

Her hair, the color of sable, had come loose from her chignon and fell over her shoulder. It was shiny and clean, and he had the urge to crawl in next to her and bring one of her curls to his nose and inhale deeply.

The freckles across her nose were more pronounced than usual, perhaps because she was still a little pale and wan from her ordeal. As he watched her sleep, he had such deep feelings for her, he almost became breathless.

"Yes," he whispered softly, "you do take my breath away, Robbie Eliot."

She stirred, opened her eyes, and turned her head. "Gavin? Is something wrong?"

"No. But I'm afraid I have to be gone again for a short time. Just to Edinburgh, and I promise it will be no more than a day or two."

She turned on her back and stretched, the movement bringing her nightgown tight over her breasts. That innocent gesture gave him stirrings.

"When will you leave?"

"If I leave now, I'll be back that much sooner," he said.

She reached for his hand; he enveloped hers in his. "Be safe. At least you get to escape the commotion if only for a few days."

"I trust Colin can handle the hens, as he calls them."

Her smile was genuine and so sweet, he bent and kissed her. That too gave him stirrings, but when they separated, he simply ran his fingers over her soft cheek. "I hope you'll be better very soon," he said.

"Godspeed."

• • •

Gavin stepped into the kitchen where the women were still squabbling about who would feed the babe at night. Or, at least Birdie argued that she shouldn't have to. He'd had enough.

"Ladies, I'm to be gone for a few days, and while I'm away, I want the three of you to stop arguing about this baby. I was just in Robbie's room, and I could hear you from there. Robbie is still healing. Remember that. Whether she acts like it or not, she is suffering from the loss, and having a baby in the house just reminds her of it."

"Oh, of course, Mr. Eliot," Mrs. Murray said. "If no one else will feed the bairn at night, I will."

"No," said Lydia. "That's not fair. I can do it. I'm accustomed to going without sleep."

They all looked at Birdie, who merely raised her eyebrows. "Then it's settled. You two can feed the bairn at night."

With that, she got up and sashayed out the door, leaving them all wondering at her selfishness. Or not.

Chapter Twenty-Three

His ride to Edinburgh had been swift. He stopped in front of the Deans' two-story townhouse, studying the gray, granite exterior with its large windows and iron braces over them. He remembered the house well. It was handsomely decorated, a show place, really, where the Deans often entertained dignitaries. Gavin had felt sympathy for their only child the moment he was introduced as her tutor. Darla, although quite a pretty girl, had a damaged arm, something that had apparently happened during her delivery. Colin had told him that there must have been nerve damage that prevented her from having any use of her left arm at all. And she was shy and withdrawn, having been overprotected by her doting parents from the very beginning.

Taking a deep breath, he handed his mount over to a footman, went up the stoop, and rang the bell.

A maid answered, and when he told her he'd come to see Miss Dean, she frowned. "Isn't no Dean at this residence."

Puzzled, Gavin asked, "Samuel Dean doesn't live here?"

"Nae, they moved."

"Have you any idea where they went?"

The maid shook her head. "I can ask me mistress if ye'd like."

He said that would be fine, and waited on the stoop for her to return. A sour-looking woman returned in her place, her nose high in the air and her silver hair piled high on her head. "What is it you wish?"

Gavin held his hat in his hand, his fingers rubbing over the felt. "I was under the assumption that Samuel Dean and his family lived here."

"They're gone."

Gavin made a motion with his shoulders. "Gone? You don't know where?"

In a haughty voice, she answered, "It's not my responsibility to discern where someone I don't even know has moved."

Discouraged, Gavin thanked her. Now what?

He made a few inquiries in the neighborhood but got no answers. He went to Samuel Dean's office where he discovered that the solicitor and his family had simply picked up and left.

Lastly, he checked with the coach company to see if they had any record of where Darla had disembarked. They did not; it was as if she had vanished into thin air.

With nothing to go on, he turned his mount toward Erskine House.

• • •

Although Robbie was content to stay in her room and avoid the others, she cleaned herself up, brushed her hair, and stepped into one of her more conservative gowns. She studied herself in the mirror, noting her paleness and the accentuation of her freckles. Anxious for Gavin to return, she tried to make herself presentable. She knew he cared for her. She couldn't sense that he wasn't interested in Birdie, but Gavin being Gavin, it was hard to tell, because he was kind to everyone.

She put her hand over her stomach, wincing not because it hurt, but because she still ached in her heart. She wondered how any woman survived the death of a child fully formed, or one she had raised, watched change from child, to youngster, to adolescent and then to become an adult. How would one deal with such pain?

She felt weepy, so she blew her nose and shook herself. *Get on with it.*

She took the stairs and followed the sounds of voices, Lady dashing down ahead of her. Inside the morning room, Lydia was folding flannels, and Mrs. Murray was rocking the cradle. The babe slept.

"Where's Birdie?"

Both women looked at her and smiled. "Glad to see ye up and about, madam." Mrs. Murray nodded toward the cradle. "Ain't she sweet?"

Robbie stepped to the crib and studied the infant, wondering just what she would feel. Oddly, she felt little. After all, the bairn wasn't hers; she'd already told everyone that you can't replace one child with another. "She's very sweet," she answered, and meant it, but she wasn't interested in doting on the infant. "Where's Birdie?" she repeated.

"She and the doctor have gone out for a ride," Lydia said, raising her eyebrows.

"I'm surprised she left without taking the bairn with her," Robbie responded with a wry smile.

"Aye, she tried," Mrs. Murray said. "It was three against one. Alice stays home for now."

"Alice? Home?"

Both women shrugged. "'Tis where she is, now, isn't it? We can't keep calling her the bairn, she needs a name." Mrs. Murray peeked into the crib and sang softly.

Robbie took a seat across from the cradle. "Remember what both Gavin and Colin said. She belongs to someone, certainly not to us."

Maureen poked her head into the room. "Ye want a wee cuppa, mistress?"

"Thank you, Maureen, that would be grand."

"And bring her some of that pudding we had fer lunch," Mrs. Murray added.

Grateful, for she was hungry, Robbie added, "And a bap, if there are any left from breakfast."

"Of course there's baps left for ye; I hid them from everyone so you'd have some if ye wished it."

"You're a dear," Robbie answered.

Maureen smiled, curtsied, and left the room.

"Maureen is a sweet thing," Lydia said.

"Aye," Mrs. Murray added. "Am glad to have her back, as I know ye are, mistress. At least she's not at yer sister's beck and call."

"Birdie doesn't care who is at her beck and call, just so long as someone is," Robbie responded.

"And now it appears to be the good doctor," Lydia mentioned.

"He says he enjoys it. We'll see how long that lasts," Robbie said. "Birdie is fickle."

The front door slammed, and Birdie rushed into the room and straight to the crib, out of breath.

"Speak of the devil," Mrs. Murray murmured.

"How is Adrianna? Is she all right? Has she been fed? Changed?" Birdie peered down at the infant.

"As ye can see," Mrs. Murray said, "Alice be fine as she can be. Now, don't go makin' so much racket; she needs her nap."

Birdie, itching to pick up the bairn, dipped in and woke her up.

"How was the ride?" Robbie asked.

The bairn was still sleepy, but settled against Birdie's shoulder. "We rode past an old castle that was near the river. Colin said it used to have a cave at the outlet where pirates stored their booty. I thought that was very romantic."

"Aye," Mrs. Murray said with a snort, "pirates, ill-gotten gains, kidnapping, and liquor. All the signs of a romance to me."

Birdie waved a hand at her. "Oh, you know what I mean." Suddenly she noticed Lady curled up at Robbie's feet. "Oh. There's the dog. I wondered what happened to her."

Robbie sensed now that Birdie had a baby to flutter over, she would forget poor Lady. Maybe she would get her pup back after all.

• • •

Gavin returned, just after dinner. Mrs. Murray prepared a plate for him and insisted that he eat it.

Colin sat across the table from him. "So, what did you find out?"

Gavin swallowed a mouthful of stew and said, "Not a damned thing. Honestly, it's like she and her family have vanished from the face of the earth." He took a long drink of wine. "I don't know what to do."

Colin poured himself a glass of wine, took a sip then twisted the stem with his fingers. "For now the bairn is fine. I think she's three or four months old, although I can't be certain. She hasn't been malnourished, and she appears healthy in every way."

Gavin finished his meal, stood and threw his napkin onto the table. "Dammit, we can't just keep her."

"I'm surprised Darla didn't leave a note or something. Odd that she would ride all the way out here and just hand the babe over to a stranger."

Gavin chuckled. "And no one is stranger than Birdie."

"Now, be nice," Colin replied with a grin.

"There's nothing to be done at the moment; we'll just have to continue on as we have been. She'll probably need a few things. Perhaps you and one of the ladies can go into Galashiels and see what you can find."

"Which of the ladies would you suggest I take with me?"

"Not Birdie, but if she insists on going along, fine. Take Lydia. She should know what a baby needs."

"You haven't asked about Robbie," Colin said.

"I stopped by her room when I came home, but she wasn't there. I thought that was good news; isn't it?"

"After you left, she dressed and came downstairs where Mrs. Murray and Lydia were tending the bairn. I took Birdie out for a ride to give the other women some relief."

"And?"

"And Lydia told me when Mrs. Murray exclaimed over the bairn's sweetness, Robbie barely glanced at her as she slept in her crib."

"I would imagine that's natural. Wouldn't that be natural?"

"I do have some concerns about Robbie."

Gavin, who had been at the window, turned swiftly. "What do you mean?"

"I cared for a few new mothers early in my practice. I particularly remember one woman who had lost her babe closer to term than Robbie's. For weeks, or even months, she had difficulty sleeping but was tired all the time. She became irritable. She avoided her family and friends. She had little appetite and she lost a fair amount of weight."

Gavin sat down again at the table and pushed his plate away. "Robbie isn't like that. She's strong."

"It isn't a matter of strength, Gavin. It's just something that goes on inside a woman's head after she's been through what Robbie's been through. Try as she might, she can't just slip back into her old skin."

"How will having a baby in the house affect her?"

"We'll have to wait and see. Just don't expect her to join the other cacklers and want her turn at holding and feeding the babe. I hear, by the by, they've decided to call her Alice. Overriding Birdie's more romantic choice of Adrianna, or Ariadne, or something like that."

Gavin looked helpless. "What can I do?"

"Just support her, Gavin. Don't bombard her with questions. Offer to take her for rides, but don't insist if she doesn't want to. Although fresh air wouldn't do her any harm. Just be a supportive husband. And when the two of you are alone, don't bring up the baby unless she does. Time will tell as to how this will all play out."

Chapter Twenty-Four

There began a routine a few weeks after the babe showed up, Robbie realized. At night when she couldn't sleep, she heard the babe cry for a short while, and then either Lydia or Mrs. Murray would feed her and put her back to sleep.

During the day, all three women took turns feeding the infant, but Birdie refused to change her, expressing pure disgust and displeasure even at the thought of it. "At least the dog did her job outside. Most of the time," she added under her breath.

Robbie had no interest in taking part. The little girl had enough people fawning over her. She had even seen both Colin and Gavin eyeing her, chucking her under her tiny chin and saying foolish things that no man would ever admit to uttering otherwise.

One day she even found Lady, paws up on the edge of the cradle, sniffing around the babe's blanket. Still, Robbie had no desire to pick the babe up. In fact, the thought of it almost made her ill—not in a disgusting way, just a bit sick to her stomach.

She tried to write. Her first story was done, and she was afraid if she tried to do any rewriting, the whole thing would become a story with a sad ending. But she made notes for another story, realizing that even if she didn't feel like it, she should at least try. It was something to do.

She moved through her days slowly and quietly, her pup at her side. Gavin had encouraged her to take a ride with him one morning, but she just didn't feel like going out. She saw the pain in his eyes, and it made her ache as well, but what could she do about it? She felt what she felt; there was no other way to put it.

Even a walk through the garden, which she always loved, did little to lift her spirits.

She did drop to the ground one day and pulled weeds with her bare hands. She got scolded by Mrs. Murray for it, and for soiling the front of her gown. Although it made more work for Mrs. Murray, something that Robbie insisted not be done, she made no move to apologize.

The fact that she hadn't done so made her angry with herself, and she started to cry.

Damn! (*Sorry, Papa*). She hated how she felt, day after day, nothing changing. Colin had told her he thought it was natural for some women to go through this. Robbie wondered why it had to be her.

And still through it all, the baby routine continued.

• • •

Colin looked over the room design Gavin had drawn of the solarium, which would be converted into a clinic. "So it's obvious to everyone that I need something more to do than coddle Birdie."

Gavin studied him. "It was Lydia who came up with the idea. The more I thought about it, the more sense it made, but you had to be agreeable, or it would come to naught. And personally, I didn't want to put a bunch of trees and plants in there; I've always believed they belong outside."

Colin appeared reluctant.

"What's on your mind?" Gavin asked.

Colin gave him a quick glance and nervously touched his face. "I'd be more likely to send patients away than see them."

Gavin leaned forward, his elbows on his knees. "I didn't see anyone running from you the night of the fire and explosion. We were so busy I don't think even you remembered that your face was scarred."

Colin nodded. "I guess I'm just a little hesitant to start seeing patients again. But then, having my baptism by fire out here in the country would probably be a good way to start."

Gavin slapped his knee. "Excellent. I'll get workmen on it immediately."

• • •

Gavin visited both villages, Galashiels and Melrose, to gather information about able workmen for his new project. Before he returned home, he walked to the inn.

"Sir." Eli Baker stood outside the inn and smiled when he saw Gavin. "I found that letter." He went inside and retrieved it.

Gavin scanned the contents, his surprise sending waves of shock through his body.

He returned from Galashiels and found Colin outside smoking a cigar. "Put that thing out and come with me."

Intrigued, Colin did as he was told.

Once in the library, Gavin handed him the letter.

"What's this?"

"Read it," Gavin instructed.

Colin unfolded the paper and read:

> *Mr. Eliot. Gavin.*
>
> *I have no place else to turn. My parents threatened to give my bairn to a stranger, and I can't stand the thought. She needs a good home; I know she will have it with you, as I learned that you recently married. And she would have to be kind, as you are the kindest person I know.*
>
> *Alice is very sweet and good natured. She is healthy. Take good care of her. I won't say outright who the father is, but perhaps you can guess. Don't try to find me.*
>
> *Very sincerely yours,*
>
> *Darla Dean*

Colin sat back and exhaled, the sound whooshing through the room. "My God."

Gavin went to the sideboard and poured them each a small brandy. "Indeed."

"Why did you just get this now?"

Gavin handed him a snifter. "Shortly after the fire, the innkeeper told me I had a letter, but when he went to find it, it was no where to be found. Today he flagged me down and said he'd found it."

"So now you have a bairn."

Gavin smothered a dry laugh. "It can't be as easy as all that."

"I'm no solicitor, but I'd say you should contact one and see what should be done. You might want to find out if there are any laws regarding such things before anything else happens."

He studied Gavin further, then said, "Illegitimacy is a horrific pall when it hangs over a family. Samuel Dean was a successful, popular, very capable solicitor. I imagine the realization of what happened under his own roof had to be close to catastrophic. And I assume from the letter, that the nephew is the despicable goat who did this to her."

"All the more reason to flee the country, I fancy," Gavin mused.

"And if the family is at all superstitious, they might feel the bairn could bring them bad luck."

"I should have noticed something," Gavin said.

"Like what?"

"The lad was always hanging about when I gave Darla lessons. I thought perhaps he was interested in the subjects." He laughed, but it was with neither wit nor humor.

"And what would you have done if you had come upon them together?"

"I would have been horrified, but knowing me, if Darla had begged me not to say anything, I just may have let the matter go. But not before taking the lad outside and tanning his backside."

"And now you have a bairn," Colin repeated.

"Something else to complicate my life. I have a wife who has no interest in the infant and a sister-in-law who wants to monopolize her."

"I do think Robbie will come around one day. In the meantime, little Alice is in very capable hands."

Gavin threw him a wry look.

"Well," he amended, "at least four of the hands are capable."

Gavin shook his head and walked to the window. The wind lifted the the leaves of the sycamores and swayed the tops of the Scots pines. Beyond, into the fields, clover blanketed the earth. There, a small herd of cattle grazed, their tales swishing lazily against the ever meddlesome midge. "I want to talk with my family's solicitor back home. I sent him a letter this morning, enlightening him about the situation."

"Will you travel there?"

"I'm hoping he will come here. I don't want to leave Robbie any more than I must. I explained that to him as well." He turned from the window. "In my naïvite I thought all women warmed to a baby, whether it be theirs or someone else's."

Colin shook his head. "I've encountered women who don't even bond with their own bairns. It's not common, but it happens."

"I've never thought about how lucky I was to grow up where I did," Gavin said. "Until I became an adult, I had no idea mothers might not bond with their own children. I really thought Robbie would change her mind about Alice."

"As I've said, give her time. She loves you; she may surprise you."

A slight pain jabbed at Gavin. "I know. I know. I just wish…"

"Good God, man, you're not still mooning over Birdie, are you? After everything that has happened?"

"No. No, Birdie is a pretty, flighty, selfish little pea hen. It didn't take me long to realize that once she showed up on my doorstep. More your speed, I'm thinking," he added.

"I know she was revulsed when she first saw me. In fact, remember the night she stumbled into the library, looking for the dog? I swear she could see, at least some things, and I am pretty certain she got a close look at my face."

"Why didn't you mention anything?"

Colin shrugged and brushed dog hair from his trousers. "I

wasn't absolutely certain, but I did watch her closely after that, and because she could see, she knew when someone was about, so she continued with her charade."

"You don't mean to say she could see when she arrived here."

"No, no, she had hysterical blindness. But upon hearing the fiasco of the proposal to the wrong sister, she apparently was shocked enough that it brought back her sight."

"You should have said something to me sooner," Gavin said.

"Why? It all came out not so long after that incident. Apparently Lydia had the same feeling that I did."

"And now you've charmed and tamed the bird. What are you going to do about it?"

"I don't think I have enough wealth to keep a woman like Birdie happy," Colin said, studying the carpet.

"Starting up your practice again will help," Gavin suggested.

Colin's head came up. "As much as I'd love to stay in the country and treat the rustics, I fear being paid in goat cheese and sheep's wool wouldn't keep Birdie happy."

"But you will split your time between Edinburgh and here. That way we get to see you regularly, and you could still have your lucrative practice in the city."

"And Birdie isn't quite your country house lassie, we know that without a doubt; she would love the townhouse, and Eve is a natural caregiver."

"There. See? We've solved your problem."

"Yes, now all we need to do is convince Birdie to marry me." Colin's voice dripped with sarcasm.

Suddenly Gavin became very serious. "Are you certain that's what you want? To marry Birdie?"

"It would take her off your hands, wouldn't it?"

Gavin shook his head. "Be serious, man. Remember, marriage is supposed to be for the rest of your life. Could you really be happy with a woman who has a temperament like hers?"

"Perhaps you couldn't; you've said before you don't want too much drama in your life. But, I tell you, the moment I saw her I was bewitched."

"I remember you telling me I had basically made the best mistake of my life."

"That was before I saw her," Colin answered. "And I'm grateful—thank you," he added with a smile.

Chapter Twenty-Five

A week before Mister Geddes Gordon, Gavin's solicitor, arrived, Robbie learned about the letter from the mother of the infant girl. Gavin had ushered her into his office.

"This isn't going to be easy, I don't know how you will respond," he began, handing her the missive.

Robbie read the letter, her heartbeat accelerating. "Why didn't you tell me before now?"

Gavin gave her a soft smile. "Do you have to ask?"

"I'm not an invalid, Gavin." Although she had to admit to herself she'd been acting like one.

"You were in pain, Robbie. I didn't know if telling you earlier would make you feel worse. I've noticed that you don't take part in the baby's care, and I—"

"Don't," she said, interrupting him. "Up until now I didn't know she would be part of the household. It's not wise to become attached."

"And now?"

Robbie smoothed her skirt, then rubbed her palms over it, as if trying to rid herself of something. "Are you telling me that just like that," she said, snapping her fingers, "we're going to raise a babe? What happens if the mother changes her mind, Gavin? What happens then?"

"I think it's highly unlikely she'll change her mind," he said, although Robbie didn't think he sounded convinced. "We'll find out what we have to do when Mr. Gordon gets here."

Robbie crossed to the window. The blackberry bramble was thickening with berries; Mrs. Murray would make jam. The hedgerows were still flowering. It was odd that no matter what drama happened in one's life, things go on as they always have, as if nothing was amiss. "Is there no way to protect people from that happening?"

"I would say that in most cases, the family is relieved to be rid of the stigma."

Robbie laughed, although there was no humor in it. "What is a stigma to one is a blessing to another, isn't that what they say?"

"Are you saying it would be our blessing?" His voice held hope.

She paused. "'Our blessing.' You say it so matter-of-factly, Gavin."

"Well, wouldn't it be? A blessing?"

She turned to faced him, fighting tears. There was an ache in her throat so fierce she could hardly swallow. "How can I allow myself to become attached? The three of them, down there oohing and aahing, taking turns with her care as if she were here to stay, how easily they fell into the trap."

"Robbie, if there is no law to protect the people who take the child in, surely there's no law to protect the mother if she wants the baby back."

Again, Robbie was close to tears. "But, she's the *mother*. She will always be the mother to that child, even if she gives her away. And us? What would we be? Her caregivers? How can we become her parents if there is no way to protect us from the mother taking her back?"

"She has a name, Robbie," Gavin said softly. "Her name is Alice."

Robbie pressed her fingers to her eyes, hating herself for the way she felt. "I know; I know."

"Would you rather her name was Ariadne?"

Robbie couldn't help but laugh. "I thought Birdie wanted to name her Adrianna."

"Either way, it doesn't matter. She could, and probably will, become Alice Eliot." He rose from the chair and went to her, putting his hands on her shoulders. She was still pale, and he realized she had lost weight. Under her flesh there was little meat and all bone. "I wish you wouldn't worry so. I know it doesn't do any good to tell you not to, but I truly want your happiness, Robbie. I truly do. And it isn't as if I believe that having a baby to care for will heal your wound; I can't begin to comprehend your pain, and you probably can't explain it to me in a way I could understand."

She leaned her head against his chest and let him envelop her. She loved the smell of him. "Does Birdie know about this turn of events?"

"Only you and Colin are aware of it."

"She will have a fit, you know, although she doesn't do any of the dirty work as it is."

"Dirty work?" Gavin smiled and raised his eyebrows.

"You know, changing the clouts, rinsing and washing them."

He was quiet for a while, then said, "I worry about her reaction."

Robbie pulled away and looked up at him. "Why?"

"Over these past weeks I've noticed how completely she possesses something. Like your dog, taking it over as if it were her right to do so, then ignoring it when the babe came. And you might not believe it, but she also holds Colin in her grip, although he would say otherwise."

"Birdie has always been like that, even when we were small."

"I've been watching her around the babe. She's almost fierce in her need to be close to her."

"What are you saying? That Birdie will resent the fact that the baby was given to you, thus to me?"

He smoothed his fingers over the hair at her temples, sending a shiver through her. "You don't think that's possible?"

Robbie shook her head slowly, processing his words. "What could she possibly do about it? Oh, I know she's difficult, but deep down I don't think she's any more devious than the rest of us. And even if you told her she could have Alice, which of course is absurd, I'm not sure what she'd do about it. Once the babe began walking and talking, she wouldn't be the needy infant she is now, and Birdie would lose interest, just like she does with everything."

He pulled her close again, and she wrapped her arms around his waist. "I hope you're right. And honestly, Robbie, she is absolutely the last person I would trust Alice with for any length of time."

• • •

The house was dark; everyone was asleep. Little Ariadne—or was it Adrianna?—it didn't matter, she had just been fed not long before; Birdie almost hoped the she was awake so she could pick her up.

With a candle, Birdie left her apartment and stole quietly down the hallway to the door of the room they were using as a nursery. She opened the door slowly, and once she was inside, she left the door ajar so it wouldn't make noise as it closed.

She couldn't help herself; she had to take just a little glimpse at the wee one. Holding her candle in one hand, she stepped to the crib and peeked into it and watched her baby sleep. How beautiful she was!

Birdie had never felt such a rush of love for a living thing. Well, perhaps the pup at first, but when the babe arrived, she admitted the pup meant little to her.

She watched as the babe, Alice—although Adrianna or Ariadne were far more exotic, and maybe she could still convince the others—lifted her delicate cupid bow lips into a smile. Perhaps she was dreaming. Birdie wondered what in the world babies dreamt about when they didn't know anything of the world yet.

Birdie hoped things stayed just as they were. She was quite certain the young mother had meant for Birdie to have her; why else had she given the bairn to her? She could have left her with anyone, but she chose Birdie.

Suddenly something brushed against her leg and startled her so, she almost dropped the candle. She turned away briefly, looked down, and saw Lady sniffing around. "Hush, you," she whispered.

The dog barked, startling Birdie more, and she tried to get her to stop. "Be quiet!" she whispered loudly and nudged her with her foot.

At her response, the pup barked again, wagging its tail and jumping up on Birdie's robe. The bairn began to cry, and Birdie whirled toward the crib, the candle teetering on the holder.

"Shhh, baby." She tried to quiet the girl, but she continued to wail, the dog continued to bark, and suddenly something bright lit up the room.

Birdie gasped. The candle had fallen, hitting the curtains, and now they were on fire.

Birdie grabbed a blanket and tried to bat the flames out with it, but the blanket caught fire as well.

The door slammed open and hit the wall. "Fire! Fire! God have mercy!" Mrs. Murray raced to the crib, lifted the babe out, and rushed from the room.

Lydia, who had been in the kitchen and heard the commotion, came in as Mrs. Murray left, with Colin right behind her. Lydia dragged Birdie from the room and Colin pulled the flaming curtains from the window and threw them on the floor where he stomped on them until the fire was dead.

Everyone was awakened. They all sat in the breakfast room around the table. Mrs. Murray made tea, which the men laced with brandy. Lydia lifted her cup. "I'll take a drop of that."

Birdie sat with her arms crossed over her chest. She wouldn't look at anyone.

Finally, Colin asked, "Tell me what happened, Birdie."

Appeased by his gentle tone, Birdie told him she just wanted to look at the babe, then the dog came in and startled her. She didn't realize the candle had fallen from the holder until she saw the curtains in flames. "It was an accident, surely you must know that," she said to everyone at the table. "If it's anyone's fault, blame the dog."

Lydia held the sleeping baby. Birdie looked at her with such angst, it actually made Robbie feel a little sorry for her.

"I guess this is as good a time as any to share the news I received a couple of weeks ago." Gavin had their attention. He told them of the letter from Darla Dean.

Those who hadn't been told beforehand sat, stunned.

Finally, Mrs. Murray said, "So the bairn is yers, then? We can keep her? And her name really is Alice?"

Lydia simply shook her head. "The Lord works in mysterious ways, doesn't He?"

The only one who was quiet was Birdie. When she spoke, what she said surprised no one. "But Adrianna was given to me, specifically. The mother could have given her to anyone, even the woman who works at the coffeehouse. Or, if she came in on the coach, she could have left her with the innkeeper. She didn't. She left her with *me*."

"So, what are you saying, Birdie?" Robbie asked, knowing her sister well.

"Why should you get her? You've got everything I ever wanted right here in this house. You got the husband I was supposed to get. The luxurious living. The carriages, horses, clothes, jewels—all the things that should have been mine. So you lost a baby; you can have another, can't you?" Tears rolled down her cheeks.

"And what of Gavin? The child was put in his care. That's in writing, Birdie. It outweighs your own wishes and desires."

Robbie saw her sister's eyes flicker around the room. Something she always did when she was processing things she didn't like. Finally, she stood. "I suppose you're right, although I don't know that I'll ever forgive you for taking my place here."

When no one responded, Birdie flounced off to bed.

"Is the crib damaged?" Gavin asked once she'd left the room.

Colin shook his head. "The fire didn't get beyond the window, but the floor is sooty and it will probably smell for a while."

"We'll put the little lamb in my room for now," Mrs. Murray announced. Then, suddenly realizing the change in the status of the bairn, she added, "Unless ye want to keep her, mistress."

Robbie pulled the edges of her dressing gown together, not

realizing that it sent the message that she was closing herself off. "You're familiar with the routine, Mrs. Murray. She'll do very well with you."

Mrs. Murray gave Gavin a worried look, then answered, "Fer now, I'd be happy tae."

They all looked at one another.

"Do you think it's safe to go back to bed?" Colin asked, only half kidding.

"If Miss Birdie wants tae take another glimpse of the bairn, she'll have to go through me first," Mrs. Murray said with fervor.

Chapter Twenty-Six

Geddes Gordon was a tall man, wide through the shoulders and slim of hip. He had a full head of light hair, much like Gavin's, although perhaps a shade darker.

Robbie joined the men in the library, where the solicitor commented quite positively on the décor, especially the books.

"I've always appreciated a well-appointed library," he replied, scanning the shelves.

Gavin agreed. "We didn't have a separate room actually called a library, but my room was stacked with books. Even after my da built me a bookcase I found it just wasn't enough space for all that I had."

Robbie envisioned a young Gavin, carefully putting his things in order, gently touching things that were special to him. Warmth burst through her; she was still so much in love with him. She wished she could slap herself, come out of the funk, and be the wife she should be and "mother" he wanted her to be to the new babe. He deserved that. Again, she felt her eyes well.

"Now, then," Geddes began. "I wish I had positive news for you regarding your situation, but although there's no good news, there's no bad news either.

"In most cases like this, no one comes forward to reclaim an abandoned child. It's done with purpose and nearly all the time, total willingness. When it happens among the gentry, it's all very hush hush because there is such a disgrace to the family. And I have not heard of any young mother defying her family and wanting her child back."

"So there's nothing to be done to protect us?" Robbie asked, fiddling with the simple gold heart she wore on a chain around her neck.

Geddes sat forward and rested his forearms on his thighs. "Imagine your scenerio. A fourteen-year-old girl, yes, still a girl by any standard, especially one so protected, becomes pregnant by a close relative. When the household learns of it, I would gather the relative involved hightailed it out of there. Could they have convinced him to stay and marry his cousin? Perhaps they tried, but young lads being what they are, he realized he had too much life to live to be tied down to a wife and bairn."

"Could they have promised him something? Like a substantial dowry?" Gavin asked.

Geddes shook his head. "I looked into the family. The lad's father owns a large shipping company out of Glasgow. Money wasn't an issue. I believe he just wanted his freedom."

"Do you think they sent Darla away to have the child?" Gavin asked.

"I checked on that as well. Yes, she was up north in a refuge for girls in her predicament. Because she had a medical condition besides the use of only one arm—"

"What medical condition?" Robbie broke in.

"She suffered from seizures," Geddes said.

Robbie glanced at her husband. "Did you know this?"

Gavin said he did not.

"The trauma of the delivery threw her seizures into unpredictable patterns. And because of that, she stayed on at the shelter for a few months, promising the staff and her parents that once she was stablized, she would turn the infant over someone who would find the bairn a good home."

Robbie pressed her hands to her mouth. "But she didn't."

"From what I can gather, she fled the shelter with her bairn one night after everyone was asleep. I traced her here, but, like you Gavin, I couldn't find any sign of her beyond that. I can have the private detective who found you look into it, if you wish."

"No, she said she didn't want me to try to find her. And even if he did, it would only stir up trouble."

"I can draw up a paper, signifying that you are the parents at the wishes of the mother. It wouldn't be a legal document, but it would be something."

• • •

After the meeting, Geddes agreed to stay for the evening meal, and although Gavin invited him to stay at the house, he said the returning coach left early, and he needed to get home.

Robbie almost dreaded the meal, for she reckoned Birdie would ask too many pesky questions about the bairn. She was right.

"So, Mister Gordon," Birdie began. "Even though the lass left her babe with me, and asked specifically that I take care of her, I have no right to say she's mine?"

Geddes swallowed the oatmeal-dipped herring, dabbed his mouth with a napkin, and said, "Unfortunately, the written word takes priority over anything verbal."

Birdie brooded the remainder of the meal, while lively conversation rumbled on around her.

• • •

During the next few weeks, Robbie noticed that Birdie was taking even more interest in Alice's care. Before she doted on her, fed her, and held her. Now she even offered to change her and get up at night with her, although those nightly sessions were more infrequent now that Alice was older. Of course, Birdie still insisted on calling her Adrianna; everyone gave up trying to correct her.

Even though there was a chill in the autumn air, Alice was bundled up and taken outdoors in her new perambulator, one Birdie had obviously chosen, for it was the most expensive to be found. Surely Gavin's accounts at the shops in Galashiels were piling up.

Colin told Robbie he thought Alice was now nearly five months old, for she could raise her head and rest on her forearms when she was laid on her stomach. And she loved to kick. Her favorite toy was a homemade rattle that Mrs. Murray had fashioned, and Alice put it in her mouth the moment she was handed the toy. The expensive silver rattle that Birdie had picked out went untouched. Actually, Lady Perlina seemed to enjoy pushing it around the floor, listening to the jingling noise it made.

Chapter Twenty-Seven

Robbie noticed that Birdie began taking the small chaise into the village a couple of times a week, which was unusual because never before had Birdie dared leave the house on her own. She had been reluctant to leave Alice for any length of time and no one allowed her to take the child with her.

Robbie asked her about her trips one day when Birdie had returned.

Offended, Birdie responded, "I'm going stir crazy around here. I don't understand how people can live in the country and never long to return to Edinburgh and the parties and the gala affairs."

"But, what do you do in the village?"

Birdie looked away. "Oh, I look at material and patterns that have come in from Paris. The owner and I talk about fashion; she's really quite educated on the subject."

"You mean for someone who lives out in the provinces."

"Exactly," Birdie answered, unaware of the slight.

"I would think there would be only so much fabric and patterns you can look at before you've seen it all."

Birdie gave her sister a sidelong glance. "Of course you would think that; you have absolutely no fashion sense at all. But look." She brought out a package from her satchel. "I found this adorable dress for Ariadne."

"I thought you called her Adrianna."

"Ariadne, Adrianna, either name is preferable to Alice." She made a face, then presented a dress big enough to hold three babies.

Although it was a lovely pink satin and lace frock, it wasn't one bit serviceable. Robbie raised an eyebrow. "When do you think she'll be old enough to wear it?"

Birdie brushed the question away. "I know it's too big, but when I saw it, I knew I had to have it."

Again, Robbie wondered if Gavin even knew that Birdie was putting items on his accounts.

• • •

Later, after dinner, Robbie went into the library and found her husband dandling Alice on his knee. She stepped back into the shadows to watch.

He was singing softly to her, a tune that she had heard so many years ago, from her nanny.

> *Gee up on the horse.*
> *The horse going to vallay.*
> *The high tide will catch us,*
> *It will catch us by the legs.*
> *It will catch us by the head.*
> *Gee up on the horse.*
> *The horse going to vallay.*

Robbie hadn't thought of that ditty in years, and now, hearing the words, wondered at how soothing it would be if the babe could understand them. The tune is what she always remembered—a lilting, sad little melody.

Gavin stopped bouncing Alice and brought her to his chest. "Ah, little Alice, you are a sweet little babe, aren't you?"

Alice pulled away and grabbed Gavin's nose. He snorted like a pig, making her laugh. Such a sweet sound it was, a bairn's laughter. Robbie blinked away the sting in her eyes. Would she never stop bawling?

Suddenly Gavin pressed his face into Alice's tummy and made sputtering noises, causing Alice to squeal with laughter and grab at Gavin's hair.

Lady Perlina darted past Robbie into the room, pushing her nose against Gavin's leg. Alice's arm dangled close by, and the dog licked it repeatedly.

"So you like Alice, do you?" Gavin asked the dog. "I do as well."

A sharp feeling stabbed at Robbie's chest. Could she do this? Could she be a mother to a child that was not hers? Alice would have a good life with them, Robbie knew that.

"Robbie?"

The sound of her name startled her.

She came forward. "I didn't want to disturb you; you are so good with her."

His expression was pained. "Will you not hold her, Robbie?"

She took a few hesitant steps toward her husband. At that moment, Alice saw her and she beamed, holding her arms out for Robbie to take her.

Robbie was stunned. "I...I don't think—"

Gavin stood with Alice in his arms. "Don't think, Robbie, feel. Just feel." He lifted the child toward her.

With excited hesitancy, Robbie took Alice and automatically returned her smile. "Well, hello, Alice." She glanced at Gavin, whose eyes looked misty. "With everyone else taking such good care of her, I just didn't think—"

"There you go, wife, thinking again."

She snuggled Alice against her chest, breathing in the sweet baby smell of her, touching her fine, feathery hair, feeling her smooth cheek against to her own. Tears finally spilled. "Oh, Gavin, I don't know what to say, how to apologize for my behavior these past weeks."

Gavin encircled her and Alice with his arms. "Then you think we might be a family, the three of us?"

Robbie felt a pull at her skirt. "I think there will be four of us," she corrected, as Lady Perlina urged herself closer to the threesome.

Gavin pulled away briefly. "I have a surprise for you." He went to his desk and retrieved a letter, handing it to Robbie after he took Alice.

Curious, she took it. "But it's addressed to you."

"I think you'll find the contents to your liking."

Frowning, she opened the letter and read the message. Her head came up, and she nearly gasped. "They want to publish my little book? How did they get it?"

Slightly embarrassed, Gavin replied, "I found it on the floor one day and read it. It's a very good story, Robbie. It has all of the things youngsters enjoy: humor, animals, and…birds who get their comeuppance."

Robbie read the letter again. "But what about pictures? It must have pictures in it."

"My friend at the publishing house said they would have their artist do them and send them on to make sure you approved."

She dropped the letter and put her hands to her cheeks. "Oh, Gavin, this is the most exciting thing!"

"And they want more of your stories, Robbie."

"My dream." She sniffed and smiled through her happy tears. "I can't wait to get started on another."

• • •

Everyone was delighted that Robbie had apparently overcome most of her downheartedness, and they were equally excited about the sale of her book. She took part in Alice's care, still regarding the others as part of the baby's "team." But whenever possible, she took Alice with her into her quiet room, sat with her in the rocking chair, and told her stories until she fell asleep. Her own stories, of course, anxious for the day Alice could read them for herself. Like the others, she was reluctant to put her down to nap, eagerly enjoying the moments she held Alice close to her heart.

One fine autumn day she bundled Alice up in her bunting, wore her warmest hat and cloak, and took the baby outside.

Mrs. Murray stopped her. "Don't ye want the perambulator?"

Robbie shook her head. "I want to hold her. I want her close to me. We'll be fine." They stepped outside and Robbie pulled in a deep breath of cool, fresh air. Alice was staring up at her.

"You know," Robbie began, "the first time I came here the air was so fresh I nearly fainted from the pleasure of it. And it still affects me that way." She grinned at her daughter. "Oh, don't worry, sweetheart, I wouldn't dare faint with you in my arms."

Alice gurgled, blowing a spit bubble.

"One of the first things I remember were the gardens. Oh, Alice, I can't wait until you are old enough to see the gardens in full bloom! We'll pick some flowers, of course we will. And you'll help me weed the garden beds, won't you?"

Alice made a sputtering noise.

"No? You don't want to get your pretty frock dirty?" Robbie clucked her tongue. "Now you sound more like your Aunt Birdie."

As they walked the path toward the stable, Robbie realized that Birdie's reaction to all of this surprised her. She had expected the same old rants about Robbie already having what should have been hers. She wasn't particularly exuberant about it, but she was pleasant enough, for Birdie.

Ben appeared at the stable door and when he saw Robbie he hurried over and peeked at her charge. "So this be the wee lassie? She be quite a bonny one for certain."

"Yes, Ben, she certainly is bonny." Even though Robbie didn't want to end this little stroll, her arms grew tired, and she bade Ben goodbye and reluctantly returned to the house.

• • •

One evening, when Gavin and Robbie had taken Alice out for an evening stroll, Lydia, who was mending a quilt, asked Birdie if she had finally come to terms with the fact that her sister's life was not hers to envy.

Birdie put down *Jane Eyre,* which Colin had begun reading to her before her sight returned. She traced her fingers over the cover and studied Lydia. "I suppose everyone expected me to create a scene."

Lydia never minced words, especially with Birdie. "Yes, I do indeed think everyone expected that."

Birdie plucked at her skirt. "Maybe I've changed. Maybe I've come to the realization that Adelaide will never be mine."

"I thought her name was Adrianna."

Birdie shrugged. "Adelaide, Adrianna, Ariadne, what does it matter now?"

"If you truly believe what you're saying, you've come far."

Birdie gave her a stern look. "Everyone can change, even me."

On a smile, Lydia replied, "Yes, I suppose even you."

Birdie tossed the book on the settee and stomped from the room.

When she learned that Robbie had taken to the baby, she had nearly climbed out of her skin she was so upset. She watched her sister, envy and anger boiling through her veins. Then, because she could stand it no longer, she formulated her plan.

Chapter Twenty-Eight

The nursery had been remodeled after the fire. Fresh yellow paint brightened the walls, and to everyone's surprise, Colin, an artist hiding inside a physician's skin, painted animals from Robbie's book on the walls. Although Mrs. Murray was reluctant to put Alice back in her own room, she knew it was best. Everyone agreed. Even Birdie. And to everyone's surprise, Birdie was quite contrite about her role in the fire.

Alice, now an estimated five months, slept through the night, rarely waking for any reason at all.

Truth to tell, everyone, even Mrs. Murray, was grateful for that. "She is the most perfect bairn," the housekeeper praised as the women sat at the table with their tea. "Sleeps through the night, don't have colic, keeps her food down. Can't expect more from a babe than that. Of course," she added, "when the sweet thing starts teething, that'll be a different story."

Birdie, who had returned from another trip to the village, glanced up from the scone on her plate. "Why is that?"

"'Cause it'll pain her when them teeth start breakin' through her gums."

Birdie appeared uncomfortable. "But it isn't always the case, is it?"

Mrs. Murray shrugged. "I suppose there are those who don't fuss, but I hae not ever seen one. And once she starts to teethe, we'll need to keep a pinafore on her, else her clothes will be wet all the time."

"Why?" Birdie asked.

"Because she'll drool like a puppy, she will."

Birdie made a face. "Adelaide will be the first to have no pain and not drool, then."

Lydia and Robbie looked at one another.

"Lan' sakes, girl, if ye can't use her correct name, don't call her anything at all." Mrs. Murray lifted the teapot and offered the others refills.

"You know," Robbie began, "she could get confused if you keep calling her something other than Alice."

Birdie made a moue. "She's too young to notice."

Lydia clucked her tongue. "And I'm sure you're anxious to get on with your life, Birdie, if not here in the provinces, then in Edinburgh or Glasgow."

Birdie cocked her head. "Yes, I suppose I will."

Her answer surprised everyone, for not once had Birdie even hinted that she might be leaving.

• • •

A few days later, Lydia straightened Birdie's room.

She opened a drawer in the wardrobe to put a shawl away, and was puzzled by what she saw. Stacks of clouts and baby shirts in various sizes. On further searching, she also found buntings, booties, pinafores, and a lot of clothing that appeared much to large for Alice.

Curious, she was eager to approach Birdie and ask her why she was stockpiling things for the bairn.

"Lydia!"

Lydia straightened, hearing the panic in Mrs. Murray's voice. "I'm in here."

Mrs. Murray scurried in, her face red from exertion. "Come quick! Ben hae cut himself somethin' awful. He's bleedin' bad. And the doctor ain't here."

Lydia followed Mrs. Murray to the stable, where Ben, who took care of the horses, sat with a rag around his arm.

"Lord, boy, what happened?" Lydia peeled back the cloth and

saw the cut, deep and jagged. She told the housekeeper to bring her water and clean cloths, plus her bag of medical supplies from her room.

Mrs. Murray quickly brought her water then went to retrieve the medical bag.

Ben was breathing hard, his face white.

"Put your head down between your legs, Benny, you're breathing too hard." Lydia was worried that he could go into shock.

Again she asked, "What happened?"

Ben inclined his head toward the table, on which lay a saw. Lydia noticed the teeth were red with Ben's blood.

She cleaned the wound and pressed a cloth against it until Mrs. Murray arrived with her bag. After treating the wound, she bound it tightly and tied the ends together. "What were you doing?"

Ben rested his back against the wall and closed his eyes. "I was making a box."

"Well, you sure did this one up good and proper," she scolded. "You need to rest that arm for a spell. You're lucky you didn't hit an artery. If you had, you'd be dead by now."

Ben gave her a crooked, gap-toothed grin. "Thank ye so much fer the sympathy."

She gave him a withering look and left him sitting on the bench.

Ben glanced at the box he was making, hoping he could use his arm enough to finish it when Miss Birdie had asked him to. He wanted to please her; what young lad wouldn't?

• • •

When Lydia returned to the house, she found Mrs. Murray in deep discussion with the local butcher, haggling over his price for mutton. After they had concluded their business to Mrs. Murray's liking, she invited him to sit down for a cuppa.

He put two jam tarts on his plate. "I see that red-haired beauty in town a lot these days."

"Yes," Mrs. Murray answered, pouring the three of them tea.

The butcher spooned generous amounts of sugar into his, then stirred.

"She's getting itchy feet, out here in the country. Not used to so much peace and quiet, I'd imagine."

"Me wife is friends with the dressmaker, Myrtle Ferguson. Says the redhead comes by nearly every time she's in town."

"That's what we've heard," Lydia responded.

"Course she spends a good amount of time at the coffeehouse, too," he added.

Lydia glanced around. "Where is Birdie, anyway?"

"She put Alice down for a nap a bit ago, and then she was off to the village again."

Lydia excused herself, pushed away from the table and hurried to the nursery. Little Alice slept peacefully. Lydia wondered why she had worried.

· · ·

Robbie, Gavin, and Colin had pleasant conversation over a glass of port in the drawing room.

"I've contacted a detective, even though I had told Geddes it wasn't necessary. I don't want to find Darla if she doesn't want to be found, but it would be nice to know Alice's birthdate, and I'm sure the haven where Darla delivered her would have that on record."

"Oh, Gavin, that's a wonderful idea." Robbie was quiet for a moment then said, "In cases such as these, I wonder how much to tell the child as she gets older. Do we pretend that she's ours?"

"She is ours, Robbie," Gavin corrected.

"You know what I mean. There is a girl out there who bravely gave her baby away so it could have a good life, not just with anyone, but with us. Shouldn't Alice be told at some point?"

Gavin reached over and squeezed his wife's hand. "I think there will be plenty of time to worry about that, don't you?"

. . .

Later, after the household slept, Robbie, restless, rose from the bed she now shared with her husband and got ready to shush Lady, who stirred at the bottom near Gavin's feet. The dog wagged her tail but didn't follow Robbie out the bedroom door.

Anxious to look in on Alice, Robbie tiptoed to the nursery and opened the door. She stepped to the crib and found it empty.

Swinging around, she rushed to Birdie's apartment, not bothering to knock, but discovering that the door was locked. "Birdie," she whispered, not wanting to wake the household. "Birdie, is Alice in there with you?"

When she got no answer, she remembered seeing a set of keys in the kitchen by the back door. She rushed to find them, and after trying several, she found one that fit.

She opened Birdie's door and went straight to her bedroom. Her stomach dropped when she discovered it was empty. She threw open the wardrobe doors, noting it, too, was nearly empty. Even Birdie's valise was gone.

Chapter Twenty-Nine

"Gavin! Colin!" Robbie rapped soundly on Colin's apartment door as she passed.

Gavin opened the door and peered out at her. "What is it?"

"She's gone! Birdie has taken the baby and is gone!"

Gavin tried to calm her. "She can't just have disappeared."

Robbie marched back and forth across the hallway carpet, hugging her chest. "She isn't here. All of her things are gone."

Colin came out of his rooms, shrugging into a dressing gown. "What's this?"

Gavin explained. "Robbie says Birdie and the baby are missing."

The three of them rushed downstairs and into Birdie's apartment.

Lydia and Mrs. Murray, both awakened by Robbie's screams, were close behind.

They lit a lamp and surveyed the room.

Suddenly, Lydia went to the wardrobe and flung open the door, and gasped.

"What? What is it?" Robbie was beside herself with fear.

Lydia turned to everyone. "Just yesterday I was in here straightening up. And this wardrobe was filled to the brim with baby things. I had meant to ask Birdie why she was buying so much, but then Ben got cut, and I went out to help..." Her voice faded.

Robbie continued to feel panic. "But if she did take Alice, how did she do it? Birdie doesn't know anyone around here, and how would she have gotten all of this stuff out of here without any of us noticing?"

"And where in the hell did she think she was going?" Colin all but shouted.

They all pondered the questions.

"How long do you suppose she's been gone?" Robbie asked.

"Hard to guess, since she didn't come to dinner." Lydia clucked her tongue. "My, but she must have had some plan to pull this off without any of us having an inkling."

"And I'm thinking she probably had help," Gavin added. "But I can't imagine who."

Robbie just stood there, shaking her head. "How could she do this, knowing..."

"Knowing she's doing it to her own sister?" Lydia finished for her.

"I knew that lassie was trouble the minute she stepped into this house," Mrs. Murray proclaimed.

They filed out of the apartment and, just to make sure, each peeked into the empty crib as they made their way toward the kitchen, where Mrs. Murray set about making tea.

Robbie collapsed into a chair. "It's my fault."

A cacophony of denials filled the air.

"From the very beginning, I knew deep down in my heart that Gavin had made a mistake proposing to me, but it was such a wonderful fairy tale, and I'd loved you forever," she said, throwing him a glance.

Gavin slid his chair closer to hers and took her hands in his. "Robbie, if there is one thing I'm certain of, it's that no one but Birdie is to blame for this. And be comforted in knowing that had I not made that mistake, I assure you I'd be the most miserable man alive right now, baby or no."

Colin slapped his palm on the table. "I can't believe she actually did it. What was she thinking? How will she care for Alice? She has no funds, no other family, and certainly no way to earn a living."

Gavin stood. "She will not get far, I promise you. Colin, after we dress, we're going on a hunt. For a kidnapper, and a sweet, innocent baby."

"I want to go with you," Robbie announced, eager to join them.

Gavin turned to her. "I know you do." He took both hands in hers, brought them to his lips and kissed them. "But we need you to stay here. There may be a message of some kind, and I want you here in case such a thing occurs."

She knew he was right; but it was hard to sit by and do nothing.

• • •

Naturally, Gavin and Colin's first stop was at the inn, where, because of the early hour, it was still dark inside. Gavin pulled the emergency cord beside the front door, and in a few moments, the innkeeper arrived in his nightclothes, carrying a candle. He peered up at the two of them. "Yes?"

"I'm sorry to bother you Mr. Baker, but my wife's sister has disappeared with our baby. Have you by chance seen them this evening, perhaps boarding a coach?"

The innkeeper opened the door and allowed the men inside. He made his way to the counter where he lit a lamp. "I haen't seen them, sirs, but let's check the schedule, just to make sure. I could have been doing other chores at the time."

All three crowded around the coach schedule. Gavin's disappointment was clear when he didn't see Birdie's name on the list.

"Ah, but she could have used a different name to throw us off her trail," Colin said. He turned to the innkeeper. "Are you familiar with all of these passengers on the schedule?"

Mr. Baker squinted at the names. "Aye, those were the only travelers. The Carmody family and a parson on his way to Edinburgh."

Gavin rested his elbow against the counter. "Truthfully, I had never thought Birdie bright enough to pull something like this off."

"I will admit she doesn't seem capable, but, as much as I'm drawn to her, she is deceitful."

The sun was attempting to break through the clouds on the eastern horizon. Gavin glanced across the street at the coffeehouse. Colin followed his gaze.

"Are you thinking what I'm thinking?" he asked.

With a shake of his head, Gavin replied, "At this point, anything is possible."

They thanked the innkeeper and strode across to the coffeehouse, which, surprisingly, was open. They stepped inside, and Gavin called out, "Faith?"

An older woman wearing a colorful scarf over her gray hair came out from the back, wiping her hands on a towel. "Ye be lookin' for my Faithy?"

Gavin had met Faith's mother some time ago and didn't readily recognize her. "Yes. We're looking for Faith. She's not working today?"

The woman pulled in a sigh and sat down at one of the tables. "Faithy took some time off. She waited until I was better; you see, I've been a bit under the weather. But now I can work, so Faithy has gone on holiday."

A peculiar feeling tunnelled into Gavin's gut. "Do you know where she went, ma'am?"

"Aye, we have family in Lairg, in the Highlands. She be visiting them."

The men thanked her and stepped outside.

"I'm getting an awful feeling," Gavin admitted.

They walked toward the livery to fetch their mounts. "Do you really think Birdie could have had Faith as a conspirator in this whole matter?"

"It's starting to make sense. We never knew where Birdie went when she left the estate. Her answers were vague at best," Gavin replied. "But for Faith to do such a thing..."

"It's what I've been saying all along, Gavin. Faith Baker is not a good woman; she is, however, a fine actress," he added with a snide smile. "With Birdie's selfishness and Faith's scheming mind, they make a formidable duo."

"So, we're off to Lairg."

• • •

Robbie paced. She couldn't think. She couldn't write. She couldn't do anything constructive, so she paced.

Lydia looked up from her cross stitching.

Robbie said, "I can't believe it. I don't want to believe my own sister is capable of such a thing. Oh, my whole life she has been a bit of a thorn in my side, but because of our differences, that's natural, I suppose."

"I came from a family of eleven; I'm the youngest. Truth to tell, there wasn't a nasty person among us."

Robbie gave her a quick glance. "How is that possible?"

Lydia put down her stitching. "For one thing, we were dirt poor. Everyone, including me, had to work to keep everything together. Guess there was no time for shenanigans."

"I guess both Birdie and I had too much time on our hands," Robbie recalled.

"But it didn't turn you into a selfish woman," Lydia replied. "Your sister, on the other hand…"

The return of Gavin and Colin from Galashiels brought both women to attention. "What did you discover?" Robbie asked, her fingers crossed in the folds of her skirt.

Gavin shrugged out of his topcoat and laid it across the back of a chair. "No good news, I'm afraid." He told the women what he'd learned from the innkeeper.

"How did she get away without alerting anyone?" Robbie wondered.

Suddenly Mrs. Murray was at the door. "Benny here to see you, sir."

Gavin nodded and Benny entered, his arm cleanly bandaged and his hat in his hands.

"Yes, Ben?"

"I heard ye say that Miss Birdie has gone with the bairn."

Alert now, both men straightened. "Do you know something?"

Ben shifted from one foot to the other. "She come to me

193

askin' fer a box." He shrugged his shoulders. "I didna' ask why, I jes wanted to please Miss Birdie, so I made her one."

"How big?"

Ben continued to study the carpet. "Big enough to pack a lot of things, but I had no notion of what she was plannin', sir, ye've got to believe me."

"Good God. Even Birdie wouldn't try to hide a live baby in a box!" Gavin strode the room nearly rubbing the back of his neck raw.

Colin added, "No, but she may have used it to pack some of that stuff Lydia saw in the wardrobe. Birdie's luggage was gone, wasn't it?"

At Gavin's nod, Colin continued. "Suppose she was in cahoots with Faith—"

"Faith Baker?" Robbie interrupted. "What does she have to do with all of this?"

Gavin went to her. "We checked the coffeehouse and learned from Faith's mother that Faith had taken 'a holiday' and her mother wasn't sure when she'd return."

Robbie's fingers were at her lips. "And you think she has something to do with getting Birdie and Alice away from here?"

"It wouldn't surprise me one bit," Colin responded.

Feeling defeated, Robbie sank into a chair by the cold fireplace. She rubbed her arms, hoping to warm herself. "Now what?" Her voice was thin.

"We were told she went north to the Highlands, to see family. It's possible that was just something she told her mam in case someone," Colin said, gesturing to himself and Gavin, "came asking for her."

Wanting to reassure her, Gavin said, "It's a place to start."

• • •

Robbie watched as the men put some things together, and then followed them to the stable. As they began saddling their mounts, she asked, "Why don't you take a carriage? If you find them, you'll need to bring all of them back here."

Gavin answered, "Not *if* we find them, Robbie, *when* we find them. And when we do, we'll rent something to bring everyone, including our daughter, home safely."

"In the meantime," Colin added, "we need to travel as quickly as possible. A carriage would be cumbersome."

As the two men rode away, Robbie wondered at the legal ramifications of this stunt of her sister's. Surely it was kidnapping, and that being the case, Faith Baker was an accomplice. At this moment, as Robbie pressed her lips together to keep from screaming or crying or both, she hoped they would get the most that the law would give them.

Chapter Thirty

Gavin and Colin rode steadily, stopping only to rest their mounts. Along the way they stopped at inns where coaches took on passengers, asking if anyone remembered two women and a bairn. So far they had had no luck.

As they rode north, Gavin felt the chill. Flipping up the collar of his greatcoat, he said, "I haven't been this far north in a long time; it's colder here."

"You spend too much time with your books and maps. You should get out more."

Gavin tossed him a quick glance. "I admit I've not really been interested in traveling myself, other than to study the old cairns and Viking lodgings that might still be around."

"Ah, the Vikings." Colin looked at Gavin's nearly white hair. "Is that where your mam came from?"

Gavin nodded. "She was working at an inn in a small town outside of Helsinki when my da came in with his crew of fishermen. And the rest is history."

"You mean just like that? What did he do, ferry her away?"

"Mam always said it was 'love at first sight' for her, because she'd never met anyone as handsome as my dark-haired da. So, not long after they met, she became Linnea Pietela Eliot."

A strong gust of bitter wind whipped around them, fanning out the tails of their coats and causing their mounts to toss their heads and snort into the squall.

Gavin pointed into the distance. "There's an inn. I'm ready for some food and a drink."

After leaving their horses at the livery, they entered the inn and were met with warmth from a roaring fire and the smell of meat juices. It made their mouths water. They took a seat at a rough-hewn wooden table by the fire and each ordered dinner and a pint of ale.

The owner stepped up to the table. "Ye be strangers, aye?"

"Aye," Colin responded. "Looking for someone."

The owner crossed his beefy arms over his powerful chest. "Escaped the law, have they?"

"Nothing as serious as that," Colin answered.

Gavin raised an eyebrow. "I disagree," he said under his breath.

The innkeeper looked from one to the other. "Well, which is it?"

"We're looking for two young women and a child," Gavin told him.

The barkeep/innkeeper frowned and shook his head. "There's been only a sma' number of travelers this time of year. Dinna recall any bairns."

Gavin cocked his head. "Have you seen two young women?" He turned to Colin. "It's possible they somehow waited until Alice was asleep in her basket then covered her with a blanket to hide her."

Now Colin frowned. "I keep forgetting we're dealing with two devious women."

With a lift of his tawny brow, Gavin answered, "How can you?"

"Nae, gents," the innkeeper broke in. "No single lassies on the coaches that hae passed through my inn, not in the last two months."

Their ale and food came, and all the while they ate, Gavin felt as though they were being watched. His gaze wandered the bar, where numerous men of questionable ages were either drinking alone or in deep conversation with another. At the far end, closest to the door, sat one man alone, nursing an ale. His gaze caught Gavin's, and he didn't look away. With a movement so slow Gavin wondered if he actually saw it, the man flicked his gaze toward the door.

After they had eaten and paid for their meal, they thanked the owner and left. Before they got too far, Gavin put a hand on Colin's arm.

"I think there's a fellow in there who might want to talk."

Colin glanced back but saw nothing.

"Let's walk toward the livery; maybe I was wrong."

Once inside the livery, they waited. And it wasn't in vain. The man from the bar hurried toward them, stepped inside, and tucked himself into a shadowy corner.

"Ye be lookin' for lassies, right?" His voice was raspy and deep; he smelled of tobacco and ale.

"What do you know?" Gavin asked.

He put out his hand and rubbed his fingers together.

"You'll get paid if you have some valuable information," Colin said sharply.

The man glanced around him. "Yesta'day the coach brings in a family what departs it and leaves two lassies inside." He looked at the door. "Barkeep comes out wi' a basket and leaves it wi' the lassies."

"Why would he say he hadn't seen any such young women?"

The stranger shrugged. "'Dunno. Mebbe he be bribed, mebbe he be related."

"Why are you telling us this?" Colin asked.

Again the shrug. "Don't make no diff'rence tae me; Donal, the innkeeper, ain't no friend of mine."

"Where was the coach headed?" Gavin pulled out his leather money sack, hefting it in his palm, the coins making lucrative noise.

The man rubbed his hands together. "Up toward Braemar, I'm thinkin'. It's the usual Tuesday coach."

"Near Balmoral Castle," Gavin said, almost to himself. He reached in and fished out some coins and tossed them to the man. As he hurried away, Colin's voice was in his ears.

"If we find you've misled us, we'll come back and take care of you proper."

Gavin snorted a laugh. "Take care of him proper? Have you ever hit a man?"

Realizing the foolishness of his threat, he answered, "Maybe I have, and maybe I haven't."

Gavin slapped him on the back. "Come on, let's be off to Braemar."

• • •

Robbie tried not to worry, but it was no use. Ever since she bonded with Alice, she had thought of little else. She was furious with Birdie, but was she surprised? Perhaps a little. One particular memory pecked at her mind, one that had involved Robbie, Birdie, and a colorful doll that Robbie had been given by a friend.

"But it's so pretty," Birdie said with a pout. "Why did she give it to you and not me?"

Robbie stroked the doll's yellow yarn hair. "Maybe because you call her names."

"But I can't help it. Her name rhymes with 'butt.'"

"It does not," Robbie argued. "Lizbet does not rhyme with 'butt.'"

Birdie got into her sister's face. "Lizbutt, Lizbutt, Lizbutt!" Then she grabbed for the doll, but Robbie hung on. All at once, Robbie was holding only the head, and Birdie had the doll's torso in her fist.

Of course once the doll was ruined, Birdie was no longer interested. Even after the housekeeper stitched the head back on, it was no longer the perfect little plaything. In spite of that, Robbie had treasured it for years.

Now, Robbie walked through Alice's nursery, touching the crib, lifting the blanket to her nose, inhaling the scent of a bairn she had just begun to love.

A sudden twist of anger coiled in her stomach. How long would it take Birdie to tire of Alice? And if Faith Baker was truly involved, what would they do with her when they both tired of her?

Chapter Thirty-One

Birdie clutched her hands over her ears. "Make her stop!"

Faith bounced the child in her arms, trying to quiet her. "What's wrong with her?"

"How in the bloody hell should I know?" Birdie was nearly in tears.

Suddenly the bairn burped, sending a string of coddled milk out of her mouth, onto Faith's shoulder. Then she was quiet.

Faith held the child away from her and wrinkled her nose. "God, that stuff stinks. And now it's all over my gown." She plopped Adrianna into her makeshift crib, tossed a blanket over her and stepped away to clean herself up. "She has a load of something in her clout, too."

"That's your job, not mine."

After wiping baby puke off her gown, she said, "Just what is your job anyway? You don't feed her anymore, you never change her. She might as well be mine."

Birdie dipped into the box of chocolates she had picked up in the village, popped one into her mouth, wiped her fingers on her handkerchief, and answered, "If this keeps up, I'll give her to you gladly."

Faith looked at the bairn. "She's flushed." Pressing the back of her hand to the bairn's forehead, she added, "I think she has a fever."

Birdie shoulders slumped. "That's all I need. A sick bairn."

"Maybe she's teething," Faith offered. "I noticed that the front of her sleeper was all wet; I guess they drool when their teeth come in."

Birdie put her hands over her face. "She wasn't supposed to be like any other baby."

With a shake of her head, Faith said, "A baby is a baby is a baby. They all puke, poop, pee, and drool. They all cry and scream for no reason at all."

"God, they can't do anything for themselves," Birdie bemoaned.

Faith gave her an odd look. "Of course not, Birdie, they're *bairns,* not dolls."

"But even baby birds learn to fly quickly, don't they?"

"You can't compare baby birds and human babies; that's just dumb."

"I'm not dumb!" Birdie whimpered.

"I didn't say you were, but what you're saying is dumb." She went to the washbasin and dipped a cloth into the water, wrung it out, and dabbed at Adrianna's forehead. "Maybe this will cool her off a little."

Birdie sat up straight. "Do you really think she's sick?"

"I don't know. Like I said, maybe she's getting her teeth. Let's hope that's all it is," she warned.

"What do you mean?"

Faith turned and faced Birdie. "If she's really ill, she'll need a doctor. Can you convince anyone that this bairn is yours?"

Birdie pressed her lips together. "I don't know, but you could," she added hopefully.

Faith shook her head. "Like I said, she might as well be mine."

After a moment, Birdie asked, "Do you want her?"

Faith expelled a snort. "Do I want a baby? God in heaven, no. How would I explain it away? Matter of fact, how would *you* explain her away?"

"I wouldn't have to. The mother gave her to me, remember?"

Faith continued to dab the bairn's face with the damp cloth. "Have you even thought about how you're going to take care of her?"

"Something will happen; it always does."

"Why do you even want her, Birdie? You don't want to care for her, you've lost interest in motherhood."

Birdie's eyes lit with fire. "Because she belongs to my sister." Her gaze trapped Faith's. "Everything I've ever wanted, she now has. Have you any idea how that feels?"

On a short laugh, Faith replied, "Yes, I believe I do. I had high hopes of having Gavin to myself." Her own eyes became angry. "But then, that was before that horrible friend of his, the ugly doctor, discovered my sordid secret."

Always interested in the "sordid," Birdie perked up. "What happened?"

Faith redampened the cloth and contined to nurse the baby. "If you must know, I had, well, I had a little fling with a student and ended up having to get rid of, you know…"

Birdie gasped, but she was smiling. "You had an abortion?"

"Yes, and that bloody doctor threatened to tell Gavin about it. That would have been such an embarrassment for me. I mean, Gavin is so straitlaced."

Birdie rolled her eyes. "Don't I know it. But he's a far better catch than Robbie's fiance, whom I stole and married."

"And your sister has no secrets?" Faith weedled.

"If she does, it doesn't matter. I did hear that she once wrote scandalous things for a magazine, but when Gavin learned of it, he merely told her to stop and write what she wanted." Birdie made a face. "He didn't even have the decency to toss her out on her backside."

Faith glanced at the bairn. "She's asleep, but she still feels a little warm. We can only hope it's just her teeth bothering her."

Birdie crumpled her handkerchief into a ball. "Maybe when she wakes up she'll be all right."

Faith expelled a long, slow sigh. "We can only hope so."

Both women wondered what in the name of heaven they would do with the baby if she actually was sick. It almost made them sick themselves.

Chapter Thirty-Two

Balmoral Castle rose in the distance, an imposing granite fortress sculpted against the cold, blue sky. The backdrop of beeches and spruce trees burning orange and gold in the crisp autumn air.

"I wonder if the queen is in residence." Gavin admired the building and the grounds.

"Possibly," replied Colin, "although it's rather late in the season."

As they crossed the bridge over the River Dee, which sparkled blue in the sunshine, Gavin mused, "Now what? It's like trying to find a needle in a haystack."

"Despite what the fellow at the inn said, I think we should ride to Crathie. If memory serves, I know a physician there, or at least he used to be there. It's a place to start."

Alarmed, Gavin asked, "Why? Do you think—?"

"No, it's just a place to start. But even those two women would know enough to get Alice to a doctor if they had to."

Gavin swore. "And to think I once held both of them in such high esteem. I must have been insane." He thought of the years he had pined for Birdie, painting a picture of her in his mind that was clearly a fantasy. And Faith? That she would do this to him was even more painful than Birdie's betrayal, because he had truly thought they were friends.

"Not insane, my friend, just naïve," Colin reminded him.

• • •

While the men hunted the kidnappers—Robbie had difficulty even thinking of the two women as anything but that—Robbie received a welcome visitor.

She met Eve Innes in the foyer, where Mrs. Murray took her satchel, cape, hat and gloves.

"What brings you to us, dear Eve?"

Eve, plain and serviceable, had warm eyes and a gentle smile. Her face was rather long, and her hair an undeterminable shade of brown, but her personality made up for every bit of it.

"Well," she answered, allowing Robbie to take her elbow and walk with her into the morning room, "I've known the dressmaker in Galashiels for many years. She once had a small shop in Edinburgh, but then her husband became ill and died, so she quit the city and moved to the provinces, closer to her other family. And, I had little to do at home, so, on a whim, I thought to visit both of you! Plus, look in on that brother of mine," she finished with a kind smile, though her eyes twinkled as she mentioned him.

"I hope your visit with Mrs. Ferguson went well, because I'm afraid your brother and my husband are away at the moment, and I have no idea when they will return."

They sat together on the settee, knees touching. Eve studied Robbie. "I fear I see sadness in your eyes."

Robbie rubbed her temples. "Is it that noticeable?"

Eve's palm covered Robbie's hand. "I'm a pretty astute judge, my dear. I hope what's eating at you isn't too serious."

"I'm afraid it is," Robbie confessed. She went on to tell Eve of the bairn, how Alice came to live with them, and how everyone had come to love her. As eager as she was to paint Birdie with a dark brush, she held back, and instead just said that Birdie had become obsessed with the child and had absconded with her.

"Oh my," Eve replied, a worried frown creasing her forehead. "And Birdie is your sister? I find it difficult to believe a sister would behave in such a manner."

Robbie chuckled. "You have not met Birdie. To be kind, she's beautiful, flighty, self-centered, terribly self-absorbed, and often doesn't think any farther than the next moment or two. Consequences usually mean little to her."

"And you're not angry with her?"

"Angry? I'm beyond angry. She has an accomplice, and I hope they both suffer a little for what they've put all of us through." She paused and then added, "I only hope Alice is all right..."

Eve gave Robbie's hand a squeeze. "Well, I know my Colin, and I know your Gavin, and truth to tell, if anyone can find the bairn, it's those two."

Robbie wondered how much to tell the woman. "I don't know if you're aware, but since the moment Colin met Birdie, he's been smitten."

"I guess I'm not surprised," Eve answered. "I don't imagine anything will come of it. If she's a shallow beauty, Colin's deformity would surely put her off."

"Yes, I think for the most part it has," Robbie said. She went on to tell Eve about Birdie's initial blindness, and now she had attached herself to Colin because of it, and how Colin, patient man that he was, had read her nearly all of *Jane Eyre*. "I'd find them curled up together on the settee in front of the fire, Birdie's expression wistful and sweet as she listened to Colin read." She shook her head. "I haven't seen her that way often, truth to tell."

Eve appeared thoughtful. "I do want Colin to find someone. I don't have any interest in marriage, I never have. But Colin—he would make such a wonderful father, don't you agree?"

"Yes, I do agree." Robbie recalled how besotted both men were when it came to Alice.

"Now," Robbie began, "you will stay with us a while, won't you? I would love your company, so please don't disappoint me," she added, her voice warm.

Eve glanced around the well-appointed room. "I am rather curious about the house. Colin spoke of it often, but men usually don't know crocheting from crossbows when it comes to furnishing such a fine place, or even attempting to describe it."

Mrs. Murray popped her head in. "Will the lady be staying?"

"Indeed she will. Ask Maureen to fix up one of the apartments for her, will you please? And when you have a moment, some tea and scones?"

"With pleasure." Mrs. Murray briefly studied the two women before leaving them alone.

"Do you have much help here, Robbie?"

"Besides Mrs. Murray, we have one full-time girl and a couple others who come in daily, who live either on farms or in the villages. We have a stable boy, and other employees who take care of things outside, and then there's Lydia of course, whom you met after her son died. She became Birdie's nurse and chaperone while she couldn't see, but now she will be helping Colin with the clinic Gavin is having built."

"A clinic? How interesting. I haven't seen Colin in a while; this must be a new venture."

"It is, and I hope you don't mind that he'll be staying out here a couple of days a week, seeing patients."

Eve chuckled. "He's rarely at the townhouse anyway. I'm thrilled he's willing to see patients again, after, well after that horrible accident with the bairn, the mongrel, and his nasty owner."

"I didn't realize there was someone else involved," Robbie mused. "He's never said as much, at least not to me."

Eve raised her pale eyebrows. "I suppose it isn't my place to tell, but somehow I feel it wouldn't hurt for you to know. Even Gavin doesn't know the whole story."

Her interest piqued, Robbie leaned in to learn more.

• • •

Except for Adrianna's tiresome cough, it was quiet in the little apartment that Faith's auntie had given them, rent-free until they made more permanent arrangements. And just what would those be, Birdie wondered? She was glad she had Faith on her side; she was the kind of person who could make decisions. That had always been hard for Birdie; someone usually took care of her, and she'd become accustomed to it.

Adrianna had coughed so hard she vomited. With Faith at the market, Birdie had to clean it up, and she was not happy about that, not one bit. The smell made her gag.

She glanced outside, bored. There was nothing to do here, nowhere to go.

Faith entered the room. "She's still coughing?"

"Yes," Birdie nearly hissed. "And she threw up all over herself; I had to clean it up." Her tone let Faith know she wasn't happy about that.

Faith put her packages on the table and walked to the crib. "Birdie," she said, her voice low, "I think there's something terribly wrong with her."

Birdie sat up. "Just because she's coughing?"

"Just listen to it. How can you not hear it? It's not a normal cough; it's deep and disturbing. And her skin is hot and her lips are cracked. She's really ill."

Birdie's eyes grew wide. "What will we do?"

Faith didn't remove her coat. "I saw a doctor's sign in the village. We've got to take the babe there, we have to."

Birdie swallowed hard. "I can't. You do it, Faithy, you can convince them she's yours. I just can't. I just can't."

Knowing better than to argue with her, Faith wrapped the baby in a blanket and tucked her close to her chest as she left the apartment to find a doctor.

Chapter Thirty-Three

Robbie was amazed at the story Eve had to tell. "So the owner merely stood by and watched as his cur attacked Colin. Fortunately, someone came by carrying a board and smacked the dog on the head. Only then did he release his hold on Colin's face."

"What reason did the man give for not intervening? Surely he could see how Colin was suffering."

"That's what was so troubling. He swore at the man who hit his dog, lifted it into his arms, and hurried away. He didn't even stop to acknowledge Colin's wounds. And," she added, "to make things worse, Gavin's mentor, Professor Baker, stood by and did absolutely nothing to help."

Robbie glanced at the window; wind blew the birches, their leaves flailing in the air like drunken butterflies. "What a terrible story. And to think he can be so calm with my pup racing around the house. That has amazed me from the time I learned how he'd gotten the scar that he isn't afraid of dogs."

"Colin doesn't let things bother him for long. He's awfully patient, even with himself. I think the only time he got truly upset over the whole ordeal was when he couldn't save the bairn."

"My husband is a very patient man as well. He can be naïve, although I think everything that has happened since Birdie perched on our doorstep has made him realize people can do bad things."

Eve nodded. "Even I could see that Faith was not a good woman. I watched her face; her expression could change from deviousness to concern to adoration in seconds. Whatever the situation called for."

"And now that woman is an accomplice in Alice's kidnapping." Robbie stood and paced, rubbing her arms with her hands.

"We have to hope that although she has many bad qualities, harming a child isn't one of them."

Robbie strode to the window; leaves continued to blow from the trees. Autumn was coming with a vengeance. "I wish we would hear some word from Gavin and Colin. Any news at all; I can barely stand not knowing something is happening."

● ● ●

It was late in the day by the time Gavin and Colin sought out the doctor, only to learn that there wasn't one in Crathie. A merchant selling wood carvings told them they may find one in Braemar, which was more than ten kilometers away.

Again, as before, they arrived in a village too late to learn anything and had to find an inn and rest their mounts.

As they sat in the pub next to the inn, they were quiet.

"What are you thinking?" Colin asked.

"I'm trying not to think at all," Gavin replied. "As each day passes, my hopes for finding Alice dwindle, and I can't imagine going home to Erskine House and telling Robbie we have failed."

Colin clapped him on the shoulder. "We haven't failed yet. Yes, I had thought my doctor acquaintance was in Crathie, but let's not give up hope. Braemar gives us another chance at finding them."

"What if they haven't even been this way? What if they're long gone, perhaps even out of Scotland?"

"I doubt they could have gotten all that far. And as far as I know, neither has much money. Anyway, it's too early; we've only been searching a few days." He clapped Gavin on the shoulder again. "Chin up, my friend. Chin up."

"All right, let's say we find them—"

"We will," Colin interrupted.

"When we find them, what will we do with the two of them?"

On a sarcastic smile, Colin answered, "Well, we can't wrap them in a sack and toss them in the river like unwanted kittens."

"They can't go unpunished," Gavin murmured, sensing that even Robbie would want them to suffer a little for what they've done.

"Let's find them first," Colin suggested.

• • •

Faith hurried into the apartment; the door slammed soundly behind her. "Hurry up," she said to Birdie. "We're getting out of here."

Birdie sat up. "Where's Adrianna?"

"She's safe, all right?"

Birdie felt an odd pressure in her chest. "We can't just leave her here...can we?"

Faith was throwing things into a satchel. "What did you think we could do? She's too ill to travel, and it's not safe for the two of us to be found, and don't think they aren't searching for us."

"But..." Birdie stood and glanced around the room, too befuddled to move. "But what could they do to us? We did nothing wrong."

Faith tossed her a cynical smile. "Does the word 'kidnapping' mean anything to you?"

"But the mother gave Adrianna to *me*. How can I be charged with kidnapping my own property?"

Faith tossed Birdie her traveling bag. "Pack up."

Slowly Birdie began folding items into her bag. "It isn't fair."

Faith put all of the babe's things into the crib, then shoved it into a corner. "This was ridiculous from the onset. I don't know what made me think we could do it. Maybe I just wanted to get back at Gavin and your sister, and this was the perfect way." She tossed some clothing for Birdie to pack. "I certainly didn't think things through, and of course, I don't think you ever do." After a moment, she added, "Revenge is not as sweet as they say it is."

Realization slowly entered Birdie's mind. "But they won't do anything to us, will they?"

"Whatever they do, it won't be a slap on the wrist, Birdie. And if the babe doesn't survive..."

"Doesn't survive?" Birdie was suddenly alarmed and alert. "You said she was safe. You *said.*"

"Yes, yes, she was alive when I left her. But if she doesn't survive, they could say we killed her. Or at least that her death is on our hands."

Birdie's knees buckled, and she nearly fell to the floor. "Oh my God. What have we done?"

Impatient, Faith shoved Birdie's clothes into her bag. "Someone is waiting to take us to Crathie, where we can catch a ride to—anywhere."

Birdie still appeared to be in shock.

"Birdie, get yourself together or I'll bloody leave you here!"

Preoccupied with fear, Birdie mechanically put on her coat, picked up her valise, and followed Faith out the door.

Chapter Thirty-Four

The streets of Braemar were busy; it was market day. Wagons and carriages, peasants and noblemen peppered the walkways, crossing wherever they could, sidestepping as much garbage and manure as humanly possible.

Gavin studied the throng. "As messy as streets are out here, they are nothing compared with the city." He and Colin crossed to the other side of the road where a physician's sign hung, swinging in the wind. "And when I think of the years Robbie had to endure the slums of Edinburgh, my whole being shakes with rage."

"You found the most patient woman in the world, you lucky man."

"Indeed. And if it's the last thing I do, I will bring our little Alice home. Robbie was just beginning to warm to her, did you know that? As much as she used to scold the other women for holding Alice too much, she's responsible for that very thing herself." Gavin wondered what kind of life they would have if Alice were never found. Would Robbie stay, or would the surroundings be too much for her to bear? And what in the name of God would he do if she left him?

• • •

Lydia found Robbie pacing in the foyer, Lady trailing along behind her. She took Robbie's arm and led her away, into the small room where Robbie took her breakfast. A teapot, its spout wafting steam, sat on the table. Two cups and saucers were in place. A variety of sweets covered a plate. Eve had gone into Galashiels once again to visit with Mrs. Ferguson, the dressmaker.

"Sit. Have a cuppa. That's an order."

"Why haven't we heard anything?" Robbie took a seat but ignored the bounty on the table. Lady curled up at her feet.

"Someone once said that no news is good news," Lydia suggested, helping herself to tea and a freshly baked oat cake.

"Nonsense. People say that just to keep others from worrying themselves ill." She let Lydia pour her some tea. "I haven't even said this out loud, but what happens if—"

"I'd tell you to keep it to yourself, but you probably wouldn't listen."

Robbie rubbed her hands over her face. "If, God forbid, Alice isn't found, what am I doing here? Why should I stay here?"

"Because you have a husband you love, a beautiful estate, and if you leave, I'd have to go as well, so that's reason enough to stay."

In spite of herself, Robbie smiled. "Leave it to you to make light of my departure."

Lydia put her hand on Robbie's arm. "I'm not, believe me. I feel your angst, dear. I have not lived your pain, but I understand it. You love Gavin; you have since the first time you saw him."

Robbie swallowed. "Aye."

"And months ago, he admitted to you that he cared for you. He hesitated to say he loved you, and he still hasn't."

"Nae, he still hasn't. So what is my purpose here? To merely be on his arm when he entertains? To make sure the staff is working the way they should be? Join inane clubs and circles, make quilts and knit clothing for the indigent? Is that what an unloved wife does with the rest of her life?"

"For many wives, it's enough," Lydia reminded her.

Robbie's fist came down on the table, making the tea slop over into the saucer and Lady scoot out from under her feet. "It isn't enough for me."

"You are putting the cart before the horse, Robbie dear. You don't know how he feels now; don't start assuming things before they even happen."

It was as if Lydia could read her mind, Robbie decided. "I do love it here. I love the countryside, the people, the clean, fresh air, the fact that I can write whatever I want, and not have to write swill, and I will always love my husband, no matter what occurs."

"Now," Lydia began, "have some tea, and then we'll go over to see how the workmen are doing on the clinic. Won't the men be surprised when they return with little Alice, to find things are almost ready for patients."

• • •

Colin realized the man who stood before them was not the man he remembered. His friend was in his middle thirties, tall, with a fine head of auburn hair. This man was short, stubby with a ridiculous comb-over of gray hair. And he didn't appear happy. Nevertheless, Colin stepped forward and introduced himself and Gavin. After telling him their story, and who they were looking for, the doctor continued to frown, removed his glasses, and pinched the bridge of his nose.

"So, you be looking for a female bairn."

Trying to contain his patience, Gavin nodded.

The stubby doctor paced in front of his battered desk, "Interesting you should come by," he began.

"Why is that?" Colin asked.

The doctor seemed happy to prolong giving them any information he might have. He went to the window and studied the street. Finally, he said, "I happened to return to the office two nights ago; forgot some important papers, and there was a box on my doorstep."

Gavin's heart took a leap in his chest. "A bairn?"

"Aye," the doctor replied, but offered no other explanation.

Gavin grabbed the man's sleeve, "Was it a girl?"

"Aye, a girl, and in very poor condition, indeed."

"But she was alive?" Gavin hardly dared ask.

"Alive, aye, with a barking cough like a sea lion, if truth be told. And a fever to beat all." His perpetual frown deepened. "I don't know who would do such a thing to an ill bairn, but whoever did," he said turning his frown upon Gavin and Colin, "doesn't deserve to have her."

"We agree, certainly," Gavin replied.

"Croup, then," Colin interjected.

Gavin gaze swept the room as if she might appear to him out of thin air. "Where is she? I must see her. I must be sure she's my Alice."

"My missus took her to the house," the doctor said. "She's a midwife and has dealt with bairns such as this. But—"

"Please," Gavin nearly begged, "I must see her."

"Maybe 'tisn't the bairn you're looking for."

"I must see her to find out; you understand that, don't you?" Gavin could barely contain his frustration and anger. Colin put his hand on Gavin's arm, as if he were afraid Gavin would attack the man.

"So you have no idea how she got here? Who left her here?"

The doctor studied Colin before answering. "Nae, no idea." He went behind his desk and drew out a blanket. "She was bundled in this, but the missus put her in a clean one to take her home. Now—"

Gavin grabbed it. "Look, her initial."

And there it was; the big, intricate "A" crocheted in the corner.

Gavin and Colin looked at each other. Finally Colin said, "You go. Take her to Erskine House as soon as possible. Both Robbie and Lydia are capable of her care."

Gavin glanced at the doctor. "Is she well enough to travel?"

The doctor took out his timepiece and look at it. "I'm sorry to say that by now, she and my missus are half way to Dundee."

"Dundee!?" Gavin thought his heart would leave his chest. "What on earth—"

The doctor took his greatcoat and hat off the hook by the

door. "It was the right thing to do. She needed more care than either my wife or I could give her. She was left on my doorstep as a foundling."

"A foundling?" Gavin all but shouted.

The doctor's defenses went up. "How was I to know? 'Tisn't the first bairn I've had to shuttle off to Baldovan."

Now Colin was shaken. "Baldovan Orphanage…and," he almost completed the title, for Baldovan was also an asylum and school for imbecilic children who were unfit to learn elsewhere.

Gavin looked at Colin, his gaze pleading.

"Aye," the doctor said, defiant. "'Tis what we do with foundlings."

"Go," Colin said to a pale Gavin. "If you ride hard you may even catch up with them. In the meantime, I'm going to find those women, and god help them if something happens to Alice because of this outrageous stunt."

"Do you know where the next coach is going?"

With a shrug the doctor answered, "Prob'ly Crathie, if 'tis a coach they're wanting."

It was the only clue they had.

"Is the telegraph office open?"

The doctor shook his head. "But I've got a key, in case of emergency."

"Well, dammit," Colin all but shouted, "this is one big god-damned emergency."

"What are you going to do?" Gavin asked.

"Wire Erskine House and tell them what we know." When Colin saw Gavin's face, he added, "I'll tell them we've found her and that you will return with her shortly."

Gavin snorted a dry laugh. "Shortly?"

"Better to tell them that than have them know the exact truth, don't you think?"

Gavin agreed, and nosed his mount toward Dundee. How often had he said he didn't like drama in his life? Well, like it or not, this was one drama he would follow through until the very end.

• • •

Faith paced the floor of their room at the inn. "I wish we didn't have to wait another whole day for the coach," she grumbled.

Birdie sat by the window, listless. Her hair was in a snarl of messy curls, and she had not changed her gown in three days. "Where are we going?"

Faith pulled her sweater close around her. Truthfully, she had no idea but Birdie was close to breaking, and Faith knew it. "My uncle at the university will take us in for a short while, until we can find our footing."

Birdie blinked away tears. "I never imagined my life would be like this." Her chin quivered and she wiped away tears with her fingers, her lacy handkerchief long gone; she didn't know where. "And you're sure Adrianna was okay when you left her?"

Faith heaved an impatient sigh. "Birdie, I told you she was. When I left her at the doctor's door—"

"You left her on the doorstep? Like a foundling?" Birdie sputtered incredulously. "How could you? She might have died before she was found. How do you know she didn't die alone, scared and sick?"

"I know the doctor was in the office when I left her at the door," Faith lied. Actually, the office was completely dark. But again, Birdie was fragile. "And I knocked on the door before I left, all right?" Faith shrugged her coat on. "I'm going out. I'll bring you something to eat."

"Maybe some chocolates, if you can find any." Birdie watched Faith stride down the street toward the mercantile. How had things come to this? Why had she thought she could care for a bairn? To be sure, it had been exciting in the beginning. It was something that needed her, and it gave her a great sense of purpose. But even now she didn't think of the bairn as a real person; she had been a toy for Birdie to play with. She actually felt a stab of shame.

As she observed Faith, she noticed a man on horseback riding into town. She squinted to get a better look, and her stomach fell. God in heaven, what was he doing here?

Chapter Thirty-Five

Colin left his mount at the livery and crossed to the inn. He questioned the innkeeper and learned that two women of Birdie's and Faith's descriptions were checked into a room down the hall. Colin tramped to the door and, without knocking, flung it open.

Birdie sat, wide-eyed, and stared at him. Even though she was disheveled, she was still lovely, but Colin was irate.

"Where's Faith?" he growled.

Birdie, appearing unable to speak, weakly tossed her hand toward the window.

"Then I'll wait." He settled into a chair across from her.

Birdie studied her hands and bit at her lips.

Finally, Colin asked, "What in the devil were you thinking?"

Suddenly she spoke, her voice anxious. "Did you find her?"

"We hope so, with no thanks to the two of you," he answered. When she didn't respond, he added, "How did you happen to hook up with a viper like Faith Baker? Talk to me, Birdie!"

And Birdie told him her story: She had been bored. She hated being in the country, and her only escape was to go into Galashiels and visit with the dressmaker, with whom she had much in common fashion-wise.

"One day I crossed to the coffeehouse. I had met Faith before on the night of the fire, when I was given Adrianna by her mother."

"Her name is Alice," Colin reminded her.

She waved his comment away. "Faith and I had much in common, I discovered. We loved fashion and gossip and pretty things. She was a regular visitor in Edinburgh at her uncle's home, and her uncle was Gavin's mentor." She gazed at Colin. "Did you know that?"

"I've met him."

"She agreed with me that the bairn should be mine, and over time, we talked about how exciting it would be to have the child to raise, to watch her grow and all..." Her voice faded away. "I began purchasing things for her, things she could wear as she got older. I hid them in my wardrobe." She thought a moment and then asked, "How did you discover I had taken Adrianna and gone away with Faith?"

"Robbie went in to check on her and found her gone, you gone, and your wardrobe empty. Lydia had found the things the day before, but you fled before she could ask you about them." He waited a moment. "And then..." He didn't need to finish the sentence.

Birdie appeared contrite. "It seemed so easy at first. Adrianna slept a lot, and Faith found milk for her, and it all seemed like such an adventure. Then, even though people had told me how hard it was to raise a bairn, I had no idea."

Colin watched her face, knowing her nuances, her theatrics, her phony feelings of affection. Strangely, she looked penitent.

"Go on."

Birdie dug into her pocket and pulled out a handkerchief, seeming surprised to have found it there. She twisted it in her hands. "She said she knew of a way to take her and get away with it." She gave Colin a poignant look. "It was all I needed. I wanted that bairn. She was mine before she was Gavin's or Robbie's. And Robbie has everything I ever wanted. Why should she get the bairn too?" Her voice ended as a pathetic squeak.

Colin shook his head. He imagined she couldn't have gotten this far without Faith Baker's devious behavior. But she was in no way innocent.

"Do you realize what will happen to you if Alice, who has a terrible case of croup, doesn't survive?"

Birdie's lips were pressed together, and she nodded. "We could go to jail, I guess."

"Birdie, people have been hanged for lesser crimes than this."

"I wasn't the one who left her on the doorstep," she pleaded. "And Faith told me the doctor was in there, and she knocked to let him know there was someone outside—"

"There was no one there, Birdie. The doctor was at home. It was only luck that brought him back to his office that night."

Birdie sagged back against the settee. "This is all so vexing," she said, nearly sobbing. "How my life would have changed if…"

"If you hadn't always coveted something that wasn't yours? If you hadn't stolen Robbie's fiance? That was the beginning of your downhill slide, I'd say."

"And if that dunderhead Gavin hadn't proposed to the wrong sister," she added.

Dunderhead? "But by that time, you had already married your sister's beau. What good would a marriage proposal be to a married woman?"

She waved her hand to indicate it wasn't important.

"Then you weren't angry because you were in love with him yourself, you were angry because he made an honest mistake?"

She made a face. "In love with Gavin? Lord, no. He was merely one of many lads who followed me around at home."

The door swung open, and Faith Baker stepped into the room and froze, her gaze locking with Colin's, and looking every bit the trapped animal.

• • •

Gavin rode his mount hard, stopping briefly when he realized he was exhausting the animal. At the next village he swapped his own horse out for another at the livery, and kept riding on toward Dundee.

He met no one on the way nor did he overtake anyone. Although he had not been to Dundee in years, he had studied maps and streets and knew where the Baldovan Orphanage was, on the northern outskirts. Orphanage! He had never felt such outrage. Such helplessness. In his entire life he had not found anything worth getting himself worked up over, until now. Until now. Like a knife twisting in his chest, he thought about Robbie and Alice, and the life they were just beginning to enjoy as a family. Would it all come to naught? No. He couldn't think that way.

His good sense having abandoned him, he didn't notice the log in the road until he and the horse were upon it, and the horse stopped short, sending Gavin over his head, onto his back on the ground. The fall took his breath from him and he stared into the night sky, gasping for air.

• • •

Robbie paced; it had become her natural manner. "No word. I can't understand why we haven't heard something. Anything at all." Her own fear was so great she didn't see the fearful glances between Lydia and Mrs. Murray.

"I'm sure we'll hear something soon," Lydia soothed, although even to her own ears the words sounded false.

"Ladies," Eve said, rushing toward them and out of breath. She raised a missive in her fist. "The innkeeper found me at Mrs. Ferguson's and I came straightaway."

Robbie took the letter and, with shaking fingers, opened it. She sagged against the table in the foyer, nearly knocking over the vase of flowers. She read it quickly.

"It's from Colin. He says they have found Alice, and Gavin will be returning with her shortly!"

Joyously, all four women read the letter again, just to make sure it was real.

"Shortly," repeated Robbie. "He'll be here shortly with our beloved Alice!"

But shortly was not to be. A day went by, then another, with no word from either Gavin or Colin. Robbie could do nothing but pace, her faithful Lady Perlina herding her this way and that, keeping Robbie from straying off toward the woods.

• • •

Colin watched as Faith's expression changed from alarm to distaste. "So, you found us. I guess I'm not surprised; you have the face of a bloodhound."

"Faithy! What a thing to say! He can't help it, you know."

Colin glanced at Birdie; she looked truly horrified. It soothed him a little to know she wouldn't say something so cruel about someone else, at least not out loud.

"You're lucky that cur wasn't rabid," Faith continued. "There are dozens and dozens of strays roaming the streets of Edinburgh, you know."

Colin continued to stare at her. "Oh, this wasn't a stray. This dog had a master."

Faith gave him an unpleasant smile. "One who stood on the sidelines and watched his pet devour you, I imagine."

"Yes."

Faith lifted an eyebrow. "Well, I must find him and commend him for teaching his dog to attack people I don't like. You must introduce me."

Colin stepped to the window, watched the activity in the street. "Yes, that would be an appropriate introduction. One self-absorbed stalker meets another."

"I don't stalk people," she shot back.

Colin turned from the window. "No? You prey on the weak and innocent, sniffing around for places where you might tunnel in and drop your poison."

Her gaze narrowed; hate spread across her features. "And you are a feckless has-been who can't even get up the nerve to practice medicine again."

"I admit to being ineffective of late. But I can change. You, on the other hand, are and will always be a nasty-minded viper."

"Colin?"

Birdie's voice was soft, but it drew his attention. "Yes, Birdie?"

"What's going to happen to us?"

He clasped his hands behind his back and paced in front of her. "What do you think should happen?"

She screwed up her face; tears rolled down her cheeks. "I don't want to go to prison."

"Oh, don't be a fool," Faith scolded. "He wouldn't do that to us."

"I'm afraid it isn't up to me," Colin said. "Gavin is the one who must decide. If I were to be in a position to do something, trust me, you two would not get away without some form of punishment. And you, Miss Baker, undoubtedly became her accomplice to get back at Gavin for ignoring you and marrying someone else."

Neither woman spoke, so Colin said, "Pack up your things, both of you. There's a coach waiting to take you back to Galashiels."

Birdie, contrite, did his bidding. Faith, belligerent, tossed him a killing look before she began filling her valise.

• • •

Gavin opened his eyes. He must have lost consciousness, because the night sky was filled with stars. He could breathe now, but felt paralyzed. He studied the the heavens, noting the tail of the Plough was pointing directly toward Polaris, the North Star. Oh, he knew where he was; he just wasn't sure *how* he was. He attempted to move and gasped as pain pierced his side, taking his breath away once again.

He tried to get up, but the pain left him flat on his back. He told himself to relax, to stay calm. Again he studied the sky, a place he knew better than the land around him. The three stars in Orion's Belt caught his eye. Zeta, Epsilon and Delta. And there was Cassiopeia, on the opposite side of the North Star and north of the Plough.

He turned his head to the side and saw the mount standing

nearby, calmly grazing. He had to get up, get going. How much time had passed? He struggled to get his timepiece from his pocket, but wasn't able to complete the task. The pain was too excruciating. He had no time to waste; he had to get to his daughter!

With all of his strength, he rolled to his good side and heaved himself to a sitting position, gasping for breath once again as he fought through the discomfort. Would the mare cooperate? He struggled to stand, his hands on his thighs as he waited for the pain to dissipate. Slowly, there was no other way for him to move, he stepped toward the horse, and when he reached her, he inhaled sharply and pulled himself into the saddle, clinging to her mane as he waited for the acute pain to wane. Then, he gave the mount a gentle nudge with his heels, and they were once again cantering toward Baldovan.

Some time later, Baldovan Orphanage loomed ahead of Gavin. English Tudor in style, it was built of rubble stones with Caen stone dressings. The roof held black and red tiles. It did not appear threatening, but Gavin had recently learned that what's on the outside is not necesarily what one would find on the inside. Thoughts of both Birdie and Faith pecked at his brain, and had they been nearby, he might have threatened to strangle them. He cursed them for their disloyalty and himself for his naïvete.

• • •

The coach carrying Colin, Birdie, and Faith pulled up to the inn in Galashiels. "You two are not off the hook," he reminded them. "Until we know that Alice is all right, you are to stay where I tell you to. Faith, with your mother at the coffee shop and Birdie, you will travel to Edinburgh with my sister, Eve, and stay there until further notice. If the two of you were anyone else, I'd have you locked up to make sure you didn't run off."

"But the bairn will be all right, don't you think, Colin?" Birdie's voice was remorseful; Colin didn't think he'd ever heard her speak so contritely before.

He studied her; she was still disheveled. Probably for the first time in her life, she thought of someone other than herself. "We won't know anything until we hear from Gavin." He refused to give them false hope; giving Robbie a measure of hope is what he had to do right now.

"I don't want to go to Erskine House, Colin," Birdie said.

"I'm sure you don't. You have created a perfect mess for yourself, and I don't doubt you'd rather not face anyone else's wrath but mine. However," he added, "I think it's time you realize that the world doesn't revolve around you."

"But they'll all hate me!" Birdie put her face in her hands.

"What did you expect?" Colin asked, feeling little sympathy for her.

Eli Baker, the innkeeper, came out and retrieved Faith's valise from the coach, then waited for her to alight. He said nothing, and for once even Faith wasn't able to look her uncle straight in the eyes.

Her aunt, the innkeeper's wife, stormed out of the inn and grabbed Faith by the arm, pulling her along with her. "Foolish, foolish lassie," she sputtered. "Yer mam just gettin' better, now you pull a stunt like this. Ye want to kill her, do ye?" The woman dragged her into the inn.

• • •

Once at Erskine House, Birdie hurried off to her apartment, locking the door behind her.

After Colin explained everything that had happened to them, learning where Alice had been taken, finding Birdie and Faith, he had to admit he was surprised he hadn't found Gavin already at the house before him.

Robbie continued to be anxious and worried. "Why doesn't he let us know where he is? I expected him long before this."

Colin pulled her with him into the morning room and led her

to a chair. "I have to admit I thought he'd be here too, but until we hear otherwise, we should keep hope and wait."

Robbie flung herself out of the chair. "I can't! I've waited and waited, since the very moment you and Gavin left to find Alice, all I've done is *wait*, and the waiting is exhausting."

At Colin's silence, Robbie suddenly realized she hadn't asked where they found Alice, only that she'd been found. Robbie rounded on him.

"Where did you find them, anyway?"

"Birdie and Faith were at an inn in Crathie, waiting for a coach."

"What about Alice?" Intense panic climbed her throat.

Colin stood and went to the window. Autumn had arrived with a vengeance. Beeches were coloring to rust, leaves were dropping, the air was cool with the promise of winter. "Isn't it enough to know that Gavin went to get her?"

"No! It is not enough." Sick with worry, she replied, "Tell me, Colin, and tell me now. I want to hear the entire ugly story, warts and all, and don't leave anything out."

After he finished, Robbie was so angry and upset she was sick to her stomach and nearly speechless. "Baldovan? They took her to an orphanage?"

"I won't pretend to understand it, Robbie, but according to the local doctor, it's where they take all foundlings."

"But she isn't a foundling! She's my daughter. My sweet, innocent—" Her lower lip quivered, and she could not finish her sentence. For the first time since the entire incident happened, Robbie allowed herself to cry.

"What must she think?"

"Robbie, she's not old enough to form those kind of—"

"That not only did her birth mother pass her off to another, but the parents she'd been given to allowed her to be taken from her crib and…" She pulled in an angry breath. "Those two. How could they? How could they?"

She rounded on him once again. "What's to be done with them?"

Attempting to placate her, he replied, "Let's wait for Gavin to arrive with Alice before we make any big decisions." Although in his mind, the decisions were made, even though the punishment did not nearly fit the crime.

Unable to control her anger, Robbie stormed to Birdie's apartment. Her sister sat at her dressing table, examining herself in the mirror. She looked up and caught her sister's angry gaze. She immediately looked away.

Robbie refused to do the same. "How could you?" Her anger was palpable in her voice.

Birdie looked back at her sister from the mirror, her eyes filled with tears, but her expression not tearful. "You have everything I've ever wanted."

"But what were you thinking? How did you plan to care for Alice? You have no way of keeping yourself fed, much less a bairn."

Still on the defensive, Birdie replied, "I didn't think that far ahead, all right? All I knew was that she was given to *me*, and therefore she was mine. And I didn't expect her to get so sick that we'd have to take her to see a doctor."

Robbie clung to the back of an armchair to keep her knees from buckling out from under her. "She was sick?"

With a defiant gaze, Birdie replied, "She coughed all the time and kept me awake. She threw up on both Faith and me, and when she coughed she sounded really bizarre, like a barking dog with a frog in its throat."

Robbie pressed her hands to her stomach. The agony her child had gone through at the hands of Birdie and Faith cut deeply into Robbie's heart. "What you did wasn't just selfish and cruel. It was foolish and irresponsible." She swung away, one hand on her forehead and one on her hip and paced. "Are you ever going to learn to think of someone other than yourself, Birdie? Are you?"

Birdie sniffed. "Well, if it makes you feel better, I am sorry."

Robbie stopped pacing and stared at her sister. "You're sorry? That's it? Birdie, she could have *died*." She had to turn away, or the urge to grab her sister's shoulders and shake her senseless would have overcome her.

"I know! But how was I to know that bairns needed so much care? I know it was foolish of me, but I had no idea how much work went into raising one of those things."

Robbie tsked. "You hardly raised her, Birdie; you didn't even have her a week, and you couldn't even do that right."

Birdie collapsed into sobs, perhaps meant to soften Robbie, perhaps real, but either way, Robbie wasn't taken in.

"What will happen now?" she asked meekly.

"God knows what I'd do with you," Robbie answered. "But it's up to Gavin to decide your fate, you foolish girl." She gave her sister a stern glance. "What would Papa say if he were alive? I think even he would have scolded you proper, Birdie."

Papa had been both girls' champion in spite of what they did or how much trouble they got into, although Birdie's antics always outweighed Robbie's.

Through eyes fraught with tears, Birdie wailed, "I don't want to go to jail."

Robbie lifted an eyebrow. "No, you wouldn't do well there, would you?"

"I wouldn't survive there, Robbie. You know how fragile I am."

"You should have thought of that when you concocted this foolish, impetuous, and very stupid scheme."

As she turned to leave, she warned, "You're going to Colin's townhouse. Eve will be your companion. If I hear any word that you have treated her as poorly as you treated people here, I'll find a solicitor who will make you pay for your mistake in a way that will surely make you realize how lucky you have had things up to now."

Contrite, Birdie asked, "Can I stay in my apartment? I don't want to see anyone. And, if Mrs. Murray or Maureen could bring me dinner, I'd be ever so appreciative."

What Birdie needed was to be forced to face the entire household, but even Robbie knew that that would just be cruel. "I'll see that you're fed, Birdie."

"And Robbie?"

Robbie turned, her expression masked.

"I am sorry."

Robbie left her, wondering how true her sister's statement was. Of course, she could be sorry; she had done something appalling and gotten caught. Robbie wondered if Birdie would ever really change.

Chapter Thirty-Six

Gavin was led into a waiting room, and wait there he did. Perhaps it wasn't as long as it'd felt, but because of his fears and worry, it seemed interminable, and the pain in his side didn't help his dispostion.

Eventually the door opened, and a formidable-looking woman entered, gray hair pulled back so tightly into a bun that he wondered if she could blink her eyes. She gave Gavin a once-over, noting his disheveled appearance, and her lips pursed into a flat line.

He explained why he was there, relating Alice in detail, who had brought her in and what the circumstances were. He described his daughter's dark, downy curls, her approximate age, the fact that she was ill with croup, and even the daisy-shaped birthmark she had on her left thigh.

The matron was unmoved. "We'll have to make some inquiries—"

"No!" Gavin put his hand on his side and pressed, hoping to ease the pain there. "I want to see the babies now. She was brought here by a midwife. If you don't cooperate, I'll have the law in here faster than you can sweep your secrets under this faded Persian carpet I'm standing on."

Alarm registered on her face. "I beg your pardon?"

"No place such as this is without its secrets, madam. Trust me when I tell you that if I am not ushered into the room where the most recent babies have been deposited, I will go to the ends of the earth to discover your secrets and make sure you pay."

Suddenly the matron appeared to realize she was not dealing with some nobody. His threats were not empty. Although he was disheveled, she saw beneath his soiled clothing that he was a gentleman of some means.

She demurred. "Follow me, sir."

• • •

Three weeks later, Gavin and Robbie sat together in front of a roaring fire, Alice on Gavin's lap and Lady Perlina curled up next to her mistress.

Alice had been cared for at the orphanage; for that Gavin couldn't take them to task. But to find her there in a room bare of anything but a crib made his blood boil. Twice she had been abandoned. Twice. She was still so very young; would there be scars? When he had ridden up in the landau with his daughter, Robbie had come running from the house, her skirts lifted high, her face wreathed in smiles and tears.

Colin had ministered to Gavin's broken ribs, binding them so they would heal properly, and Gavin refused anything for his discomfort except a good shot of brandy.

"My life is full," Gavin said, bringing Robbie's face to his and kissing her.

"As is mine," she replied, her eyes warm and shiny with happiness. "Your decision about the women was very generous, you know that."

"I do know that," he responded. "But what good would it have done to punish them? The villagers and everyone in the surrounding countryside knows what they did; that is probably punishment enough. I'm surprised Faith can show her face, although I did hear that she's planning on returning to Edinburgh for good."

Robbie wanted no secrets between them. "Eve told me something about Colin's accident, that your mentor came along when it happened but didn't intervene."

"Yes, I know."

She shot him a look of surprise. "How did you know?"

He squeezed her shoulder. "I'm not as out of touch as everyone thinks I am. I began having second thoughts about him when I learned that I had been the first choice for a position I had badly wanted in Athens. The position went to another of his pupils, one I knew did not have the qualifications I had. I looked into it and discovered he'd been bribed to pick the other fellow."

"And how did you learn the truth about Colin's accident?"

"I thought it strange that he should have such bitterness toward Faith, whom, I thought, was nothing like her uncle." He gave her a grim smile. "Yes, I admit to being naïve about her. But I had learned where Colin was treated and wanted to make sure he got all of the help he needed, medically and financially. The doctor who treated him told me in confidence what had actually happened."

"And you didn't admit to him that you knew?"

Gavin shook his head. "If he had wanted me to know, he would have told me. I suppose he was trying to protect me, but by that time the halo I had envisioned over Professor Baker's shiny pate had tarnished quite a lot."

Robbie snuggled close and watched Alice sleep in her father's arms. "And now Birdie is living at Colin's townhouse. I hope Eve is as patient as I'd suspected she was."

"Colin wants to marry her."

"Has he asked her?" Robbie touched Alice's dark curls, her fingers gentle.

"Do you think she'd accept if he did?"

"I don't know. He should have threatened her with prison or marriage." Although Robbie didn't truly believe that. "I got a note from Eve the other day. She has introduced Birdie to some of her customers, ladies with connections. Hopefully Birdie will be content, at least for a while."

"And Colin and Lydia are running a fine clinic down the hall." Gavin paused, then asked Robbie, "Have you made a decision?"

Robbie knew what he was alluding to. One thing that had eaten at her since she left Edinburgh was the condition of the girls, the runaways who so often ended up in prostitution. "Yes. With Mrs. Murray and Maureen here to help with Alice, I think I can afford to spend one, no more than two, days a week counseling any of them who might come to see us." She turned and looked at her husband. "All of this activity in your home must be disturbing for you, yet you act like it's the most normal thing in the world."

"With you by my side, I'm calm and steady. Whatever else goes on here is just an added blessing." He was quiet a moment. "I do love you."

Surprised, she turned to him. "You do?"

"I've fallen headlong, madly, deeply in love with you, Robbie Eliot."

Robbie's heart nearly burst with happiness. "And I love you more than ever."

They sat quietly, enjoying each other's company, the warm fire, the dozing pup, and the sleeping bairn. Their thoughts were entwined. Life was impossibly good.

Epilogue

FIVE YEARS LATER

A young woman sat in a chaise, accompanied by a nurse who held the reins of a pretty painted mare.

"Do you want to get closer?" the nurse asked her.

"Nae. I can see from here," she answered, her voice holding an eagerness about it that wasn't lost on her companion. They were in the shadow of a clump of scrubby oak, well hidden from view.

Across the lawn, a family was enjoying the summer weather. The father, a handsome man with very light hair, was pushing a six-year-old girl with dark curls in a swing that was hung from an enormous oak.

"Higher, Papa," she screamed with glee. "Higher!"

As if responding, two dogs raced around the tree, barking into the wind.

The mother, a pretty woman, now very pregnant, sat nearby, watching her family; she had a notebook on her lap and had just looked up from it. Her smile was warm as she studied the other two. "Be careful, Gavin," she cautioned. "Not too high."

"Ah, but my Alice is a brave girl, aren't you, my sweet? And today is your birthday; you are a big six-year-old."

Alice laughed into the wind, her curls lifting and blowing into her face as she soared. "I'm brave, and I'm six! Higher, Papa!"

Darla Dean fought back tears. Her baby was safe. She was

happy. She was loved. Darla had known it would be so, but to see for herself made her content.

"We can leave now," she said to her companion, knowing she would never look upon her child again.

Gavin caught a glimpse of the chaise as it moved slowly out from behind the trees. Although he had felt they were being watched, he had not felt alarm.

The front door opened, and Lydia came out holding his and Robbie's three-year-old daughter. He stopped pushing Alice on the swing long enough to give Linnea a kiss on the cheek. "Did you have a good nap, sweetness?"

Linnea—who had her father's light hair, though it looked more like puffs of clouds than actual hair—rubbed her eyes with her fists. "I dream of Lady."

Responding to her name, Lady Perlina bounded toward them, tail wagging and ears perky. Linnea reached down to touch the pet, and Lydia put her on the ground. The dog, who had been a protector of both girls from the very beginning, gently nudged Linnea's tummy, which made the child giggle.

The other Corgi, Lady's daughter, Miss Sallie, joined them and pushed Linnea to the ground. Instead of being upset, the child laughed and rolled around on the grass with the dogs.

"Papa, it's my birthday, swing me!" Alice ordered, trying without success to swing herself.

Gavin and Robbie exchanged glances. Their daughters were as different as the colors of their hair. Alice was a little lady; she loved dressing in pretty dresses and having tea parties with her dolls, often requiring her little sister to join them—or serve them.

Linnea, on the other hand, loved the grass. She loved the trees and the flowers, and whenever she could, she would attempt to climb into the oak that held the swing. Mrs. Murray always complained about the grass stains on Linnea's clothing, but everyone could tell she wasn't as upset about it as she tried to be.

"Papa!"

Lydia moved to the swing. "Here, birthday girl, I'll push you."

Robbie let out a yelp, which brought Gavin to her side immediately.

"It's nothing; just a good, swift kick in the ribs," she explained with a soft smile.

"So our dinner guests won't flock around the bed to welcome our new son?"

Robbie raised an eyebrow at him. "You have your mind set on a boy, don't you?"

Gavin gave his wife a loving look. "Not really. I'm just grateful you're healthy."

"When do the guests arrive?" Lydia called, continuing to push Alice on the swing.

Colin, Eve, and Birdie, now his wife, were coming to spend a few days in the country to celebrate Alice's birthday. Birdie had not been to visit for many months. No matter what excuses she gave, everyone knew it was because she had had enough of the provincial life when she'd lived at Erskine House years before. And now, with her new social status, she rarely pulled herself away to visit her sister and the family. It upset no one.

Although Birdie had softened since her marriage to Colin, her basic personality was still the same. Both Robbie and Gavin wondered how either Eve or Colin could abide by it day after day, but as long as they didn't complain, no one brought it up.

Linnea toddled to her father and he reached down and picked her up, snuggling her in his lap. She immediately put her thumb in her mouth.

"They should be here any time," he replied. He gave his wife another glance, one she returned with a sly smile. "What's that look for?"

"For you, my darling husband; all of my smiles are because of you."